Guests of Chance

Also by Colleen Curran

Novels

Overnight Sensation

Something Drastic

Plays

Casa de Mary Margaret

Something Drastic

Cake Walk

Sacred Hearts

Triple Play:
Amelia Earhart Was Not a Spy
A Sort of Holiday
El Clavadista

Senetta Boynton Visits the Orient

Sibyl and Sylvia

Local Talent

Whale Watch

Maple Lodge

The Pillbox Hat

Guests of Chance

Colleen Curran

Edited by Laurel Boone.
Cover illustration by Lorraine Buchanan.
Jacket design by Julie Scriver.
Book design by Lisa Rousseau.
Printed in Canada.
10 9 8 7 6 5 4 3 2 1

Library and Archives Canada Cataloguing in Publication

Curran, Colleen, 1954-
Guests of chance / Colleen Curran.

ISBN 0-86492-438-0

I. Title.

PS8555.U67G84 2005 C813'.54 C2005-904171-4

Published with the financial support of the Canada Council for the Arts, the Government of Canada through the Book Publishing Industry Development Program, and the New Brunswick Culture and Sports Secretariat.

Goose Lane Editions
469 King Street
Fredericton, New Brunswick
CANADA E3B 1E5
www.gooselane.com

For Katie McGlynn Curran,
my wonderful mother and our Duchess of Donegal

’Twould be a wildish destiny,
If we, who thus together roam
In a strange land, and far from home,
Were in this place the guests of Chance:
Yet who would stop, or fear to advance,
Though home or shelter he had none,
With such a Sky to lead him on?

— William Wordsworth,
“Stepping Westward”

Love can read the writing on the remotest star.

— Oscar Wilde

Chapter One

It was my first trip over so much water, and for so long. It could've been worse and been even longer, across an ocean way wider than the Atlantic, it might have been the South Pacific over atolls where Amelia Earhart got lost. I couldn't stop thinking about how much water and nothingness, civilization-wise, was down there, and how much there was of it, and how far down it was. When the pilot said we were still 3,195 miles from our destination, I was afraid of getting an anxiety attack. I didn't want to have to breathe into one of the air sickness bags or stick my head between my knees to calm myself down, and how does anyone do that in airplane seating anyway? So I gave myself positive thoughts: How grand it'll be to be in England now that April's no longer there, because it's May, which is way better than Heidi's original wish, February. I didn't take that travel date suggestion well.

"February? In England?"

"I know, but I'd like to be there for Valentine's Day. Because that's when Miles and I met last year."

She didn't admit it, but I knew Heidi thought of it as their unofficial First Anniversary. I was glad Concordia didn't have spring break in February in one of the not-so-grand-to-be-in-

England months. Instead we would go in May, when all their lovely gardens would be in bloom and their houses not full of the damp.

We were hours and hours away from England. I told myself, I can do this, I must, I have no choice, I cannot freak out. I couldn't believe it: no one paid attention to the flight attendants' demonstration of what to do in an emergency. They would have to rely on someone like me, the only one who memorized the safety precautions. I'd be the one yelling, in a calm manner, "It's under your seat, put on your oxygen mask first and pull to release air before assisting anybody else, yes, even your own child!" I'd be the one who knows which way the pulley goes to activate the emergency chute in case we landed on water. I wouldn't be surprised when it turned into a huge raft. I'd be the first one to blow the whistle that comes with our life jackets that I knew how to inflate. Why, we could wind up flying on automatic pilot because the captain and crew ate a different meal from us, got felled by food poisoning and needed someone to fly the plane. That always happens to stewardesses, look at Karen Black in *Airport '75* or Doris Day in *Julie*. I hoped some other passenger on the plane might be a former pilot, captain, or flight attendant on a courtesy ticket, they'd know how to fly the plane, unless they'd been drinking because they're flying off-duty and for free. I worried we'd be shaking some drunk pilot or tipsy flight attendant, they'd be useless, and suddenly everyone would be looking at me: "You'll have to fly this plane." Just because Viola thinks I have an I Will Survive face, ever since I was a day extra in a lifeboat on *Gamon de Pycombe, Dog of the Titanic*. They'd given me too much time to dwell.

They announced the in-flight movie: *A River Runs Through*

It. Were they trying to kill me? A movie about a whole lot of water? AN OCEAN RUNS UNDER YOU, LENORE. Why didn't they just put on *Airport* '77, with Jimmy Stewart's luxury airliner going down into the Bermuda Triangle, and make me watch Lee Grant's dead husband float by her window? I had my rotten ex, Fergie, to blame for so many of the movie scenes that rot my brain. He taped *Airport* '77 when it was on CFCF. He loved all the airplane disaster movies. *A River Runs Through It* when *EnRoute* magazine said eastbound overseas flyers would watch *Strictly Ballroom* or *A Few Good Men*. Heidi promised we'd be asleep by the time they put the flight entertainment on. She sure would be, with the strange plane reading she brought: *The Pillow Book of Sei Shônagan*. The journal of a tenth century Japanese court lady.

"It's famous for her lists. Look: Elegant Things. Unsuitable Things. Things That Cannot Be Compared. Things That Give a Pathetic Expression."

Heidi brought a work book to read on the plane. I had a *People* and an *US*. I read about Goldie and Kurt while Heidi read List 16, "Things That Make One's Heart Beat Faster." For Heidi, it was Miles Farnham of Near Sheffield. She could change the list title to Things That Make Us Travel Across the Atlantic Ocean to See If There's Anything to This Romance. Well, I was getting a London Show Tour as my Christmas present out of it because she was nuts about him but needed to find out if it's mutual. Of course, he couldn't know that, that's why I wasn't just there as the fellow traveller, I was to be the beard/chaperone.

I told myself, focus on all the Good Things This Journey Means: I'm going to a foreign land, I'm going to Europe. We'll be in London where "Eng-a-lund swings like a pendulum do, bobbies on bicycles two by two," there'll be the Changing of the

Guard and Big Ben, and everywhere we look will be something old and famous, and maybe we'll see royalty coming out of someplace; we can find out where Diana exercises and maybe see her running down the street in her gym clothes to her little car, dodging the press. "Decades ago" Heidi saw Princess Margaret coming out of the Royal Ballet starring Nureyev when she went to England after graduating from college. Maybe if I'd gone to college I might have gone to Europe, that's what they all did. Elspeth proclaimed it was the best time of her life, especially in Greece, that was the only time she was "truly free and truly happy." It's one thing to think that life's all been downhill since then, but to say it out loud in front of her kids? Poor Frieda and Northrop. Elspeth didn't even care if the kids were listening, her complaint was all directed at Douglas the Husband Horrible, who Heidi said "was most definitely a Post-Europe Acquisition."

Good Thoughts of My Journey were interrupted by some turbulence. And then a big dip. The Fasten Seat Belts sign lit up. And I told myself, change the record, forget thoughts of the journey, turn to Sei Shônagan. "Heidi," I said, "Benoît makes my List of Things That Make One's Heart Beat Faster."

"Of course he does, Lenore. My mother is so disappointed."

"Your mother wants me to be happy."

"But with her bachelor son Daniel, not with Constable Benoît Archambault. She saw how serious you're getting at Mirabel Airport."

"She can't. We don't even know that."

"Sheila Flynn Knows All. She said, 'Oh, it is serious. I hoped Lenore was just grateful he caught the man who was leaving mash notes on her car.' I told her they were hate mail."

"Oh yes, the weird Blake Farnham."

"I told her, 'And don't forget the serial killer next door. Lenore helped Benoît apprehend Madame Ducharme.'"

"He sure did."

"'There's more to a lasting relationship than just being involved with criminals,' my mama says. 'What did all that dancing and flirting Lenore was doing with Daniel at our anniversary party mean?'"

"We weren't flirting."

"'And now they share that restaurant they inherited from Daniel's roommate Gaëtan?' Lenore! She still believes they were roommates."

"Daniel thinks it works best, the roommate story works for your mother."

"I'm fed up. She's pathetic. You've moved on, why can't she? She told me I'm in the way and to stop our $2.50 Tuesday Movie Threesomes."

"Doesn't she think if Daniel and I were a couple we'd make you stay home sometimes?"

"'Daniel's shy,' she says."

"He is not."

"About being a gay man with a concerned mother he is. That's got to stop. So I dropped a big clue, just before we went through security."

"You were that mean to your brother-in-mourning and your unsuspecting mother? Right before you left the country?"

"If I get my wish, it will all be out in the open when I get back, all the tears and recriminations, and I'll only need to deal with the aftermath. Maybe a little post-meltdown."

"Benoît's driving your folks back to Montreal, and he'll have to break up a family fight in the police van."

"It wouldn't be the first time his paddy wagon taxi became

a cause célèbre. Viola's birthday party?"

That notorious celebration caused Viola to get in tune with her Artistic side. Everyone in what Elspeth called our Circle thought Viola was finally getting over the break-up with Charlotte till she invited us all to hear her perform at the Yellow Door. I'd never been there, I'd heard of it, I always thought it was some beatnik place in the McGill ghetto, I was half right.

"It's a coffee house, Lenore," Heidi assured me. "For artists, musicians and poets."

The last career title really scared me, it's one thing for super-depressing Sylvia Plath poetry to get published, poetry by somebody just off the street is another.

"We have to be supportive." Heidi's famous last words that always mean I wind up at some weird feminist collective or dog school. This one would mean handmade poems. Viola was going to be part of Open Mike Night. That's a You Are Warned promise, like the Waitress Wanted sign you see as you head into a restaurant.

"They're not all poets. Yellow Door sometimes hosts fiction writers. More often than not, it's folk music artists. Jesse Winchester often played there, you like him. And Bruce Cockburn. And I'm sure possibly even the McGarrigles."

I knew she was fishing with the McGarrigles. She'd say k.d. lang and Anne Murray got their start there too, just to get me to go. I wanted to help Viola through this crisis, but I had a bad feeling.

Heidi managed to park on Aylmer, on the actual street, and took this as a good sign. And when we got to the Yellow Door, which has one, along with green steps, she pointed at the tree hanging out sideways over the street in front that made her think of a banyan, to me it looked like something Hayley Mills would climb out her window to escape on. Heidi asked the studenty guy at the front door with a cash box if it was a good house.

"Oh yeah. At least sixteen people, thereabouts, so far."

Heidi was thrilled.

"Of course, it will really get full up later for the Open Mike."

"Later? It's not right now?" I asked. He couldn't smell my fear.

"No, there are the Writers, Poets and Guest Artist first. Our scheduled program."

"What time does Open Mike begin?"

"After eleven."

Eleven? It wasn't even eight o'clock yet.

"Maybe my friend and I will go out for a bite and come back later," suggested Heidi.

"You can, but you probably won't get a seat or even get in. We fill up fast. We have food here."

So we decided we couldn't not be there for Viola, and we headed toward what I thought must be the café part.

"No, it's downstairs, Lenore."

We had to go down a flight of narrow stairs, and oh yes, there was a faded poster of Jesse Winchester, and suddenly it's the seventies, we're in somebody's basement in the suburbs. There's an upright piano and a music stand and lots of uncomfortable-looking black chairs next to poles that block the view but keep the building and the low ceiling up.

"There's the toilet if you need it," said Heidi, pointing to a little bunch of steps. "You'd better use it now because there'll be no getting near it once the Open Mike crowd storms in," she said, and laughed at how witty she could be under my duress.

She promised coffee and anything else I wanted, on her,

but the child of hippies at the kitchen counter stated, "There's no coffee, just tea bags, if you plug in the kettle." They do have little milk cartons, with straws, like the ones kids get in elementary school, and some nice cookies.

"Homemade?" asked Heidi, trying to be a sport.

"No. Voortman's. From a bin."

When we got back to our seats, they'd been taken.

"Excuse me? I think you have our seats?" Heidi said.

"We didn't know whose coats they were," a long-golden-haired fiftyish peaceniky man replied.

"They seem to be gone . . . ," said Heidi.

"No one was sitting here."

"We were."

"Not when we got here," said Golden Hair. I was distracted when his companion starting to braid his hair while we stood over them, half-pints of milk with straws in our hands.

"Coats on chairs indicate they're taken," said Heidi.

"Don't panic. Try chilling, babe. Your coats are on the church bench by the back wall. And there are still chairs left."

"Yes, and *you* can go look for some."

"She said take a seat, we took a seat, what's your problem?"

"You are," shouted Heidi.

Mister and Sister Golden Hair picked up their stuff and moved to really bad seats behind a pole. Under his breath he muttered, "Milk Maid has to have her seat back," and Heidi responded, "Goldilocks has to learn he can't take other people's chairs."

People all around pretended they didn't see this, except for Child of Hippies at the no-coffee-but-tea-bags counter. She was horrified, such an aggressive scene in this laid-back place.

"I'm sorry, Lenore, I just couldn't give in," Heidi said. I didn't blame her; it was shocking to see that kind of bad seat-etiquette from someone you'd expect all he is saying is give peace a chance.

There was no sign of Viola or any of her Sisters when the show started. The mistress of ceremonies welcomed us and apologized because two of the poets scheduled to read couldn't make it (HURRAY!), but she's happy to announce that the Guest Artist has agreed to share some of his new poems-in-progress so we won't be deprived. He'll bookend this Written Word evening along with four experienced local writers. "There are still four local writers? There would have been six?" I don't think I can take this much creative writing in closed quarters. "I am going to kill Viola," Heidi snarled to me.

The MC is pleased to welcome our Guest Artist, who lives just outside of Peterborough, Ontario, "a back-to-the-lander immigrant, he's originally from the States, we're so glad he could make it, he's just been nominated for a Triller Award, a great honour in Toronto literary circles, but he's here with us tonight, aren't we fortunate, welcome him, please." And then who ambles up from the bad seating behind the pole but our Seat Stealer.

"It could be worse," whispered Heidi, "he could have turned out to be Jesse Winchester."

Seat Stealer's name is Titus Vanzetti.

"My cat's name was Sacco," he tells the crowd.

"So they were Sacco and Vanzetti?" I say to Heidi.

"It's a long story, yeah, we took their names," Titus says to the crowd, "but there are some people here tonight who turn fascisti over people appropriating anything, even chairs. Just like my namesake, I was wrongfully accused. I've only been here half an hour and it's been a fractious time, as some of you may have witnessed."

And many eyes try not to focus on us, but they all know we

are the ornery ones.

After what seems to be a lot of silence, Titus takes out a little tape recorder. "This is man's best friend on the 401." He lifts it up to the ceiling, not a big reach. This, he tells us, makes it possible for him to drive and compose at the same time.

"Couldn't his girlfriend drive the car if he gets inspired on the highway?" I say to Heidi.

Titus pushes the play button for the poem he "wrote" on the way here. The title is "Rendezvous with Atwood."

And it's about how he cornered Margaret Atwood when he spotted her having coffee in a Futures Toronto café on Queen Street. She'd been the celebrity judge for the CBC Literary Competition that passed over his work. But she finally remembered his piece, and when he forced her to be honest, she told him it was pretentious. She turned away, putting two-percent milk in her Nigerian Blend, and the poem ended: "Who in hell was she anyway, to spurn me, to judge me, who the hell is she?"

"The Governor General's Award winner for *The Circle Game*, that's who," shouts Heidi.

"Hey, you get your own gig if you want a soapbox, Milk Maid," Titus shouts back.

The MC intervenes. "We must respect the artists and not interject. If anyone needs further expression, please find the sign-up sheet for Open Mike. You can share your opinions then, but not during an Artist's Forum. Thank you."

"Can I borrow his little tape recorder to catch all my impressions now for later?" Heidi calls out. They pretend not to hear her.

"Drink your milk," I say to Heidi, and she laughs, thank goodness, it makes her stop picking a fight with the entertainment. Titus Vanzetti had written three other poems on his way to us on the 401, sometimes with his companion asking, "Should we turn off here?" or "Pee break?" in the middle of them. These poems were awful, one was called a haiku, at least I knew who the first one he played was about. I wished he'd had a rendezvous with Nancy Greene or Margaret Trudeau. It wouldn't have been pleasant for her, but it would have made his pretentious poetry more interesting for me. His finale was an entire chapter from his Triller-nominated novel. (How that happened is Toronto's fault — they must be desperate for nominees.)

The other four what Heidi called *soi-disant* poets and writers followed. I thought, they find obscure things to write Broadway musicals around, but this stuff? Fifteenth-century war in Japan and animal husbandry? I did like the "exploration in sonnets series" about the ice castles people used to build on the St. Lawrence; I'm not a complete new poetry snob.

Written Word Lovers kept coming down the stairs during the readings, as well as a calico cat who definitely knew her way around. I asked Heidi, "Is that Sacco?" but the cat never strolled near Vanzetti, so we figured not. When the Writers part of the evening was finally finished, Titus came over at the break and asked Heidi where could he get some real food in this town. She suggested the Bar-B-Barn, unless his companion was a vegetarian. "My lady friend is bushed and went to her sister's, she's left me solo. I hope you'll change that scenario." Yes, but of course, he asked Heidi out. She said no thank you; she's only here tonight for Open Mike.

"Ouch! I guess I'll be raked over the coals."

"No, our friend Viola's ex-girlfriend will be."

"I didn't take you two for Sapphists."

"No, but you took our chairs."

He glared and lurched away, and I stared at Heidi.

"We're better off if people think we're lesbians, Lenore. That way creeps think we have an agenda and won't hit on us."

Cash Box Student was right, the place filled up for Open Mike, tons of people came down those stairs, and finally one of them was Viola. Heidi had been counting to make sure they weren't breaking the fire code. Viola took off her red duffel coat, and that's when we saw, in addition to lots of makeup and her hair tied back, she was in a long black tuxedo jacket and a Colonel Sanders tie, with black stockings and spike heels.

"Judy. *A Star is Born*," she said.

"Of course," said Heidi.

Then we noticed the guitar.

"A guitar, Viola?"

"Well, yes. I'll be singing. My own composition."

MC Woman overheard her. "Only one piece on your first visit, you know."

An original song on original guitar. This was going to be very scary. Viola would be second on the bill. And her only sympathetic audience was going to be Heidi and me, where was the rest of the Circle? Elspeth of Concordia? Beth of McGill? Friends from Viola's lab? Any of her Sisters of Sappho?

The first Open Mike performer was a "La Bolduc"-like singer who was back by such popular demand that she would do two songs. When she sang the first one, we could see why, this lady could sing les bleus in joual. Her second song was a ballad about the Laughing Lady in the Haunted House ride at Belmont Park. This brought back such wonderful memories, even though the Wild Mouse ride there scared me because I always thought the little rattly coaster would go off the rails and crash. I guess that's what made it fun, maybe that's what amusement rides are all about: they make you think they might kill you.

Then it was time for the Number Two spot: Viola Turcotte. You could tell her costume was a surprise to all.

"It's not exactly Yellow Door attire," said Heidi.

Viola in a poncho, swirly peasant skirt and sandals would have been just as bizarre to me.

"This Open Mike Night is a golden chance for me to share some of my pain with you, the horrible, relentless pain inflicted by someone I thought loved me but abandoned me," began Viola, in what was going to be a rant.

The MC looked at her watch, then showed Viola five fingers.

"It took nine years of my life to forge this song, but I'm being given the five fingers. I'm only granted three hundred seconds of your time to sing you the words I never got to say to Charlotte, once my own true love," said Viola.

She picked up her guitar and started to strum and then to sing. I wish I could say it sounded Joni Mitchell-y, but it didn't.

You've left an empty room
In the home
You called your heart
But now it's occupied
By a selfish, skinny tart.
O you say she's beautiful,
O you say she's fine,
But when I look into your soul,
I know your heart is lyin'.

There was nowhere to hide, we were stuck there, we were the friends of the Artist Formerly Known as a Pretty Normal Human Being. We would not get out of the Yellow Door alive. Casualties of Open Mike Night. Viola was sincere but she was terrible, we never knew she had such a scratchy, out of tune and angry singing voice. Heidi whispered, "Lenore, you may have to go in there. Sing over her, drown her out." There was silence from the audience. Viola forged on, yelling out:

Pain, pain, pain
Is all that's left for me?
Now that my room is taken
By another
And you've thrown away my key.
Your heart is occupied
By one who won't be true
Because I'm the only one
Who is truly meant for you.

That's when the Yellow Door began to fill with shouts. But not Go home! Who let her in here? No: "You tell it!" "So true, so true!" All white women, badly acting as if they were in that movie *Say Amen, Somebody!* The more Viola sang, the more they cheered and called out, "You're not alone!" "I hear you!" agreeing, repeating the words, and by the next time Viola got to "Your heart is occupied," they were all singing or crying. There were a lot of people in pain in that room, "selfish, skinny tarts" were not safe to walk the streets. When Viola finished, they stomped and cheered. The MC followed by the cat came to the Open Mike.

"Every so often, something this rare happens at Open Mike, and I must ask the first-time performer if she will share a second piece."

"I only completed this one. It took so much out of me," offered Viola.

"Can you do some Indigo Girls?"

"No, but I do have a piece I'm working on, it's in rough draft," Viola said.

"If you would do us the honour."

"First, maybe you all need to know Charlotte's a professional photographer in Toronto now," Viola told the crowd.

"Toronto . . ." people now murmured, as if she'd said Charles Manson.

Heidi had her head in her hands as Viola started to sing the piece she called "Charlotte's Web"

There's always someone taller,
There's always someone younger,
There's always someone skinnier
Waiting around the corner,
But I'm someone who's here.

The crowd shouted out, "But I'm someone who's here!"

There's always someone blonder,
There's always someone richer,
There's always someone wittier
Waiting around the corner,
But I'm someone who's here.

The crowd stood up for this and sang out, "I'm someone who's here!" As her song took a greater turn for the personal, the cat sat on the brown stool by the piano observing her.

Someone who's here
When your day in the darkroom's been doomed
Cause someone opened the door by mistake
And all your negatives got ruined.
If I could get an in-vitro dish
To whip together the perfect wish

And then give birth to the me who's best for you,
Don't you think that's what I would do?

Then she stopped and said, "Sorry, that's as far as it goes right now."

An elderly lady shouted, "It resonates my sinews! My old man left me for a bottle blonde!"

"Sing the first one please again!" the Child of Hippies called from her no-coffee counter.

"I'll sing it again and again if it takes all night," promised Viola, and she did, and the place went berserk. "It's like some Pentecostal revival meeting frenzy," observed Heidi. The all-male trio going on after Viola left, they knew they couldn't follow that act.

"Go share some show business adage to make her stop," Heidi told me. "This much adulation is not healthy."

This was a big task: who could get someone off the stage when the audience loved her that much? But I had enough training from Jamie and my short life in community theatre to know what to say. I went up and whispered to her, "Always leave them wanting more."

We led her away from the stomps and screams, up the stairs and out of the Yellow Door to the street. We took the diva back to her home at Madame Ducharme's house, her new digs since Charlotte who threw away the key had sold their beautiful Westmount home so she could move to Cabbagetown with the selfish, skinny tart. Viola said she had champagne in the fridge.

"It's been sitting there waiting for a celebration, you know, the one I thought I was going to have," she told us.

"Well, let's pop that cork!" said Heidi the Hypocrite, "because there's cause to celebrate: tonight a Star Was Born!"

"I think it may mean I'm over Charlotte," said Viola.

"Really?" I asked, Hypocrite Number Two, because that song did not sound to me like I'm Over You and Can Move On.

"Definitely over her. But it was amazing to see how others responded. I think I performed a group exorcism." All I could think was, she'd opened a lot of wounds.

Heidi and I kept it to ourselves, but we both wondered where everybody else was tonight, especially Elspeth. She called Heidi to explain the next day when she didn't know I was there. Daniel had given Heidi his speaker phone, so I got to hear the whole discussion.

"So where were you, Elspeth?"

"I was without car. Douglas has For Womyn Only."

"Why would he use your van?"

"Because he needed it for one of his inventions. And he's still not home. By the time I realized he'd purloined my means of conveyance, it was too late to make the train."

"There are buses. She needed you," Heidi dared to scold the Godmother.

"We can't all live in the heart of the city! I am stuck in Baie d'Urfé. No train, no van, no can go. I'm sorry I missed it."

"You don't mean that."

"Of course I do, it was a triumph!"

We both stared at the phone, then Heidi managed to ask, "Says who? Did the *Gazette* review it?"

"No, Viola said so, on her answering machine message. She even does a snatch of her song, very Melissa Etheridge. My inspired gift to her of *The Artist's Way* was not wasted. Her lyrics are so Week Three: Recovering a Sense of Power. Julia Cameron was right: Anger is fuel. Maybe Viola can do her song at my Pot Party."

"Pot Party?

"Yes. You and Lenore are invited. And any of her serving

wench sisters from Festin. I note second Saturdays are her night off, so I chose that."

"Maybe she's doing something with Benoît."

"She won't be."

"She could be. They may have plans."

"But they don't."

"How do you know?"

"You'd be more specific. You'd say, They're skating at Beaver Lake. He has Canadiens tickets. They're going to some policeman's ball. You'd know if there was anything special planned. If she can't come, she can't come, but you must, I need you to be here. You need to buy things to beautify your surroundings."

"By Pot Party you mean pots? Like Tupperware?"

"Tupperware? Never! This is highest end goods. Elijah's life-enhancing one-of-a-kind pottery and sculpture."

Benoît was on duty that second Saturday, so I was going to have to find another excuse. I didn't want to go near Elspeth's house ever again, not after the last time. She was monstrous, nothing could be more twisted than that Great Escape evening that had caused Viola to put that champagne on ice. Poor Viola had been through hell. Charlotte was pretty merciless about the break-up, she had had the house when they got together. "Viola's contributed, all these years, to all the decorating, renovating and maintenance, but it's always been Charlotte's house. So it was hers to sell without even listing it," Heidi told me when I found out Viola was being put out on the street once Charlotte moved permanently to Toronto.

"Couldn't Viola have rented it from her?"

"Charlotte said she could buy it, which is of course impossible because it's now worth over $300,000."

"So where is Viola going to go?"

"Madame Ducharme's house is free again. It shouldn't stay

empty. Viola would be a better tenant than your wannabe philanderer-if-you'd-let-him Wilder III."

Yes, I'd been pretty infatuated with Wilder III, but I hadn't fallen for him in the end. He was bad news for me, but he was a happy tenant and he did pay his rent. The Ducharme house had been empty since he fled back to Boston and his psycho girlfriend.

So my next visit to Tanguay prison to see Madame Reine Ducharme was once again about renting her property to someone we thought was a good bet. And for such une pauvre femme en need, Reine agreed right away. "Mais, elle a les prospects d'une autre blonde?" I said there was no new girlfriend in the picture yet for Viola, we think Viola's hoping Charlotte will leave the twenty-two-year-old child model and return to her. "Oh, oui! Et Cabbagetown, c'est pas Montréal!"

Madame said this was her lucky day. "Un jour formidable!" I was visiting, her house was rented, and today's mail had brought three interesting items. Numéro un: "les photos d'Hollywood de mes bébés." Jamie had sent the latest Polaroids of her miserable, spoiled little dogs. "Brioche et Montcalm semblent être contents en Californie," and she'd made the right decision when she let a star like Cotton Brady take her beloved petits chiens with her to live in Lotus Land. They had performed so realistically as this vedette's pets in *Garden of Secrets*. Was it possible that the téléroman would be rerun? She hadn't been able to tape it when they all watched it in the prison common room, which she calls le centre de cultures et de loisirs.

Why hadn't I recorded it? Why, I did not say: because the character loosely based on her goes free and the one based on me goes to the electric chair! Benoît was so cross when we watched it together, he said that's what comes of my associating with bad women. He doesn't like me visiting Madame because les femmes in here are not locked up just because of "les cheques bouncés et l'amour avec les gens méchants."

Numéro deux: Reine, it seemed, had a letter from the Feds: she would be moved to Joliette. "Joliette! C'est un beau penitentiary!" She might even get her own bungalow cell. It would be a much better place "pour composer mes mémoires." Because, numéro trois, Randall Kingfisher's *Saturday Night* magazine exclusive interview with her swung him a publishing contract he'll share with her. They're going to co-write her autobiography, in the form of letters from her to him.

Isn't there a law against benefiting from your crime? Randall Kingfisher claims her memoirs "ne sont pas sensationalistes," so publishing them is "un service au publique." A public nuisance is more like! Heidi was really mad when I told her about this development, but she was happy we got Viola a place next door to live, at an impossibly reasonable rent for Westmount, where we could keep a suicide watch over her.

The plane kept making me anxious. I was going to spend over two weeks away from home, but if I had too good a time abroad, I might have to pay for it, that's Heidi's Bad Travel Karma. I hoped not to catch it. Every time Heidi had a great holiday she paid for it when she got back. Her 1989 trip to Ireland was so fabulous all her house plants died because Beth got carpal tunnel syndrome and was in a wrist bandage and was so incapacitated that lifting anything was "pure torture," even putting a key in Heidi's door or dialling the phone to ask somebody else to look after Heidi's plants. And Beth didn't pick up the mail either, it was all over the hallway, including a letter from Revenue Canada that Heidi was being audited. It turned out all right, as it usually does whenever Heidi is aloof or huffy with men, the auditor asked her out and she had One Date. "He mistook my terror for flirtation," and she only had to pay a little bit of interest on her badly filed return. They went out to Eduardo's Bring Your Own Wine restaurant on Duluth; Mario was very handsome but "such a sad accountant stereotype." When the bill came, he pulled out a calculator and figured they'd made a mistake, and then he did the tip "to the pennies, Lenore" and put it on his credit card so the waitress couldn't get away with not declaring it, so that was it for Mario Fragapane.

Heidi had to endure the Visit of the Tax Man, but Viola had to put up with Elspeth's constant drop-ins. Suddenly, Elspeth declared that the next full moon we all had to be together for Viola's sake at her house in Baie d'Urfé. And we should be prepared to stay over. Heidi was suspicious.

"Is it going to be some sort of go-down-to-the-river cleansing ceremony?"

"It's too cold for her to expect us to Moondance in her garden." I hoped, anyway.

"It's never too anything for Elspeth, every visit gets weirder and weirder, have you noticed?"

I wish Elspeth had tried to make us Moondance or even break the ice in the Baie of Urfé because the ritual plan she concocted this time was so much more bizarre. She brought it up right after she boasted about her college days and how much better her life was in Greece before she wound up stuck with Douglas. He gave a nasty smile and filled his wine tumbler. Again. Elspeth looked directly at Heidi and me as we sat on big all-that's-missing-is-the-hookah pillows by the fireplace.

"Viola and I have been in deep discussion for some time now, since the divorce," said Elspeth.

Viola nodded.

"And what she revealed to me is that she wants a child," said Elspeth, and then she looked over at her own children, Northrop and Frieda.

A chill went to my heart; her tone suggested that all Viola had to do was pick one and he or she was hers.

"As you see by my progeny, I birthed the best of both species, a boy child and a girl child," Elspeth boasted.

"I have no preference, as long as it's healthy and it's mine," said Viola.

Heidi and I couldn't believe we were hearing this, and we were the ones who brought Viola here. She'd want to take one of these species home in Heidi's car.

Elspeth stared at Douglas and said to him, as if he was some servant, "It's time for Frieda and Northrup to go."

"Not yet," he said.

"Yes, yet. Now," Elspeth commanded. "Prepare them."

Douglas got up and the kids followed him out — to pack their little bags, I thought, so whichever one was chosen could leave right away. Elspeth threw two big birch logs into the fire, logs too pretty to wind up as firewood. "Viola has made inquiries," Elspeth said and beckoned to Viola to join her to address us from in front of the crackling fire.

"Inquiries where? Of whom? When?" Heidi asked. We knew that Viola had desperately wanted children and Charlotte hadn't, and that's what she thought had broken them up until she found out about the Child Model. But we figured the dream had stopped there.

"I've been so despairing because I want to have a baby," began Viola.

"So I told her to stop brooding and start breeding," Elspeth said.

Viola had talked to doctors and sperm banks and had all the details. She'd even looked through a catalogue of donors.

"A Book of Dads?" I asked.

"Yes. But there are no pictures, just basic details. Hair, eye colour, height, etc. But he would still be a stranger. And it can be very expensive, until it takes," Viola said.

"Up to $15,000, depending on the procedure," Elspeth said.

"Do you want us to help finance it? Is that what this soirée's about?" Heidi asked. Usually I'm the one who doesn't know what's going on, I couldn't believe Heidi didn't know where this was heading.

"We want you to finance it with your positive spirit, we want you to endorse it, even assist with this undertaking," said Elspeth. "We need you to be attendants, timing is everything, this is a very delicate procedure when not done conventionally, we want it to take the first time, and we've calculated that it will, tonight," said Elspeth.

Heidi stood up, she'd figured it out. "Oh no. No, no, no."

"Look at the beautiful children Douglas provided Elspeth," Viola said.

These two children from these two parents are one of the great mysteries of our age. If they didn't look so much like both of them, we'd be sure they were adopted. Viola, I wanted to say, you've always said Douglas was a repulsive user ne'er-do-well creep. Viola, I wanted to scream, he has no job, he makes his wife finance his patent schemes, he drinks too much, he never shaves or seems to have a bath, he wears awful shirts, he has that sneery laugh. No, don't! Don't do this. I would have said all this and Heidi would have said more, but his wife was in the room. His wife, the monstrous mastermind behind this fertility ritual.

"The full moon will bless us this night," Elspeth said.

"It will not!" said Heidi.

"Oh, don't be so Catholic, Heidi," said Elspeth.

"It has nothing to do with being Catholic. Okay, maybe it does, but Protestants, Jews, Hindus, Muslims, Buddhists, even feminists would agree that this is wrong, Viola, so wrong."

"This does not require her to do the deed with Douglas, if that's what's bothering you," Elspeth said calmly, and then she began to explain how the deed would be done.

It was like the scene in *The Big Chill* where Glenn Close offers up her husband, Kevin Kline, to her friend Mary Kay Place. Only in this movie of Viola's Life, it wouldn't be Kevin Kline, it would be Douglas. And it was going to involve a baby food jar, a hypodermic syringe, a diaphragm and Heidi or me running back and forth between bedrooms with the donation.

And Viola keeping her legs up in the air for an hour.

"This is depraved! We won't!" Heidi announced.

"You must," Elspeth said.

"No means no," I said.

Elspeth was disgusted with us. Fine! she would "help" Douglas, and then she would help Viola.

Douglas wandered back to the fireplace.

"What time do you think we can begin?" Elspeth asked him.

"By eleven o'clock. They'll be asleep."

"What if they wake up? How are you going to explain?" I wanted to know.

"They won't wake up. In any case, they've got very sophisticated minds," Elspeth declared.

I wanted to call Children's Aid on them that second. I grabbed Viola by the arm.

"Hey! Lenore, he's been good enough to offer!"

"For free?" I asked.

"Of course for free. He's capable of being a giving person."

"Not that giving," Douglas said with his weird laugh. "I mean, if a stranger gets $18,000 . . ."

"Fifteen. That's the whole price, the top price," stated Elspeth.

"And that's in US funds, eh?"

"No. It can be done in Canada. And that total fee includes the doctor and the insemination and all kinds of steps," said Viola.

"Which we won't be taking. Hey, do they throw in dinner with your friends? I think $8000 Canadian is a fair price."

"But this changes everything," said Viola.

"I expect it does," said Douglas.

Elspeth said, "You are vile."

"I'm still the best chance she's got."

"No, you're not! There will be other full moons," said Viola, who grabbed her duffel coat and marched out to Heidi's car. We followed her as Elspeth and Douglas started a screaming match sure to wake up the sophisticated-minded children.

"Why don't you ask your lover boy Elijah to help out?" was the last thing we heard Douglas shout at her.

"He's truly horrible," said Heidi as we drove away.

"I knew that," Viola said, "but they have such great kids. And Elspeth offered him up as a father. I didn't know he wanted money. I thought he wanted to help me out, that he could be pure of spirit."

When I told all this to Madame Ducharme on my next visit to Tanguay, she wanted to know why Elspeth hadn't offered up her amour Elijah. Certainly he might have been purer of spirit, and that way there would be no children in common. She wished Viola well. She'd heard stories about do-it-yourself-at-home pregnancy schemes but "avec les basters de turkey, pas les hypodermiques!" Maybe Viola should consider "La Chine." Many Quebecois had adopted beautiful girls from China, but they didn't come free either. She sighed.

Then she wanted my advice: did I think she should include in her memoirs the fact that she had a serious love letter pen pal?

"In the year she's had in prison, she's had more boyfriends than I have," lamented Heidi.

Reine and Heidi had something in common, they both had letter-writing beaux. Heidi's was Miles of Near Sheffield, Mme's was a nutcase in Utah who falls in love with women behind bars.

Our flight attendant was pregnant, really pregnant, at least seven months along. A sleazy man in an aisle seat kept asking her for "a more substantial pillow" and a better headset. I thought she could go into labour in the aisle and he'd lean over and say, "My pillow?" I was cranky, being judgemental of strangers, so this was what transference felt like, I transferred my fear onto something else. A Trip to England might mean romance/relationship for Heidi, but for me on that plane, it meant sheer terror! I could have taken one of those tranquilizers Madame Ducharme recommended, "Les Poppers," but I'd seen what mood-altering prescriptions can do, and I wanted to be a good flight companion and not comatose, I couldn't let on to Heidi that I AM TERRIFIED. We're over a very big ocean! We're going over it for hours and hours in the pitch dark. Even though I had crossed America twice in a plane — across the Grand Canyon and I'd just been to Hollywood and back — but that was in daylight.

I couldn't give in to an anxiety attack, I was there to have a good time, and once this flight was over, I'd be stuck on the other side of the ocean for sixteen days. I was already missing things, we'd only been gone an hour and forty-five minutes and I was already so homesick. I had to leave behind mon gars Benoît, my house, my competitors, my restaurant. It was the first time I'd left Festin du Bois alone since it became half mine. Dependable, smart managers were in charge, Daniel would look in every day. Benoît promised to keep my house "under police surveillance," and I was pretty sure he wouldn't run off to try and get into the Tourist Industry in Florida and put me into debt the way Fergie did or fall in love with somebody else while I was away.

I didn't go into much detail with Benoît about what didn't happen to Viola at Elspeth's Full Moon ceremony because I was afraid he might see it as illegal, somehow, and he can't stand Elspeth anyway. It's also pretty insulting to men and women, that whole scheme. I did tell him Viola had decided to celebrate her first birthday without Charlotte at Festin du Bois. Benoît said to make sure it was the best birthday she'd ever had. I was planning it as the most Judy Garland birthday she ever had, Judy always makes her get happy.

Viola was so loyal to me she did not choose to go over to Montreal's new theme restaurant sensation Les Nuits des Chevaliers for her fête. Everybody else had. It usually takes time for a theme restaurant to catch on, but not them, they'd only been open two months and had a year-long list of people waiting to sit at their Round Tables, despite the complaints from the Society for Creative Anachronism that they were not authentic. Daniel was sarcastic when we went on our spy mission to check out the competition. He called their establishment Nights Knights and asked me, "Does the plague come with the main course?" and "When do you think they'll show us the Bring Out Your Dead dessert cart?" He was just mad that evil can prosper. Tyler Garrow had vowed he'd get back at me for not selling out Festin to his corporation, and he had. Who'd think that someone with no chivalry could take a huge warehouse that should be a Price Club and turn it into a thriving medieval banquet hall? With live horses? Knights in shining armour and jousting? Who knew there was that much chain mail in Montreal? And how those damsels-in-distress waitresses in cone hats and long wispy Camelot dresses could work, I could not figure out. And how they didn't catch on fire, letting the customers smoke. Jocelyne complained that Daniel's and my "Pas Fumer / No Smoking" anywhere policy may make Festin distinct, but it keeps customers away. "C'est ridicule! C'est Montréal!" People here smoke, she insists.

Okay, so Les Nuits des Chevaliers was the hottest restaurant in town, but could they claim they hosted a birthday party as successful as the one Festin had for Viola?

Did I even think it would be that big a hit? Elspeth had just given Viola her present: *The Artist's Way*. Viola was puzzled by this big handbook for a gift. Elspeth was shocked that not one of us at the table had ever heard of such an invaluable guide. She even had plans to include it in next year's Women's Studies curriculum at Concordia. "It's a twelve-week program with exercises to help you recover your creativity." It would make Viola an aspiring or working artist. "But I'm a scientist," said Viola.

"A scientist with a broken heart who needs to heal," coached Elspeth. "This bible will lead you on a chiropractic spiritual path to higher creativity."

We all took a look through its pages, it had nice quotes from famous writers. Heidi made up a game, she had us all choose a number and that's the week we'd have to do. I chose Week Six and got: Recovering a Sense of Abundance. That sounded like fun.

"It's not fun, it's empowering!" Elspeth said.

"Thank you, Elspeth, I will start Week One on Monday," Viola had just promised, when there was a commotion at the front entrance.

Jocelyne rushed in, she'd been having a smoke outside on the steps when she saw Benoît pull up. "Le paddy wagon est ici! Avec . . . avec . . . mon dieu!"

That Benoît! I thought, he's going to pretend to arrest us. But he was up to way more than that. Our customers with a better view oohed and ahhed as Benoît escorted in someone who looked exactly like . . .

"LIZA MINNELLI!"

Viola stared. This was the best female impersonator anyone had ever seen. Whoever it was looked exactly like Liza, it was amazing. I didn't want to ruin the magic, but I had to ask Benoît, "Where did you find him? Her?"

"Comment? C'est ne pas une drag queen, c'est le vrai deal, Lenore. Ça c'est Liza Minnelli."

And it was. She was Liza. Liza Minnelli.

"Liza, she's in Montreal to make the movie, working title *Killer Bee*," Benoît said. "They make us close Boulevard René-Lévesque et Dorchester. I tell her about Viola and how much she love her Mama Judy and her. And how ma blonde makes her fête au Festin. Liza has time between the shots, so she tells me, Let's go!"

Liza walked over to the very shocked Viola and gave her a big hug and then kisses on both cheeks.

"Hi, sweetheart. Happy birthday."

And then she turned to me and said, "I've come to your Cabaret, old chum."

She sang them all, but she couldn't take all night because she had to get back to the set "for some big chase scene. And they've got me driving the car! Ha ha."

She made everybody at Festin sing "Cabaret" with her, then asked Viola to join her in "Maybe This Time" and changed all the references from "maybe he'll stay" to "maybe she'll stay." Viola had the best birthday of her life. And I realized that maybe this time I was lucky.

"That Benoît," Liza confided. "I don't make a habit of this, Lenny, ha ha. But who could say no to this gorgeous cop who's determined to do something truly special for his girlfriend?"

"Oh. Viola's not his girlfriend."

"I know that, Ha ha, Viola's the one with the broken heart, but you're the one throwing the party at your restaurant. Benny did it for you, Lenny. That guy's so out of his mind in love with you, sweetie! But tell me, why does he call you ma blonde when you're not?"

Liza sang "Mein Herr" with Jocelyne and got me to sing "New York, New York" with her as her finale and kissed us all goodbye, and Benoît gave her a police escort back to the set in the paddy wagon. The same one he borrowed six weeks later to get us to Mirabel and then drive the Fighting Flynn Family back to town.

Chapter Two

"What's Lara Flynn Boyle doing wearing a business suit in a movie about fly-fishing?"

Heidi's Pillow Book had put her to sleep before the movie started, she woke up to discover the in-flight movie was not *A River Runs Through It*.

"Because Lara Flynn's *The Temp*. Don't get mad, get even," I told her.

"What's she doing with that knife? Not gutting fish."

"She's sleeping and killing her way to the top of the secretarial pool." If she'd been awake, if she'd looked up the *EnRoute* movies usually scheduled for westbound flights, she'd know they'd switched West for East.

"Charming. Oh well, it could be worse. Daniel got *Basic Instinct* last time he took a plane."

"I had *Alien 3* going to Los Angeles."

"Poor you. It was so gratuitous, her being bald."

"Sigourney's hair was all back for the Oscars."

"It must be strange seeing movies now after you've sat near the real live stars at the Dorothy Chandler."

"I don't think Lara Flynn Boyle was there, anyway I didn't see her, so I can take this movie as a story, a really bad story."

Heidi had a point, it is sort of unreal seeing movies now, I guess that will wear off someday. It's still kind of unbelievable that I was there. I guess Liza Minnelli was good practice for all the star-gazing to come. The Oscar nominations weren't even announced when Jamie gave me his call from Hollywood and booked me.

"You can't go to England in March. March 29, mark it on your calendar, you're coming with us to the Oscars!"

"Even if Cotton's not nominated?"

"But she will be. Or thousands will die. She's paid her dues, she says, it's her time, and I think many in the industry would agree. She was a revelation in *Night of Plenty*. And it's such a rags-to-riches saga, the film in the can for two and a half years, almost not being released. And then of course her performance!"

"But won't *Gamon de Pycombe, Dog of the Titanic* hurt her chances? When the voters see what we did in that —"

"It's got a new title, chickepen. And Hallmark won't broadcast *Titanic Dogs* till May, so we're safe. And they're already saying she'll be robbed if she doesn't get a Golden Globe nomination next year for *Garden of Secrets*."

"Oh Jamie, you don't believe that, do you?"

"Like I have a choice? I live and breathe her hype, it's exhausting, but we're ready to ride the Oscar train."

He was singing another Hollywood tune when he called me once Cotton Brady really did get nominated.

"I thought the fights with her over the For Your Consideration campaign for Supporting Actress would be the worst battle I'd go through! The studio put her up for Supporting under her protest. You saw her on the *Today Show* right after they announced the nominations?"

"Yes, she was very gracious," I told him.

"If not for me, she would have mouthed off all over NBC —

she was the Best Actress, she carried that picture. The years this has added to my age, chickepen."

"Think of how many more years if she hadn't been nominated."

"Yes, but we had a confidentiality agreement with NBC, they weren't going to interview her if she wasn't nominated, but she was, thank the heavens."

"I guess now she's even more high-strung and full of herself."

"Ego as big as the universe and still expanding. But Miss Hissy Fit is not the problem, it's this Chérie Sternschuss."

"Who's that? One of those executive producers?"

"I wish. No. Chérie Sternschuss is a stylist. And she is deciding what Cotton will wear to the Oscars. She's the frumpiest thing you've ever seen, and she's saying no Balenciaga, no Vera Wang, no Bob Mackie. Which I do agree with, Mackie did *The Carol Burnett Show*, we can't remind the Academy of Cotton's TV sitcom past."

"But by the time Cotton's wearing the gown, she's at the Oscars and they've voted, haven't they?"

"Word gets out, it gets out!"

To think that Jamie changed from an IBM engineer and a star of Montreal community theatre life into a *Sunset Blvd* press secretary/handler/houseboy in one quick step. It was always his dream to get to Hollywood, but it's all my fault he got mixed up with Cotton Brady. I kept hoping that he would wind up in TV or the movies, even though he hadn't had a walk-on or even been a day extra. The dogs and Cotton Brady had the careers, not him.

"At least he's integral to Cotton Brady's survival and not some sycophant," said Heidi, and once I figured out how to spell sycophant and was able to look up what it meant, I had to agree.

Even though I knew he was wasting his true talent.

Lucky for me, Heidi and I planned to spend sixteen days in England, so I couldn't take too much time for California. Four days there was long enough.

The studio publicist decided Cotton's bungalow in Pasadena was too TV-starish, so they'd moved into a lavish apartment hotel for all the interviews and hoopla before the awards. Cotton was thrilled to see me.

"My bijou girl! Sweetie pie! My lucky star! Monty! Bagel! Look who came to stay with us!"

Montcalm et Brioche didn't recognize me at all. These maudits chiens had lived in my house, destroyed my couch, made me enrol in dog school and wind up as their handler and an extra on a movie set, and they didn't know me, even by smell. I took pictures of them for Reine Ducharme with their cadeaux: chew toys she asked me to buy and new little sweaters she'd made on a loom at Joliette. They were for walks along the beach. She'd seen photos of Marilyn Monroe in a sweater by the Malibu surf, so she knew the sweaters could come in handy à la plage.

Cotton smoked even more like a fiend, her hands were so nicotine stained they looked as if they'd been hennaed. And she was popping every pill that came her way like they were M&Ms. "For the stress, doll."

"All prescribed! They are painkillers, Jay!" she'd scream whenever Jamie preached, "Moderation, not too many dolls, Miss Neely O'Hara!"

The afternoon I arrived, Chérie Sternschuss was coming over with the final selection of dresses. She had promised Valentino and Versace.

"What about the jewels?" Cotton asked Jamie.

"We've got to stop holding out for Harry Winston's," he said.

"No. Only Harry Winston's. That's what I deserve."

"Chérie knows all he has left are under eight hundred thousand dollars. Peanuts."

"I'm not wearing costume jewellery!"

"Exactly. That's why I've got calls out. Only to Rodeo Drive, don't fret," Jamie said.

"To who? Fred Leighton? Chanel? Gimme names."

"No. That will jinx it. But it looks very, very good," Jamie said.

Chérie stormed in. Jamie was right: she was a frump. It was hard to believe that Sternschuss, translated from German, meant shooting star.

"I have not slept in sixty-eight hours," was the first thing she said.

"Then how come she looks like an unmade bed?" Jamie cracked to me. He can be so mean.

Chérie schlumped down on the couch and almost crushed Bagel-Brioche. Soon she and Cotton were discussing gowns through a cloud of smoke.

"So where are they?" Jamie had to know.

"That's the thing, Cotton has to go to the mountain," Chérie pronounced.

"I'm not going with you to the designers."

"You haven't liked anything I picked, Cotton. It impresses them when the star does a turn. That's how everyone is locking in the best dresses. They're hiding the truly boffo stuff from the stylists. Michelle Pfeiffer grabbed, like, eight Randolph Dukes, and she's keeping them till the day, when she'll decide which one to wear," Shooting Star said.

"They can't allow that. What a hoarder."

"Well, they let her. Emma Thompson and Susan Sarandon arrived at Valentino's the same afternoon and —"

"I should have been up for Best Actress! Supporting's narrowed my gown field of choice!"

"Come with me in person and grab everything we like, and then we'll do the shoes," Chérie said, trying to pull Cotton off the couch.

"I want Lenny to come as my good luck charm," Cotton said.

"Good. She can fight off Miranda Richardson if she shows up. I hear she's a crying-game baby cause she hasn't found the perfect dress yet. And the more hands to grab gowns, the better."

I once thought that the designer came to the star with one dress he'd created especially for her, but it's not like that. Stars have to go to their upscale schmatte district, where they've got the gowns on racks. The designers let the nominees wear their dress for free in front of the entire movie-watching planet because that can make them world famous designers of evening wear, if they aren't already. Then everyone wants a copy of the gown, so that's how they make their millions. If I was ever nominated, I would not go through the nightmare of competing for the best dress left on the rack. I'd have Montreal's own Simon Tratt, who did the fabulous costumes for our musicals, design me a dress. Especially since I did just that, by mistake.

Of course, that was a big surprise, all I did was call and ask if I could borrow "The Party's Over" dress I wore as Ella in *Bells Are Ringing*. Simon scoffed, "Of course not, you silly, silly woman. I'll design you an Oscars gown, for cost. My time will be free, darling, all I ask is you pay for the material and do me the honour of wearing my original creation to the Academy Awards."

After we pulled seven designer dresses from the racks, Cotton went off with Chérie to get the shoes, and Jamie took me to the jewellers. We drove along Rodeo Drive, then down a side street — we were not to tell Cotton we were getting back-alley goods. It was still a pretty swanky place: Balakrishnan's. His specialty, Jewels of India, featured the most sparkling diamonds I'd ever seen. He was willing to loan Cotton dangling moonstone earrings, bracelets and a necklace, net worth 6.5 million dollars. The only condition was that they be seen on the Oscar telecast. And that seemed an easy promise because when they announce a nominee, the TV shows her acting as if she's not nervous, in her seat, wearing all the glittering borrowed hardware.

So Jamie signed for Cotton. He initialled the clause that said should Cotton fail to comply, Balakrishnan's would require her to purchase the jewels or face being sued for misrepresentation. Mr. Balakrishnan promised that an armoured van would bring them over on Oscar morning. "Right after the hair and makeup has been done for the leading lady."

"Uh, for the supporting lady," Jamie informed him.

"Supporting category?"

"Yes. I guess this changes everything?"

"No. But Madame's performance in *Night of Plenty* was not supporting. Without her strength of character, there was no story."

"She couldn't agree with you more," Jamie said.

It was strange to be in Hollywood but not get to see much of it. Jamie was all caught up in Oscardom so he couldn't be a tour guide, and he was so stressed out that it would have been disloyal not to help him in any supportive way I could. So my lost opportunities were Disneyland, Universal Studios, driving down the coast in a red convertible with the top down, and sticking my hands in the sidewalk at Grauman's Chinese. I did see the Hollywood sign up on the hill, but we didn't get to pose by it or on it the way I dreamed I would if I ever got to LA. My entire visit was Cotton and the interviews and the gifts and flowers and the dogs yapping around her agent or her publicist or her psychic or some suit from the studio. The Scientologists even dropped in, but she wasn't buying. Every so often somebody famous would show up to chat or lend support. At first it was a big thrill when *Salt and Pepper*'s Valerie Singleton came over. Valerie looked exactly the same, the years and years had not changed her, it was freaky. Jamie said, "Well, yes, she's had more restoration work than the Sistine Chapel."

Her skin had a weird lustre, very smooth but lizardy at the same time. They snuck her in the back entrance so as not to remind Academy voters that Cotton was actually her TV co-star who'd managed to be in a low-budget independent picture that got her nominated for an Oscar. Valerie was such a real friend to Cotton that she gave up an entire afternoon to help Cotton rehearse her acceptance speech.

"Sugar, I have to say it, I'm not hearing sincere," Valerie said, puffing away.

"She's not that good an actress," cracked Jamie.

"Nothing scripted! I'll go with, what's it called, the moment," Cotton said.

"No, no, no," yelled Jamie and Valerie.

"Why not?"

"We can't have a 'You like me. Right now, you like me!' fiasco!" shouted Jamie.

"And why not? Everyone said she was emotional and sincere. And look at Sally, TV didn't stop her, they gave her two Oscars."

"She did *Sybil* for TV, Cotton. *Night of Plenty* is your first big dramatic screen chance, anywhere," said Valerie.

"So they should give it to me for proving myself. And I'm

the only American nominated with all those damn Aussies and Brits."

"You are not," Jamie told her.

"I am so, that other one, she's Italian."

"She's American. From Flatbush. Brooklyn."

"She's nothing but a tough, cheap little Italian moll in a comedy! They better not give it to her! Or to any of those limeys with the accents, especially that Joan Plowright, she already got hers five years ago!"

"No, she didn't. You're mixing her up with Dame Peggy Ashcroft," Jamie said.

"Is there any more Zinfandel? Anyway, we all know my only real competition is Vanessa Redgrave."

"Sweetheart," Valerie said, "you think the Academy will let *Red*grave back on her soapbox after 1977? The way she mouthed off about the PLO?"

"Oh yeah, the PLO," said Cotton, who had no idea what the letters stood for. "In '77? That was a long time ago, you think they remember?"

"They remember us, don't they? I mean, other than Lucy and Ethel, who else do they name first as a classic female comedic duo? Huh?" And that's when Valerie looked at me.

"Hmm?"

"Name one, go on, Lenore. A female TV combo more beloved than us."

"After Lucy and Ethel," Cotton said.

"Mary and Rhoda?"

"Mary and Rhoda!" Valerie repeated it over and over, and she and Cotton laughed like it was the biggest joke they ever heard.

"I told you she was refreshing," Cotton said to Val, wiping tears of laughter from her eyes.

It's interesting and scary to see two people in mutual self-delusion. This was how they've survived Hollywood so long.

"They remember everything, Cotton, and you, you are an American icon. The Oscar's yours. So no winging your speech. In my humble little ol' opinion, for what it's worth, I mean it's up to you, darling, but I think you should leave out thanking your grade school teacher and the pooches —," advised Valerie.

I was taken in, I told Jamie they had real rapport. Valerie was a loyal friend.

"Yeah, a friend who wants to make sure Cotton thanks her in her acceptance speech," said Jamie, too jaded by Hollywood to believe in women's friendships. He refused to see how we can bond, especially instantly the way I did with Casey McCordick.

One of the many things the studio let Cotton spend money on as a Supporting Star was a dog-walker. Casey would show up twice a day to exercise Brioche et Montcalm. I started joining her just to get a breath of smoke-free air and talk to someone who was a real person. On our first walk, she had some questions she wanted answered about her clients.

"Do you call Bagel and Monty French names because you're from Montreal?"

"Yeah, and because they're from Montreal, too. I knew them before they were the Hollywood stars they are today."

And that's when Casey found out their real owner, Madame Reine Ducharme, was in maximum security prison because she had poisoned six people she served jury duty with on the trial of a vicious serial killer who got a not-guilty verdict.

"No way! Has someone done anything with that scenario yet?"

"*Garden of Secrets* for ABC. Starring Cotton Brady as Mrs.

Charmin and Bagel and Monty here as her pets. I got stuck being their handler for a dog picture they got cast in last year about the *Titanic* and starring Cotton. She wanted me to come to Pasadena to be her assistant, and I said no."

"Smart move," said Casey, "but Jay got stuck with it. How come he calls you chickepen?"

"It's a nickname from *The Unsinkable Molly Brown*. We met doing community theatre musicals together, he adores show business too much."

"He must, to put up with her."

Dog-walking was of three jobs Casey kept to support "her habit": believing she could make it in Hollywood. "As an actress?" I asked her. "No, worse," she said, "as a screenwriter. A trashy mind like mine can't go wasting away doing something useful in Cable, Wisconsin." She'd been told you had to be in LA to get an "in," but that had proven wrong so far, even though there was hope, her play *Frankenstein in Ireland* got a staged reading in January.

She was too young to have ever seen Cotton and Val in *Salt and Pepper*, but, she figured, "Cotton must have been pretty funny. Because she's funny now. She's so self-involved and almost horrible. Quite campy. Only I don't think she knows it."

She agreed with me: Valerie and Cotton had a bond.

"One might even dare to say that what they have is genuine, or as close to genuine as you can get in this town," Casey said.

"Jamie thinks Val only wants to be thanked from the podium."

"Who wouldn't? A billion people will hear it. A billion people!"

Casey has given herself three years. Then at age thirty, she'll face facts. "If Casey has struck out, she's struck out. I'm not going to be one of the Do You Know the Way to San Jose people. Staying on when their chances are past."

"If you leave, bring Jamie with you."

Casey saw how much of a doormat Jamie was for Cotton. But she wasn't sympathetic.

"Don't Cry For Me, Argentina. He's a grown boy. He can say no. But sometimes it's impossible once you get sucked into this vortex."

When she said vortex, it made me homesick for Heidi. This was the first time since I arrived that someone had used a smart word like vortex. "Jamie's not cleaning pools. Or houses. He doesn't have to wait tables, pack boxes in a warehouse, do telemarketing or pull a midnight-to-six shift at a 7-Eleven, or even be her gigolo to be in Hollywood. He's got a sweet if shallow life going for himself."

The day came, and Chérie Sternschuss had come through. They'd made the final choice, and Cotton had the designer dress of dresses, it was exquisite, along with an Armani purse and the seventy-five-thousand-dollar shoes and ten-thousand-dollar stockings with diamonds in them that no one was going to see. The Brinks truck arrived on time with the jewels for Madame. Cotton would look like a goddess, everything was going so well. But. Except for. She'd downed the first anti-depressant at eight a.m. with her vodka and cranberry juice. Her reason: she was angry that she'd been denied the *Entertainment Tonight* "Day in the Life of Oscar Nominee" feature in which *ET* follows you, the nominated star, from morning till night, how you get ready, if you win, if you don't, what you say at the parties afterwards. I told her I always wondered about letting people record this big day, as if it wasn't extreme enough. Imagine if you lose? "But I'm not going to lose, Little Typhoid Molly!" Cotton shrieked that she'd been "slighted! slapped in the face!" *ET* was the reason she had her first tantrum of the day. And her first Xanax.

"It should be ME! Denzel Washington did TV once too! Have they ever forgiven him for *St. Elsewheres*?"

"*Elsewhere*, Cotton, and it was a good show," Jamie said.

"So was *Salt and Pepper*, Jay. And what kind of day in the life can Denzel show them better than mine?"

"I think he has a lovely wife and family. And they pray and go to church."

"Wife and kids. Who cares? Does he have cute little woofy doggies like these?"

Brioche et Montcalm barked in unison from their seats at the table. Jamie changed the channel that had made the "Tomorrow on *ET*" announcement.

Five minutes later, Cotton was mad because Nick the Greek had handicapped her at ninety-to-one.

"Go back to Mount Olympus! Or Athens! Wherever you're from!" she screamed at the TV.

"I believe he's from here," Jamie said.

"Oh, we're all from here now, Jay. Where we're from before is what counts," she said, then fell into a nap.

We roused her in time to get her into the limo with Chérie for the hairdresser and makeup artist, she was mad and pouting because they weren't coming to her. She tried to take a Valium, but this time Jamie headed her off at the pass.

When Cotton got back she looked sensational, she went straight to her boudoir and started yelling, "Where are they?"

"Down the toilet," Jamie yelled back. I knew he wasn't lying because I'd helped him.

"We tossed your crutches, Cotton. You're going to do this sober or as straight as I can get you, you're an actress for heaven's sake, pretend."

"I need my dolls! Gimme my dolls!" she whined.

"You don't need them, Cotton," Chérie said. "I'll show you some simple yoga exercises, they'll help centre you."

"Yoga? I don't have time to learn yoga now! Doesn't it take years and years just to be able to cross your legs?"

Chérie somehow convinced Cotton to follow her out, alone, to the sundeck for Quick and Easy Yoga. And it worked, because Cotton was way calmer when Chérie left her with these parting words: "You're so beautiful, Cotton, but what you've got ahead of you, ich bin asoy off spilkis — I'm on pins and needles."

The stretch limo picked us up at three o'clock, even though the awards didn't start till six LA time. The limos are so lined up it can take forever just to get to the Dorothy Chandler. The only VIPs allowed in the limo were Cotton, Jamie, me (special dispensation) and a studio exec. But not one exec wanted this honour, Cotton was just too high maintenance for any of them. Chérie attempted to get the empty executive position, but Cotton nixed that, she insisted Brioche et Montcalm occupy that spot. However, Calhoun the driver refused, he had no clearance for animals and anyway, he said, it wasn't fair to the dogs, being left in the limo for such a long time. Cotton pronounced, "We'll pick up that Casey, she can get out and walk them if they have to do their little widdles. Call Casey, get Casey!" Jamie said, "Her gig is over. And the dogs won't let us leave them behind. You'll have to take them on the red carpet, and they'll steal your focus, Cotton."

That did it, we handed the dogs off to the hotel bell captain for return to the suite, and off we went. That was a lucky escape because we were stuck in the limo for two and half hours, usually not moving. All you can do is wait and get more nervous and, in Cotton's case, drink all the champagne.

She and Jamie had a screaming tug-of-war that made Calhoun yell at them.

"Hey, hey, back there! Don't make me stop this car."

"He won't give me my Moët!"

"Give Miss Brady the Moët!" Calhoun told Jamie.

"No more till after the awards ceremony. Then she can have all the Moët she wants. She can drown herself in it!"

"I won't thank you in my acceptance speech."

"Then I'll say it myself. I'll be there, anyway, propping you up, Miss Days of Wine and Roses," Jamie said.

"Don't be so mean. It's my big night, Jay. My Big Night of Plenty. One more glass. One little glass." Jamie gave in, the way he always does. He poured her more bubbly, but Cotton didn't want it in one little glass, she grabbed the bottle and held it like a baby.

"It's mine, all mine, even if the studio's only splashed out for this cheap fifty-dollar-a-bottle plonk, they think I wouldn't notice? " she slurred. "Jamie! I'm nervous! And I am going out there in front of the world."

"Stumbling? Mumbling? You wanna be rolled along on the red carpet?" Jamie shouted.

"I wanna be brave enough to walk on it. I am terrified, Jamie! To them I'm a TV star. Cotton Brady. Cotton Brady Bunch is what they think."

"They do not!"

"I'm not Hollywood!"

"You are too Hollywood. You're nominated for an Oscar for God's sake! You're stunning, Cotton. You look like 7.5 million bucks."

Even this cheerleading didn't help. Cotton had stage fright, or red carpet fright. All her obnoxious bravado and divadom was to hide the fact that she was scared to death. Mad as she was when they had snubbed her, she was even more scared they finally noticed her. She chugged the rest of the champagne. And then she passed out.

"I've got to get her to Cedars," Jamie said, slapping her lightly on the face.

"The hospital? Can't we just drive around some block three or four more times? Or go to the back of the line? Till she revives?"

"She's gotta revive now. Cotton, wake up, honey! Wake up! Oh, dammit! They've got to pump her stomach, not a pretty sight. It's happened before. The week before the nominations were announced, she overdosed," Jamie confessed as Cotton sort of came to.

"But all she's had is too much champagne. We flushed all her dolls away," I said.

"Or did we?" Jamie said and grabbed Cotton's $64,000 Armani handbag.

Jamie pulled out vials of pills. He read the labels: "'Prozac . . . Ativan . . . as needed. Chérie Sternschuss.' So much for Quick and Easy Yoga. Sternschuss Feel Good."

"I'll go with her to Cedars. When we pull up, you get out, you've always wanted to go to the Oscars, Jamie," I said.

"I know. But I owe her, Lenore. Besides, I can't wear these jewels in the crown on camera."

That's when he started taking the Balakrishnans off her.

"Will we drive up anyway and ask some star to wear them?"

"A star is right here," he said handing the necklace and earrings to me.

"Me? I can't wear 6.5 million dollars worth of jewels."

"If you don't, Cotton has to buy them, remember? Play or Pay."

"But no one will see them on me, I'm in the balcony."

"Not anymore, gorgeous, you're in the house, you're in Cotton's seat, and a very lucky seat sitter will be in the other." Jamie slipped the bracelets on me and handed me Cotton's Armani evening bag.

"You'll join me, somehow, later?" I said.

"No way. This is gonna be a long and bumpy night, and I can't leave her," Jamie said. "You go. You know her speech. If they ask, say she's had an allergic reaction to cough medicine."

The limo pulled up to the curb, and I got out to walk along the runway of world fashion that's the Oscars red carpet wearing 6.5-million-dollar baubles and bangles and a thirty-two dollar dress.

Everyone was trying to figure out who I was, especially security. But I had all my papers, the official invitation and three tickets. Even at this moment, I knew I could not let the extra tickets go to waste. I walked over to the stands set up for the cheering fans, thrusting their hands out for me to shake even though I was nobody anybody knew, until I heard, "Lenore! Lenore!"

It was Casey McCordick.

"Casey! Casey. Cotton was just asking for you."

"Where is she? I'm here to wish you all good luck, send good vibes, it's insane up here," Casey shouted back.

"It's gonna get even more insane if you can come on down here, cause you're going to the Oscars with me!" and I flashed Jamie's ticket at her for proof.

"Oh my God! Oh my God!" she screamed and finally got down to me, but we couldn't head in yet.

"I still have my ticket for the balcony. Do you know anyone else here?"

"Everyone I know had to work. But whoever gets it from these stands has to deserve it," Casey said.

She looked up into the crowd and shouted, "WHO IS OUR GOOD NEIGHBOR TO THE NORTH?"

"Oregon!" a man shouted.

"Alaska!" another patriot yelled.

"Canada! Canada!" a very smart girl yelled.

"What do you do for a living?" Casey asked her.

"I'm an actress-model. Waitress. I'm a waitress," the girl yelled.

I shouted up to the waitress, "Come on down! You're sitting in the balcony!"

"Is this really for real?" the smart waitress asked when she joined us.

"None of this is, but let's go with it, eh?" I said and handed her the balcony seat pass.

"Thank you, thank you so much! I didn't know you were from Canada. Oh, you should have been nominated this year. You were robbed!" she said, hugged me and ran off to get her balcony seat.

"My God, you do look fabulous, Lenore. But I'm not dressed for the good seats," Casey said, in her University of Wisconsin Green Bay cut-off t-shirt.

"Sure you are, you've got this," I said and handed her Cotton's Armani purse. "Let's go."

I was asked by three different television gossip reporters where I got my dress. "Simon Tratt de Montreal," I announced clearly and distinctly.

When I told Casey the real story of why Cotton was a no show, she had some advice.

"Oh no, not the cough medicine defence. Say a tragedy has befallen her family."

"That's not true, that's bad luck."

"It's no one human, it's one of the dogs. A rare canine fever that happens to small breeds, and it's highly contagious, and Cotton didn't sleep for days, nursing Bagel, and was so unselfish she wouldn't take the dog to the vet for fear of infecting other small dogs." Casey said this in such a just-the-facts-ma'am way that even I believed her.

"You're very good and very fast," I said to Casey.

"A woman and her dog, an American love story."

It wasn't until we got into our seats that it hit me. "What if Cotton wins?"

"She won't. She can't. Impossible. Against that competition?"

"Miracles happen. And Cotton was really good in *Night of Plenty*. I didn't recognize her performance."

"Yeah, she was phenomenal, but not weighed against this calibre of actresses, one of them is Lady Olivier, for heaven's sake."

"But what if all the actresses with accents split the vote? Or they decide to go for the red, white and blue underdog? Look at *Rocky*."

"*Breaking Away*, Cloris Leachman, *Marty*! You're right, there is a precedent," Casey agreed.

"And Cotton wins? I'll have to go up there and give that speech!"

"No, forget that speech, you're not even going to paraphrase it. It's cloying, cringey, disgraceful, it's not happening, okay? What you'll do is thank the Academy, say how honoured Cotton was to be in the company of such esteemed actresses, that this is the greatest moment of her career, possibly her life so far, but she had a family emergency. Thank her director, her co-stars, then Jamie, Val, mention your restaurant in Montreal by name, and use whatever time you've got before the band starts playing to laud the bravery and vision of small independent filmmakers."

Billy Crystal rode out on a giant Oscar pulled by Jack Palance, who did some more one-arm push-ups, and the sixty-fifth Academy Awards ceremony had begun. Everything else was a scary blur till the Supporting Actress category was out of the way. I was a wreck. Since they go alphabetically, Cotton Brady was named first, and the entire Oscar viewing world saw me in the 6.5-million-dollar jewels and thought, "Wow, has Cotton Brady ever changed." As the names of the other nominees were called, I was praying, "Please not Cotton, please oh please not Cotton." Finally the winner was announced, and no one was happier than me when Jack Palance flubbily said:

"Marisa Tomei."

The "cheap little Italian gangster moll in a comedy" had beaten them all, she was more shocked than anybody, and Casey whispered, "Do you think he read out the wrong name? There was some hesitation there."

Even though I felt badly Cotton didn't win because I knew she'd be devastated when she revived, I was totally selfish and so happy I didn't have to go up there in front of the world, much as Jamie, Valerie, Festin and independent filmmakers needed the plug.

I settled down for the rest of the ceremony. When Clint Eastwood was a huge winner for *Unforgiven,* I thought of all the time I put in watching his bad movies with Fergie. Now here I was, seeing Clint in real life, only three rows away from me. Elizabeth Taylor was there, in fabulous jewels; Casey whispered, "But can she say the rocks she's wearing once belonged to a maharanee?" They presented Liz with the Jean Hersholt Humanitarian Award, and they gave another one to Audrey Hepburn for all her work with UNICEF, but she wasn't there of course because we lost her in January. Audrey was so wonderful, Heidi's made sure I've seen all her best work. It's interesting that they give movie stars Academy Awards not just for best acting but for being good citizens of the world, too. Then the Oscars were over, people were heading off to the famous lavish parties, so I handed Casey all the invitations.

"Are any of your friends off work by now? Two of them can join you at the Governors Ball," I told her.

"I'm not going without you," Casey said.

"You can make important contacts, keep the Armani till tomorrow," I said. "I can't go, I've got to get to the hospital."

"Can't I go with you? You never know when you'll need another cough medicine twist."

Since the limo was hired for the night, Calhoun was there to drive us to the hospital. He'd even managed to snake his way up to the front of the notoriously endless limo lineup, citing an emergency. When I introduced Calhoun to Casey, he said, "Casey? Hey, Miss Desmond was calling for you earlier." He found Casey's Adventures in Oscar-Going just too fascinating.

Cotton was in ICU flanked by monitors, Jamie at her side. My getup and maharanee jewels and the passes in the Armani purse convinced the nurses that we were part of Cotton's entourage. That and pretending they believed Casey's story that we were Cotton's daughters.

Jamie jumped up and hugged me and then collapsed.

"The biggest night of her life and she missed it." He sobbed quietly.

But he'd missed it too, and he looked so handsome in his Dolce & Gabbana tails. This Oscar Night was one of his big dreams dashed, but all he cared about was Cotton. Really.

"She works her entire career for something this big, and she ruins it with pills and liquor, it's all my fault," he whimpered, buried his face in his arms and leaned across the passed-out Cotton.

"Don't be such a drama queen," Casey said.

Jamie pulled himself up.

"I have to be. It's my fault."

"It's not your fault, it's hers. She took the pills, she drank the champagne. It was her choice to ruin things for herself. And face it, she ruined things for you too. You put in all this time for her, turned your back on your own life, and this is how she repays you?"

Jamie had stopped crying. He was in awe.

"Wow, are you a motivational speaker?"

"No, I had to go to Al-Anon meetings because of my brother," she said. "This might be the totally disgusting kick-in-the-pants embarrassment Cotton needs to make her get sober."

"But where does she go from here?"

"Betty Ford for starters."

"Okay. Okay, it'll be For Her Consideration."

Jamie knew Cotton hadn't won.

"I wasn't all that devoted by her gastric-lavage sickbed. They were watching the Oscars in the nurses' station, and I asked Keisha to come get me when they did the supporting category. And the Best Song musical numbers," Jamie said.

He'd had an incredible fantasy: that when Cotton came to, he'd be standing there, holding up her Oscar. (The one I would have had to accept on her behalf in front of the entire world.)

"Who thought they'd go with an American? Marisa Tomei, talk about your dark horse," Casey said.

"Even seated, you in the Simon Tratt Original and the jewels looked smashing, Lenore, sensational," Jamie said. "But were you praying? Your lips were moving."

"I was so nervous." I didn't completely lie.

Keisha came in to check Cotton's IV. "I told you, Jamie, you don't want to be here when that activated charcoal starts doing its work. It's not very attractive. You go home, get some sleep, or get out to some of them Oscar parties."

"And I told you, I'm going to be here all night, I want to be here when she wakes up in the morning," he said.

"Just like Atticus is for Jem in *To Kill A Mockingbird*," Casey said.

"I never saw that," Jamie said.

"Shame. Bet you would have, if it was a musical," Casey said.

I caught Keisha looking over at me.

I thought she was about to say, There are too many people by her side. How come you took all the ICU visitor chairs? You look like the Seven Dwarfs by Snow White's bed, waiting for her to wake up. But instead she said, "Pardon me, but girl, you've got the haute couture going, and you're so glittery, like a true movie star. I can't take my eyes off those diamonds."

"They're something, eh? Wanna try them on?"

"Oh no. All I wanted was a better look at them."

"No better way than up close and personal," I said, and Casey helped me take them all off and put them on Keisha. Her fuchsia nurse's uniform really set them off well.

"Oh my Lord," Keisha said.

"Come look at your gorgeous self in the mirror." Casey led her into the ICU bathroom. I followed them in, we all gazed at beautiful Keisha.

"I'll remember this the rest of my life. Thank you," she said when we took off the jewels. "Too bad the rest of my rounds won't be this fine and spectacular."

When Keisha left, Casey spun another story. "What if Keisha wasn't really a nurse? What if she was here to get the goods because she's a jewel thief, or worse, a Hollywood reporter? Or what if she's a nurse who convinces you to let her have her picture taken in the gems and then sells her Polaroid to *USA Today*? And that makes Mr. Balakrishnan's store so mad they sue Cotton? Or it turns out the jewels were stolen from some maharanee?"

"Does your mind work like that all the time?" Jamie asked.

"Much more so now that I'm in Hollywood," Casey said.

"You must do something with your gifts," Jamie told her.

"And you better get yourself out of Norma Desmond's mansion. Or you're going to wind up floating in her pool," Casey said. And even though she knew her gig was up because Cotton's studio gravy train had stopped, she insisted on going back to the suite to walk the dogs, on the house.

"It's been a long night for Monty and Bagel too."

"Take the limo," Jamie said.

"Really?"

"Sure, he's hired till six a.m."

"I don't think Calhoun will mind, you two got along so well," I said.

"We have so much in common. We are the hired folks, after all," Casey said.

And off she went, and Jamie and I had the first real conversation we'd had since I got to Hollywood.

"Casey's right, I'm a Joe Gillis hack, I've been seduced by Hollywood, I'm pretty pathetic," he said.

"You can come home anytime."

"I've got to get Cotton straightened out, I know she's selfish and shallow and treats me like dirt —"

"If you're going to tell me you like that in a woman, I'm leaving and going to Elton John's party," I told him.

"No. No. Being in her thrall is my fault. I've been the enabler wind beneath her wings since I got here, but I'm coming out of the shadows."

"You're leaving?"

"Oh no."

"Once you've been sucked into the vortex, it's hard to leave."

"Oooh, where'd you get that?"

"Casey. She's really a writer. Her play *Frankenstein in Ireland* was read at the Pumps garage space in La Jolla just a few months ago. She's really good, you saw her, she can come up with stuff out of nowhere right away. She rewrote your cough medicine excuse."

"Yeah, everyone in the hospital wanted to know what 'family tragedy' made Cotton 'overcome with exhaustion,' and I said I couldn't say."

"Next time they ask, tell them it was one of her beloved dogs. Bagel came down with a rare canine fever, Cotton's been up for three days and nights walking the floor with the ailing animal."

"Why didn't we go to the vet's?"

"It's so highly contagious Cotton didn't want to risk other

dogs getting it. Sometimes your pet is spared, the fever passes, but you just have to wait it out and hope."

"Wow. It's almost plausible. And puts Cotton in such a courageous and humanitarian light."

"She could win the Jean Hersholt Award next year."

"Casey came up with that, on the spot?"

"She's very good."

"I think I'll let her be my friend."

"You can attend Al-Anon meetings together."

"How about Hooked on Hollywood Anonymous Meetings?"

"There's a cure for everything."

"But not tonight. The Oscars. Was it amazing?"

"Yes, it sure was. Unbelievable."

Of course, Cotton did wake up eventually, and by the next afternoon I was their audience for a shallow, twisted discussion before I had to leave for the airport.

It scared me because I'd been there long enough to know who they were talking about, even if Cotton sometimes had no idea.

"What's with that Mollie Haskell crack about the only good role for an actress this year being Jaye Davidson's in *The Crying Game*? That Jaye's a man isn't he?"

"Yes, in real life. But, look, there's a trick with *The Crying Game* —"

"What trick? Some Linda Hunt show-offy tour de force? Davidson was up for best supporting actor, so why is someone saying he had the best role for an actress?" Cotton screamed.

"I'm not telling you, it'll spoil the movie."

"I'm never going to see it."

"Lenore might."

"Lenore can leave the room so you can tell me. Dollface, get out —"

"I don't have to, I've seen *The Crying Game*."

Jamie was surprised by that. "You did, chickepen? How come?"

"Heidi made us go because she heard it was Irish."

"So what's the big secret?" Cotton was of a mind to know. I wasn't going to make it easy for her. I had to sit through that art house movie to find out the surprise, and she could too.

"Why's some woman movie critic saying some man was a better actress than me? She's attacking my work. This was the year the Academy officially saluted Women. I think my fellow nominees and me should demand something from the paper, what's it called, a retribution?"

"A retraction."

"Yeah, one of those. That and get me a lawyer. How did Marisa Tomei win anyway? If they were going for an American, it was me they wanted. Somebody on TV said Jack Palance read the wrong name, all his push-ups went to his brain!"

That's when Casey McCordick snuck back in, thank goodness.

"You came to see me off?"

"Better than that, we're taking you off. The chariot awaits," she said. I said goodbye to Cotton and Jamie and I followed Casey outside.

And there was the stretch limo again, with Calhoun at the wheel, to give me a chauffeur-driven ride to the airport.

Casey rode up front with the driver. Jamie got upset when he realized we weren't heading to the airport.

"We're taking a little detour, one I planned to take you on last evening," said Calhoun as he pulled up near Schwab's Drugstore.

"We don't have time not to be discovered over a soda," said Jamie.

"We're not going in, there's something outside I want you to see," Casey said. We double-parked and all got out.

"Look down," Calhoun said, and there it was: Cotton Brady's star in the Hollywood Walk of Fame.

"Oh right, Cotton's TV star, she could have gotten another one for Movie Star, if she'd won the Oscar," Jamie said and almost started to cry.

Casey tried a philosophical approach. "No one will remember ten years from now who won for best supporting, even in two years."

"Marisa Tomei will remember," I said.

"Well yes, she's got the statuary to remind her."

"You know, there is a rainbow consolation in all this," Jamie declared. "For the rest of her career, Cotton Brady can put 'Academy Award® Nominee' next to her name."

"Do the Hollywood Walk of Fame engravers do codicils?" mused Casey. Calhoun took a group picture with us all pointing down proudly to Cotton's star, then we got back into the limo.

At the airport, I wished Jamie good luck with everything, especially his boss.

"You take such good care of Cotton. You're very devoted to her."

"Somebody has to be," he said. Then he changed the lyrics from the *Oliver!* torch song.

"As Long as She Needs Me," he serenaded as I went through the departure gate.

Chapter Three

An almost empty Johnny Walker forty-ouncer rolled down the aisle of the plane. The pregnant flight attendant picked it up and returned it to its owner, Sleazy "I want a better pillow" Man.

"He probably bought it at the Duty Free. He's been drinking out of it the whole flight, at least it finally kept him quiet, and he didn't get up to any shenanigans," Heidi said to me.

And at least Sleazy Man hadn't drunk it with some lady stranger, making their lost inhibitions get so much the better of them that they became members of the Mile High Club. I used to think that only happened in movies or urban folklore because the toilets on airplanes? There's not even enough room for one person. The beautiful people in the Mile High Club usually meet in the bathroom lineup or have been staring across the aisle at each other or had too many drinks and it starts up in the seats. It could happen with people who are already together and just can't wait till they land and get home or to their hotel, but how badly would they need to do this? The toilets are so small, at least on every plane I've ever been on. And how can people do Mile High late in the flight when no one's been maintaining the bathrooms and the waste receptacle is stuffed to the rafters with paper towels and everything else?

It's so unromantic and has such bad lighting. Mile High membership must require that you're drunk, you're not claustrophobic, you got to have it, and you don't care about:

1. People waiting to get in
2. Plane needing to make emergency landing and the 'Please get back to your seat' light
3. Romantic ambience

And how about:

4. If this isn't my partner, what about the one I do have?
5. What if the doors aren't soundproof? Or lock proof?
6. How many people saw us go in here?
7. How do we get back to our seats after this?
8. What if I need a cigarette when we're done and I set off the smoke alarm and I go to jail?
9. If a mile is 5,280 feet and the average altitude is usually at least 35,000 feet unless we're descending, shouldn't this be called the Twenty-Two-Mile-High Club?

Most of its members are probably honeymooners, college students, business execs or sex maniacs. I guess it also happens when you're really in lust or the plane ride is really boring or you need to relieve the stress of flying over an ocean in the dark. Would I say no if Benoît were sitting there instead of Heidi? He would never suggest it, he's a policeman, and it's so selfish when people are waiting outside the toilet door, especially some poor mother who has to get in there to change her baby's diaper, how can there be a changing table in there? It must be against the law, using an airplane cubicle as a bawdy house. You probably get arrested when you get off the plane. Well, Sleazy Man had given me lots to think about. After Heidi interpreted the pilot's latest static report, "We're fifty-four degrees north of Dublin," I popped the question.

"Do you ever wonder what kind of people are members of the Mile High Club?"

"You'd be surprised."

"Heidi!"

"Not me, my God. With some stranger? That is so depraved."

"Yeah, that is, but what if it was your boyfriend?"

"I've never been on a plane with a boyfriend." She sounded sad. I didn't make the bad joke that if she were ever travelling with a boyfriend and that boyfriend were Miles, they'd join the Miles High Club. "In any case, I was referring to a couple we know who boasted about it at a party."

"Daniel and Gaëtan?"

"Lenore. My brother? You think he'd do that, or tell me if he did?"

"Who then?"

"Elspeth and Douglas. Someone made a remark about Mile High and she gave a dirty laugh and looked at Douglas and he gave that snorty laugh and smirk, and then she chortled that they kept up their membership every time they take a plane."

"Every time? Even to Toronto?"

"She said, 'It's one of the only great family traditions we keep.' It ruined my dinner."

"Well, thanks a lot, Heidi. Now you've given my head a bad image. Lucky for me I won't have to use the facilities again before we land."

I love London. I think I love Trafalgar Square most of all, it feels to me like the centre of the world. I love all the pigeons, they make me think of Mary Poppins and Feed the Birds, tuppence a bag, even if it's not a sweet little old lady, just a man with a concession stand selling popcorn. Those pigeons fly and swirl around and land on Nelson's Monument as he looks out over it all: St. Martin's in the Field Church, Canada House, all the happy tourists. Right across from his plinth is the National Gallery, with *Sunflowers* by Van Gogh, everywhere is culture and Britishness, London is so England it's like Ottawa with a Mountie in red uniform on every corner. My first experience was so British: 10 Downing Street, Big Ben, the Tube, Picadilly Circus, Dickens's House, Madame Tussaud's, the Thames, and even a Camilla sighting.

"She's Catholic, you know, or she was, that's why they couldn't marry, it would bring down the monarchy," Heidi said. We didn't see Mrs. Parker-Bowles sneaking into Mass but slumming at the theatre. People were shooting her dirty how-dare-you-do-that-to-Our-Diana looks from the stalls. Heidi was mad that the tickets that came with the Show Tour package were "old Andrew Lloyd Webbers or tired, shoddy West End musicals and chestnuts," but I enjoyed them. Tommy Steele is a wonderful entertainer. I can't believe *The Mousetrap* has been playing this many years, and people kept the secret so well I never knew who the murderer was, what a surprise! Heidi said, and I agree, that a true sign of how civilized the Brits are is that they sell chocolates and ice creams at the interval and then let you eat them in your seat when the play starts again. It wasn't part of the Show Tour, but we got to the National Theatre for a Chekhov play because someone from Heidi's *Coronation Street* show was one of the *Three Sisters*. She was very convincing as a discontented Russian rich girl, Heidi says once she gets the theatre out of her system she can go back to being in a soap opera. And we were like groupies at Covent Garden because the actor who played Derek on *The Street* has that dollhouse boutique, but he was away. The person tending the store seemed surprised that people with Canadian accents were looking for Derek. We even got to see where it all began for Punch and Judy and went by the Royal Opera House, Heidi didn't make us go to the opera but I wouldn't have minded.

The tour on the red double-decker London bus was wonderful too. I loved it, especially the Beefeaters at the Tower of London with the ravens whose wings get broken so they don't fly away and cause the monarchy to collapse. "I guess they're Catholics too," I told Heidi. It was sad to see where poor Anne Boleyn and any other wife Henry VIII wanted rid of had her head chopped off. At least divorce got invented because of him. The guide treated me to true hospitality: when Heidi told him about Benoît when we drove by New Scotland Yard, he made the coach stop and let me have a picture taken with the sign so I could "make a copper happy." Then he said, "There is of course a major fee for that special service, my lovelies. You must take all your bleedin' geese back to Canada wif' you! Blessed birds is nuffin' but scavengers! They knows a good fing when they finds it and won't leave.

They don't fly souf for the winter, they don't fly anywhere, just hang about London, leaving their mucky mess!" Yes, our tour of London Town was pretty fabulous, it's too bad we got into a fight at the British Museum, but they started it.

It was a situation that could only end badly, it's one of Heidi's "issues," and now it's one of mine. We'd seen all the mummies, and even though they're amazing, it's kind of an invasion of privacy to look at them with their bandages off. All that trouble the Pharaohs went to, to be buried in a pyramid thousands of slaves had to build, and they wind up in a glass case with school kids staring and asking, "How did they take their brains out through their noses, Miss?"

Our Fate was to wind up in the Elgin Marbles wing. I'd heard all about them from Heidi, but whenever I heard the word marbles I pictured marbles, big green marbles the size of bowling balls. But they turned out to be statues and panels, rooms and rooms of them, even a whole temple. I was not unaware of the controversy, thanks to Dr. Heidi Flynn, about Thomas Bruce, Earl of Elgin, father of Lord Elgin the Governor General of British North America, who once lived at Villa Maria. That was way before the CND nuns turned it into a private school for girls like Heidi, who thus suffers Marbles guilt by association. She'd lectured me on how Elgin bought the Marbles from the Parthenon in Athens for a song from the invading Turks, carted them off and then sold them to the British Museum in 1816. The Greeks want the Parthenon Marbles back, but the British won't do the ethical thing and insist on keeping them. Even when Melina Mercouri is the one who wants them back the most. She's so Greek, she was so good in *Never On Sunday,* which Heidi made me watch. The volunteer lady guide was going on and on about how wonderful the British were to save these the Elgin Marbles from destruction because, left to the Turks, they wouldn't even exist anymore. Then a petite English lady asked, "Is there any chance the Elgin Marbles will ever be returned to Greece?"

"Oh no," the guide said.

"It would be perceived as a goodwill gesture and look good for the Empire," the lady's burly husband said.

"And what would be next? When will it stop? Do we return the Rosetta Stone? Really!"

"There's no need to be so dismissive," said Heidi.

"I beg your pardon?"

"It is a valid question. The Marbles belong to Greece, they are part of their heritage, the Greeks want them back. They've made it quite clear to you that they consider them stolen. Keeping them is a disgrace."

"And the Indians want the land back you Americans stole from them."

"I am not American, I am Canadian. And I never stole anyone's land, I'm Irish, your people stole land from my people."

"Let's move on," said the guide.

"Does that mean that if anything is rescued, the rescuer owns it? Does the fire department own the house they saved from burning or the person they caught in their nets?" Heidi kind of shouted after her.

We didn't intend to follow the guide to another wing, but we got stopped from doing that even if we had wanted to.

"Best stay back, both of you," Petite Lady Wife said.

"There was no need to bring up Northern Ireland," said Burly Husband.

"When did I do that?" Heidi said.

"By bringing up your Irishness," he said.

"She's giving her time to act as our guide. You should be grateful, not bring up the Irish Question and go rabble-rousing," said Petite Wife.

I stepped up. "Hey, lady, you're the ones who asked if the Empire would perform a goodwill gesture and return the Marbles to Greece. You're the rabble-rousers, not us."

"Come on, Rodney," said Petite Wife, and they marched off.

An older man had also stayed back, he came over, we thought, for Round Three.

"You are Greek?" he asked me.

"No, neither of us is," I said.

"You have Greek souls, efharisto, thank you! Parthenon Marbles don't have to be return free of cost — we will pay as many drachmas they want to buy them back, No they say! I thinking we have to come here and take them back ourselves, maybe in the night, like the Trojan Horse, but womens like you, they make me see, is not just Greeks who want the Marbles to come home. Somehow. Somehow. Kapos."

His name was Costas, and he gave us his card.

"I run taverna on Santorini, you come there one day, I hope."

"Kapos, kapos. And maybe we'll bring the Marbles with us," I said, and this made him weep a little bit and laugh.

"Wonderful womens," he said and hugged us both.

Then I remembered: "I have a taverna too. In Montreal, you come there some time, some kapos." I handed him a Festin card. If we weren't a non-smoking establishment, I could have handed him matches.

When we got back to the hotel with its twin orange bedspreads, Heidi said that that battle with the sanctimonious twits would arm us well for the next one. That reminded me that something bad would happen, we would soon pay for our almost perfect tourist time so far. Heidi's Bad Travel Karma was about to kick in.

"Oh no, Jemima Farnham. Don't make us go, Heidi."

"We have to. We'll be staying with her relatives, we can't not see her, and maybe we can convince her to do something about her golden-haired-boy Blake and his Trans Am and his drug running," Heidi said.

"We couldn't convince her when she lived on our street. She ran off here because of Blake."

Jemima the Monarchist had never been happy in Canada and always wanted to return to England. Her chance came when she offered her services to the Queen after Her Majesty's Christmas speech about her *annus horribilis*. Jemima thought she'd wind up a lady-in-waiting, so far she was running a National Trust Heritage Estate in Surrey. She knew we were coming. It was a duty call, Heidi had other Great Houses she'd much rather visit, given a choice.

"I thought if we did one of those fusty estates it could be Knole in Kent."

"Why Knole in Kent?"

"It was the childhood home of Vita Sackville-West. Amazing tapestries, garden, afternoon tea and a deer park. Vita was Virginia Woolf's lover," Heidi informed me.

"But that Woolf site's not on Elspeth's Must Do List!"

We were still smarting from what we foolishly thought was going to be a Bon Voyage card from Elspeth. She said we weren't to open it till we were settled in London. I thought it would be a beautiful card with some wonderful thing she'd arranged for us as a surprise, like afternoon tea at the Savoy or really good show tickets. I don't know why I fantasized that, I've known Elspeth long enough to know it would be something twisted and literary. It was a card all right, with an illustration painted by Virginia Woolf's sister Vanessa Bell, and inside it, Elspeth commanded:

> WHEN IN ENGLAND, MUST DO IT!
> DO NOT MISS:
>
> 1. In London: (a) Bloomsbury, Russell Square, all haunts of Virginia Woolf (1882-1941).(b) Absolute must: 23 Fitzroy Road (Yeats House plaque; building where Sylvia Plath (1932-1963) gassed herself); bring "too red" tulips.
> 2. If going south: (a) Isle of Avalon (lore, stone circles in Avebury). (b) Tintagel (two-hour hike to witches' museum). (c) Cornwall (land of our ancient goddesses); contact guide: Priestess Melpomene (to coordinate all, card encl.)
> 3. If going north (& I know you are): (a) Heptonstall Cemetery (not all that far from your pilgrimage to Brontëparsonage, Haworth), grave of Sylvia Plath (1932-1963); instructions: hack off name Hughes if engraved back on; bring "too red" tulips.

At the bottom there was a shopping list of things she wanted us to buy her at Tesco's and Boots.

"The more we get to know Elspeth, the more I'm convinced she's a mental case," I said.

"When we get home, I think we should limit our exposure to her," said Heidi.

"Good idea. Elspeth thinks everything she says is right, like it's the gospel, it's getting on my nerves."

"Yes, she is too dogmatic, and insane as well as thoughtless. Imagine almost getting Viola pregnant by her husband, then not even showing up for her Open Mike Night, all brought on by *The Artist's Way* she gave her as a birthday present?"

"And you know why we were the only ones at Open Mike Night, eh? Everyone else is cutting Elspeth off. We never see Beth anymore. She's hiding out at McGill. And she was the second in command of the Sylvias. The Professors Who Love Sylvia Plath Too Much."

"Elspeth's certifiable. A To Do List with footnotes. Heaven forbid she would mention the Brontës's dates, even though she gets Plath's in twice."

"And no mention of any shopping for her children. All that great stuff they had at the British Museum for kids."

"The hieroglyphics rubber stamp set. They would have loved that."

"It was both fun and educational. We should have bought it for them."

"But it would look strange, we're not that close."

"I know . . . but she's their mother. She should be asking us to get great British games and books for them, not Boots camomile shampoo and Vindaloo curry powder for her."

"All those beautiful collectibles in Derek's Dollhouse for Frieda. The London Transport Museum bus memorabilia for Northrup. I could spit, tremendous toys just waiting to go to bright children, Elspeth is so thoughtless."

"How have we put up with her for this long?" I asked. We'd have indulged in only half this much character assassination, of course, if Elspeth had slipped some pounds for our afternoon tea and her groceries into the envelope, instead of commands to visit two of Sylvia Plath's last sites.

No matter what, we had to make our visit to Longbreach House. The Surrey train station with its clock tower was charming, but we had a twenty-five-minute bus trip after that. I love riding on the top of a double-decker bus, especially that one in Surrey through the willows. It passed under so many willow branches, we couldn't help laughing and screaming, and that got us looks when we came down the stairs to disembark right outside the gates of Jemima's country estate, with its large storks on their columns. I'd seen pictures of Trust Estates with "eccentric accents" like pineapples and Egyptian doodads, but storks?

"Was this perchance the home of some royal personage who invented the storks bringing the babies story?" I asked.

"I daresay no, for then it would have been called Breech Birth House," replied Heidi as we headed up the cobbled road. It's an old, awesome fortress, like where the Giant might live at the top of the Beanstalk. "All that's missing is a moat," Heidi was saying, just as the big castle door opened and Jemima greeted us.

"Welcome to — oh, hello," she said.

Once again, because I never learn, I expected the impossible, I thought Jemima would be so happy to see neighbours from Canada that she'd do something she didn't do for the other visitors: give us each a hug. But no.

"You never confirmed you were coming," said Jemima coolly. "I didn't know it was today, this afternoon. You might have rung me, you know? I'm expecting a call, if you'll excuse me," she said and disappeared down a long, dark hall full of old, untouched-up family portraits. A nasally college girl in a cardigan and a wool scarf came over to us. She stuffed her used Kleenex into her pocket and sniffled.

"Four pounds twenty."

"Each?" asked Heidi.

"Unless either of you is a pensioner."

We handed over eight pounds forty without snarky comment. She gave us a National Trust History of Longbreach House pamphlet to share — "we have to conserve" — and told us to wait for Mrs. Farnham, she'd show us around. A very tall gentlemen in an ascot emerged from the shadows. Heidi told me later she thought he looked like Nosferatu, the Undead, and I had to agree.

"If Mrs. Farnham is preoccupied once again, I can escort these lovely visitors," he said.

And that's how we got a house and garden tour from the last remaining owner of a house that's been around since 1356. Sadly for us visitors, in all that time nothing much had happened there, battles had been fought on far away fields, and any restoration had been done on other paintings on other estates. You could hardly make out what any of the paintings were, they were so dark.

"That's a Titian. Its companion is in the Uffizi," he claimed. He could have said the Mona Lisa was under there.

Only once did the house seem that it could be more interesting. It was terribly drafty all over, the reason Nasally Girl was going through all the Kleenex and everyone was wearing sweaters or, in Lord Florian Peach's case, a down vest. In an upstairs wing, after he'd made us look at an awful lot of porcelain, we came to a particularly cold part of the house.

"That's the Cold Spot." He pointed to it and made us stand in it.

Heidi and I had just seen *The Haunting* and knew this could be promising.

"So Longbreach is haunted?" Heidi asked hopefully.

"No. Just poorly insulated," he said.

In the truly stunning gardens everything was in bloom for hectares and hectares, as the brochure called them, and we finally got warm.

"We nursed hopes that *The Antiques Road Show* would do programs from Longbreach, but so far, silence," Lord Peach said as he showed off his rose garden. "There was talk of some Jane Austen book being turned into something for BBC. I approached the producers about using Longbreach but they said, 'It doesn't say Lord Darcy to us.' Can you imagine?"

"Lord Darcy? They're filming *Pride and Prejudice* for television?"

"It would seem so, yes." Heidi was so excited, Lord Peach was so bored. "Of course, Longbreach would be ideal for location shooting if there was ever any interest in a Bloomsbury Group project — "

"Bloomsbury Group?" Heidi said brightly.

"You know of them?"

"Of course, I'm a professor of English," she said. "You have a Bloomsbury connection?"

"Of a sort, yes. Mary Hillier?"

"Sorry, I don't know of her."

"She was the help, a servant woman, better known as Mary Madonna or Island Mary. She frequently posed for photographic portraits taken by Virginia and Vanessa's great-aunt, Julia Margaret Cameron. Under her tutelage, Mary the maid managed to marry up."

"And she married up into your family?" asked Heidi.

"No. But my great-grandfather was acquainted with the peer she married, and we believe she was a guest here one shooting party weekend for the hunt."

"What did you hunt? Not the little foxes?"

"Bosh, no, that requires horses and dogs. Game birds."

"And with this minor Bloomsbury connection, you hope to attract Woolf scholars?"

"It's by no means minor. So sorry it's not Lytton Strachey and Carrington or even poor dear Leonard Woolf with their little monkey. But Island Mary's little rags-to-riches tale could attract certain *literati cognoscenti*, don't you think? I have to entice people to come here somehow. We're not going to survive on two visitors a week acquainted with Mrs. Farnham. These estate taxes will be the death of me. You don't see me going the thirteenth Duke of Bedford route, putting a fun fair and safari park on the grounds. What John Robert Russell's done to Woburn Abbey! Fine, yes, he's made it solvent, but at what cost? He's mistaken in thinking that it is better to be looked down upon than overlooked, even if he is getting upwards of a million and a half visitors a year. Have you any ideas what I could do?"

"Well, for starters, you could do something with this maze of roses," I began to advise him. "It's high and thorny. You could make it scarier and harder to find your way out of, like a fairytale or, I know, the creepy moving hedges in *The Shining*." Lord Peach looked utterly stumped and perplexed, we obviously didn't have the same reading list. "Okay, or you could set up tables in the middle of it, like a Mad Hatter's Tea Party? Or serve even more food, do candlelight suppers where you could play host? A Dine with the Aristocracy sort of thing?"

"Whatever gives you ideas like that?" Lord Peach asked snidely.

"Lenore owns a theme restaurant in Montreal with my brother, she knows how to keep the public happy," Heidi snapped.

"And what's the story with your storks out front?" I asked him.

"Storks?"

"Those big birds with long legs on your plinths?"

"Oh, the perelyndls, they're extinct," he said.

"Did they go extinct here? On your land? Were they the game birds your hunting party shot down?"

"No. The very last ones fell in Cheshire, actually. In 1926. We had nothing to do with their final demise," he said sadly. "I say, you weren't thinking of some sort of dinosaur park, were you? I'm hundred and sixty-seventh in line to the Crown. I can't go making my estate a circus, a tourist attraction."

"Well, you have to do something," Heidi said, fed up with him.

"Have you thought of a gift shop?" I asked.

"Mrs. Farnham has plans for one. In fact, that's how she occupies much of her time. We spent yesterday looking at dinner napkins packaged especially for the National Trust. And she's after anything with 'By Appointment to her Majesty the Queen,' even soaps endorsed by the Royal Family. I must say that is probably for the best, the few people she has guided around have registered complaints with Melinda. We've marked Mrs. Farnham's cards due to her tendency to denigrate the guests. But she works for her board and keeps Mrs. Ivy on the hop, so who am I to complain?"

We were walking through a little valley of bluebells by a millpond when he brought up the real reason he took us for the tour.

"And then, of course, there is the question of an heir," he said and looked at Heidi in a very unsavoury way, like the wolf looked at Little Red Riding Hood after he ate her grandma.

"The two of you, you're not a couple, by any chance?"

"Us? Together? No, we're part of couples but with other people. We're both quite taken. Spoken for," Heidi exclaimed.

"Yes. That's true. My boyfriend Benoît is a police officer,

and Heidi's on her way to visit Mrs. Farnham's nephew, Miles of Near Sheffield," I added.

"Pity. All the good strapping farm stock ones are taken," he said, looking at Heidi again.

Jemima finally came marching across the hectares to us. Lord Peach decided to take his leave, but not before giving Heidi one last chance, if she was really, really desperate.

"If things don't work out with the gentleman up north, please do keep in touch, you could be Lady Peach of all you survey. It's not often that I've encountered someone both Bloomsbury-informed and buxom," he said, and off he went. Heidi was not pleased with Jemima.

"That call certainly took a long time," she said.

"It was Canada, Neville actually, he dropped a little bomb, I had to take some time to myself to digest the information."

"Is everything okay on our street?" Heidi asked, alarmed.

"Why wouldn't it be?"

"Your son Blake," I said.

"Don't tell me Blake's leaving nasty notes on your car windshield again, because Neville is on the lookout, and I know any claim like that would be a falsehood. I do have another son, as you know. It seems my Alistair and daughter-in-law are expecting a baby."

"Tammy-Anne is pregnant?" Heidi said.

"Oh, yes, you were at their wedding," Jemima said, with such distaste you'd think Heidi had stood up at the back of the church declaring just cause why this pair should not be joined in matrimony.

"I didn't crash it, your relatives from England invited me," Heidi said.

"You were dancing with Miles. A great deal." Jemima narrowed her eyes.

"Yes, I was," said Heidi and blushed. Jemima stared at her.

"Well, well, congratulations, Jemima, a baby is on the way," I said.

"It seems I am to be a grandmother by late fall," Jemima said.

"That would be a good reason to come home, to set things right, it hasn't been the same since you left," Heidi informed her.

"So Neville tells me, every time he calls," Jemima said.

"Then you must know how bad Blake's been since he moved back in, he's drugged or drunk and skateboarding up and down our street after midnight," I said.

"Neville's lost control, and he's never home. Blake could break his neck without someone to guide him," Heidi said. "Sometimes a boy needs his mother."

"He's twenty-three years old," said Jemima.

"That's why it's odd that he's hanging out with local teenagers, they're a bad bunch, having underage beer parties on your front steps," Heidi told her.

"Why doesn't your latest boyfriend the constable arrest him then?" Jemima asked me.

"Benoît's never been there when Blake acts up."

"Oh, so this latest man of yours hasn't moved in yet?"

"No. And when he visits I don't want him to have to be on duty, we have to see how well we get along when there's no police business."

"He's fought enough of our battles already, and Blake's antics are under Westmount jurisdiction anyway," Heidi said.

"Surely you didn't journey all this way to berate me? Please don't let us discuss Blake again. I'd like the remainder of our time together to be pleasant. You will stay and take afternoon tea with us? Please?" And what could we say but yes, of course.

This would be our first real tea in England, we'd had some rock buns and Eccles cakes in dingy, steamy little cafeterias, but nothing like this and on such exquisite wooden garden furniture. It was a fabulous spread, created by Mrs. Ivy, a woman from town, a real cream tea with treacle sponge, scones and Devon custard, crustless cucumber sandwiches, bone china teacups — the works and this splendid setting almost made us forget how unpleasant Jemima could be, especially about her own English relatives.

"You are not to tell them you were here, it will put it into their minds to visit me, with all their unruliness and caterwauling, they'll go bothering the neighbours' dogs and use up all the Bronnley soaps and lotions in the lavatory. They'll organize the gardeners in some revolt for even higher wages to trim the topiary, and I can well imagine Miles scaling the battlements in his mountain gear and then diving off them into the ponds to cool off."

To do this Miles might have to take his shirt off, and I could see that Heidi was thinking the same thing, her face turned redder than before. He's not even around and she gets like this, what will it be like when he's before us in the flesh? Am I ever gonna be in the way.

"Why ever are you going to visit those people anyway?"

"They invited my parents to visit too sometime, my mother got on very well with Irene."

"She would, with that Irene," said Jemima.

"And Heidi got on very well with Jennie and Miles," I told her.

"Yes. Miles was asking all about one of you before he left," Jemima said, and her eyes had a far-off searching look.

"He was?" Heidi asked, thrilled like she was sixteen years old. But this infatuation was the reason we were here, this was how I got to England, this was how I got to be sitting having tea in an English country garden and got to be in on the secret of *The Mousetrap*.

"Well, you're welcome to him, to all of them, those peasants are not my relations, really, they're Neville's, I only married into the Farnhams, don't let us forget! It's in name only, once Alistair's child is born I'm suing for divorce, I need to be free to follow other avenues." She looked off dreamily in the direction Lord Peach had gone.

Then, oh where had the time gone? Was it already time to finally leave? Were we really at the castle front door?

"It was so lovely of you both to visit, do tell everyone how well I'm doing here in my milieu as Director of Longbreach, of course it is a stepping stone, word will come any day now from Her Majesty's people that I'll be moved, I believe Marquess Carnavon has expressed interest in my taking over her correspondence, if anything were to befall the hundred and nine peers before her in line to the throne, she would be Queen, and with that would come enormous responsibility for me. Well bye-bye, safe home, love to all." She headed back up the murky corridor.

We were down the path and almost at the bus when Melinda the Nasally Girl caught up to us. In the shadow of the peridnigms or whatever they were, she puffed, "You seem to have forgotten. That will be twelve pound sixty each."

"But we paid already, when we first got here. You gave us a pamphlet," Heidi said, waving it. And how had the admission price tripled?

"I know. It's for the Afternoon Teas. They're twelve pound sixty each."

Of course they were. Jemima, ever true to form. We sat on the top of the bus but didn't scream as we wound under the willows on the way back to the train station, we were too overwhelmed by the Britishness we'd been through all afternoon. And Heidi held forth on her feelings about Lord Nosferatu Peach.

"But you could be Lady Nosferatu Peach, you buxom Bloomsbury babe, unless Jemima gets a quickie divorce and beats you to him," I told her.

"Some women will do anything for a sense of en-title-ment. Imagine marrying up with him. Did you see how big that Bloomsbury wannabe's teeth were?"

"He did have really big teeth. Do you think they're actually big, or does he just have more teeth than the average person? Maybe it's from all the upper crust intermarrying."

"No wonder the rich get called the horsey set," Heidi said. "Surrey is supposed to be so beautiful, and we had to spend our day at Longbreach. For nothing. We can't even tell the Farnhams we put in time there."

"And she's not even coming back to straighten Blake out."

"She was in pretty rare form, not one crack about Canada the whole time we were there," Heidi said.

"Her accent's gotten more British, eh?'

"Very poncey now that she's back."

"Up-market. Toffy-nosed. Cut glass."

"You know what's in Surrey that we missed? Runnymeade, where the Magna Carta was sealed. And the Devil's Punchbowl. And Box Hill, where you can see five counties all at once. And all kinds of pretty villages and meadows and heaths. But what did we do?"

"We had a lovely cream tea."

"That cost us over fifty dollars."

"We could have been in London."

"We could have done one of those Original London Walks,

to think we've missed the Haunts of Jack the Ripper." Heidi sighed.

I wonder about Heidi sometimes, such a well brought up girl with such a fascination with murderesses like Lizzie Borden and serial killers like Jack the Ripper, you never know with some people. Of course, she'd say Jack the Ripper's victims were all women so that makes his crimes a feminist issue, and therefore it's okay to be obsessed with something so gruesome, horrible and unsolved.

Our campaign to get Jemima to return had failed, she thought she had a chance to become a Lady, so she chose to take care of a stranger's estate instead of seeing to her mess at home. She'd come to rue that decision!

Anyway, the day after our Longbreach ordeal, we could head north to what I thought would be Heidi's Destiny and me making myself scarce.

Chapter Four

I didn't say so out loud, but silently I was practically screaming: Why did they say they're Near Sheffield when they're closer to Leeds? When the train chugged into Sheffield, I thought hurray, we must be near, but we sure weren't! We had to change trains twice to get to Bickton-on-Curds. What kind of place name is that, anyway, for anywhere? Okay, so we have names like St. Louis de Ha-Ha and Flin Flon, but Bickton-on-Curds? I guess I would have had a better attitude if we had been met at the station by some Farnhams with a banner and balloons, or even some nice older gentleman with a horse and carriage who said, Would those be your bags, misses? But there we were, two foreigners, all alone in this grimy station. I thought it would be pretty, like the one in Surrey. It wasn't. I tried not to be prejudiced, but it was all so sooty and grey and sad-looking. When no one turned up, we decided to get a taxi. When we arrived, Heidi kept looking at the address and then at the house as if one of them had to be wrong.

"It's the Cobbles, ayup," the taxi driver said. "That's where the Farnhams is at, give a knock then, oh no need, I see a message on door, t'ra then."

Heidi was expecting a Tudor thatched cottage covered in roses, with diamond-paned windows and a greenhouse, instead it was a council row house with a graffiti-covered brick wall next to the railway tracks. Too bad we took a taxi, we could have hopped a freight right to the back door. It's not their fault they live in what looks like a tenement, it was ours for thinking they didn't. And of course after Longbreach, everything looked small.

There was a note tacked on the door:

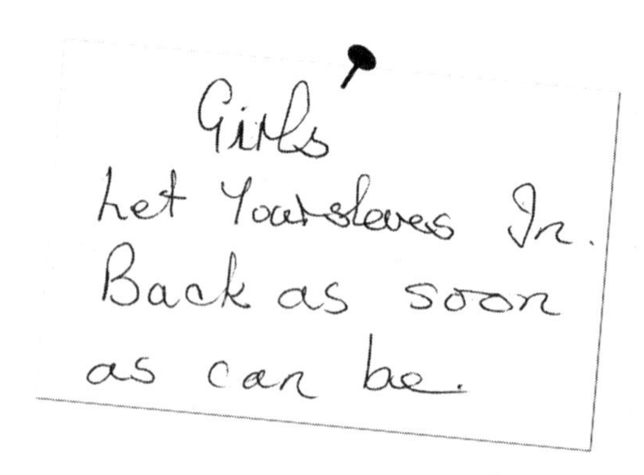

"I suppose we'd best let oursleves in," said Heidi.

We let oursleves in and got to see the house without the people who lived in it around, so we didn't have to pretend we weren't shocked.

"Oh. Oh dear," said Heidi.

Every single space was crammed or covered, there were newspapers scattered all over as if a hurricane had come through, and the living room was painted in two main colours with matching pennants and a framed print of a football stadium on the main wall.

"That must be their soccer team and the wall accents are

the team colours," Heidi said. We saw later how much of their strange, convoluted house was dedicated to the team, even the WC, with shag rug in team colours up the wall.

"They did know we were coming, there was a note of welcome on the door," Heidi said.

I figured someone must be home because the TV was on and we could hear water running upstairs.

"Miles? He's taking a shower?" Heidi hoped.

The water turned off, we heard some scurrying, Heidi called up "Hello," and a voice called down, "Damn me! You're not here already?"

It wasn't Miles, it was Jennie. She came down in a team colours bathrobe and hugged us both.

"I didn't know it was today. No one tells me anything. But then I am all at odds now that I'm back home. I've got to be at the surgery in less than an hour, glad someone's here for your arrival."

"So are we," Heidi said.

"Can't leave anything to Mum and Dad once they've got the panto."

"The panto? They're not running their newsagent shop?" Heidi asked.

"Oh, one of them will be, but not both this time of year, every spring it's the same, a crisis, but the show goes on, never fear," Jennie said.

"They're at the show?"

"They're in it. Mum runs it, with Dot. Tonight's one of the last practices," Jennie shouted as she ran upstairs to get dressed.

"Oh, they should have told us they're in rehearsals, we'll be in the way," Heidi called up.

"Never. They were so chuffed you'd be here to see it," Jennie yelled and asked were we hungry? We shouted yes, but we figured we'd wait for everyone.

"That could be ages, I'll get you both a curry," she bellowed. But first, could we see if there were any cans about? There was everything about, and yes, there were plenty of empty cans.

"To take for the deposit?" Heidi asked, picking up three.

"No, to drink. Lager." She was downstairs again, all spanky in her nurse's uniform. She went into the messy kitchen. "No, all gone, no cans in, I'll get some, yeah?" and off she went. We just sat there in shock, Heidi putting on a brave face. No one home, no Miles to meet us at the station, no food or cans in, everyone off at panto practice, this our first night in Bickton-on-Curds town.

The curry from the take-away was very good, and the cans made us feel a little mellower. So did the really bad TV. Jennie had no idea where we'd be sleeping, so she couldn't show us to our room. We said we'd be fine, she shouldn't be late to the ER. She confessed she was horrible: she looked forward to the occasional minor accident victim.

"I do love suturing, I'm mad for it," she said and sped off.

Heidi searched through their *Radio Times* television magazine to see if *Coronation Street* was on, we were way behind in Canada, she'd get well up on it, but this wasn't a "Corrie" night. Flipping channels, I was amazed how awful their TV shows are, some as bad as ours, we must only get the best British fare on Vermont PBS, Mountain Lake and CBC. They don't export their rubbish across the ocean. We wound up watching a show called *Gobsmacked*, where they shock unwitting participants. This week's show featured people who came back from holiday to discover other people had moved into their house. Later in the show they'd let us see someone from one of the football teams "get his cards," be fired on live TV. It was way after ten o'clock when Gordon and Irene Farnham came in, kisses all around. They were so sorry to have missed us, wasn't Miles there to greet us? He knew we were coming, that's ever so strange, it's marked on calendar, look see, we had checked it ourselves already, we were there:

Something must have come up, he was ever so excited we were coming, that's not like him.

"It's exactly like him, the lad's got crampons for brains," his loving dad said.

The TV was on the whole time, they never turned it off or down even. Now a sitcom was on, *Squatters Rites*, a lot of punkers with dogs and piercings, it would require subtitles if CBC ever made a big mistake and bought it.

So was our trip nice, how did we like England, had we seen much of Bickton-on-Curds? Lots of time to see it, where did we plan to go? Haworth, what was there? The Brawnteys?

"Them writer sisters, Mother," Gordon informed her. Oh yes, she said. And where else? Heidi named many more spots, we'd hire a car and drive to the Lake District, visit Dove Cottage, where Wordsworth lived? Then if we were really adventurous and had the time, get to Hadrian's Wall? Irene's eyes were glazing over, and I thought, Heidi has this vast itinerary planned so she looks independent and not really here because of Miles. Anything more local, like? Irene asked. Oh yes, Heidi had a meeting sometime in Bradford. "Oh, they do a lovely curry on the main street, they claim they got the biggest naan bread in Yorkshire. And they're not lying. And at some of the cafés they've got them Indian music videos going on the telly, from Bollywood, very lively, can they dance! Seems it's not against their Hindu religion."

Irene guessed we'd popped in to see Jemima Farnham. "Bringing her the news from your street, were you, lovies?" We confessed. Yes, we tattled on Blake the Menace, but Jemima didn't care, Neville had called with the news she's to be a grandmother come the fall — "Oh, she won't leave England for a Canadian grandchild, my ducklings. That one! With her poncey airs, lah-de-dah, thinking any day Her Majesty will give her a position in waiting to some Dame or Princess Michael! Bet she's already packed her picnic basket full of prawn cocktails and champagne for Ascot or Wimbledon. If she thinks we're lowering ourselves so she can give us an audience at Longbreach, she's got another think coming! Jemima Winterbottom's never taken to being a Farnham, only married into it. Well, then, so did I, I'm really still a Blunt at heart. Irene Blunt, that's me before I married his nibs here. And how are your mum and dad, Heidi, love? And when are they coming to see us?" Heidi couldn't give them a date, but she presented them the box of chocolates her mom had sent Irene. She opened them right away. "Oh, them lovely Laura Seconds! I'll make us tea, shall I?"

"The panto has been fraught," she yelled, clanging about in the kitchen.

"What's your panto titled?" Heidi asked.

"*Noddy in Love*."

"Naughty in Love?" Heidi repeated.

"Naughty in Love, that would be good, eh, Mother! That would get the punters in." Gordon guffawed.

"Stop that foolishness, Gordon. No, it's our beloved childhood hero, our darling Noddy, the elf. It's Noddy in the Land of Love. Noddy sings and we do some wee skits, it's lovely, but that little madam Heather Wilton playing Noddy is being uncooperative. Now she's whinging that all the singing is giving her megraines. She's in terrible pain. Thinks we'll put up with that palaver, just because she's all we've got and she's been our star three pantos running."

"And her mum's the director," Gordon said, almost a whole row of Laura Secords gone.

"Then let Dot direct the bloody thing proper. All she does is go on about perfecting her Spring Berries Roulade for the cast party," Irene said.

"Put the fear of God into them both, Mother. Tell them you've got a professional singer under roof, imported her in from Canada," he said as he finished off the vanilla cream that's just like the Laura Secord Easter egg.

"I will tell her that, so I will! That will teach little Madam Heather with her megraines! You sing so lovely for your supper, Lenore, I remember at your Feast-In restaurant, we had such a nice time," Irene said.

"You should have seen her in *Bells Are Ringing*, she was wonderful," Heidi said.

"I know she was, lovie, I've got all the crits here." Irene pulled newspaper clippings out of a stuffed drawer.

"You have my reviews?"

"Every one! Heidi sent them to Miles, he passed them over, we know all about your great success, you'll be on Broadway next," Irene declared.

"Not with those notices, our bells weren't ringing, it was a big flop, the Montreal critics hated it," I told her.

"Yes, but they loved you, Lenore, look, Heidi hi-lited them in yellow, 'Rutland is possessed of a boffo voice,' 'defied the mediocrity all around her' — Gordon, leave some chocs for the kids!"

"They're on offer anytime," he said and shoved the box at Heidi.

"Oh, no thanks, this late at night, chocolate will keep me awake," Heidi said. And now she was going to show Miles how independent she was by making us go to bed without our tea before he finally got home, but Gordon cut her off at the pass.

"Like our decorative accenting? Only house in Bickton-on-Curds what looks like this. I told mother we should invite the team lads over for one of her steak and kidneys or hot pots when season ends, they'd feel at home." Irene came in with the tea and McVitties biscuits. Gordon complained, "Is them biscuits all you have for pudding?"

Irene shot back, "Shut your gob when it's full of them Laura Seconds." The round chocolate-covered digestives must have reminded Irene about soccer because she launched into just how badly the team had done this year. They were going through "a bad patch," but Gordon asked how could they excuse last year and the one before that? Still, they loved their lads, and that's when the lad they loved the most stormed in.

Miles sure has an aura, the same aura of irresistible manliness Clark Gable isn't using anymore. I didn't realize when he was in Canada, I wasn't exposed to him that much, or he never really looked at me. He's kind of sexy in a dangerous way, with some built-in swoony effect on the ladies. "Heidi!" he mountain yelled, picked her up and gave her a big hug like he never wanted to let her go. And then he dropped her down, looked at me and said, "Lenore?" and hugged me and, I think, kissed or nibbled my ear. He did it so fast I wasn't completely sure, but that's what it felt like.

He sold a car, sorry. A Jag. Mick wanted to celebrate by driving the new motor to a favourite pub, and a match was on telly and, well, you know how it is. What match, son? Gordon asked. Oh yes, said Heidi, I wish we'd seen that, we were flipping channels, we never saw any football. "Closed circuit EFWA," Miles said, "only on the pub's satellite." Soon as it was over, Miles told Mick they couldn't stay for last orders, he had two Canadian girls waiting for him at home. Mick had just dropped him off at door, in the Jag.

"This Mick . . ."Heidi said.

"No, it's not Mick Jagger, at least I can't say it is." Miles smiled.

"Mick's driving a new Jag after drinking at a pub all night?"

"Well, yeah. Not every day you get a new Jag. Oh, Mum, is that all the bloody cans you got in?"

"The girls nicked them," Gordon said and laughed.

"You've had a skinful already, my son. You'll have tea," Irene said, and took the can he was about to open away from him.

Miles sat down on the ottoman across from Heidi and only

had eyes for her. He was within great kissing distance, but we were all there.

"How long's it been since we last saw each other, yeah? You look fit."

"Uh, thanks, it's been over a year, I guess," she said.

(Over a year and two months and three weeks, she could have told him. Or he should have told her!)

"You were off to Everest, or about to be," Heidi added.

"Oh yeah! I was! I did! Yeah!"

And he rushed out of the sitting room.

"Now you've got the boy started, you breathed the magic word," Gordon said. "I'm off to bed, I've got to do papers in morning. Night, girls. Welcome to Bickton."

And Gordon shuffled off, but he was almost knocked over by Miles coming back in with a slide projector and a screen. He began setting it up.

"Oh Miles, it's late for the girls, they've had long day, they must be knackered," said Irene.

Miles looked at us hopefully.

"You're not knackered, are you? I reckoned on sharing this with you as soon as you got here," he said.

As if Heidi had to ask. "Is it your trip to Everest?"

"Mind-reader!" he said, grabbed her face in his hands and kissed her on the forehead.

"I still can't believe he's been. Twice." Irene beamed and looked down at what was left of the Laura Secords.

"Oh good, Gordon left me what looks like the caramel centres," she said. "And there are some of the nutty ones for you, Miles. I'll put kettle back on, we'll want more tea."

"You couldn't do me a fry-up, could you, Mum?"

The look she gave Heidi and me seemed to say, My son! Is

he crazy? At this time of night? but instead what she said was, "Would you girls like one too?"

We said no thanks. And off she went to the kitchen, and Miles ran off to get his other carousel of slides.

"Heidi. Look at the time. And he's got at least two carousels," I whispered.

"But he's so eager to show them to us, he's like a school boy," she said.

"I'm going to bed . . ."

"No! That will hurt his feelings."

"It'll hurt them even more if I fall asleep. And you should have some time with him alone," I said.

"With his mother here? Stay, Lenore."

By now it was way after midnight, Heidi was too excited by seeing Miles again to be tired, and this could have been a wonderful slide show. I mean, how many times does someone show you slides of his climb up Everest? Well, if they were slides of this calibre you'd wish the answer was NEVER. I think maybe five were in focus, and they were the ones he didn't take — group shots of him and lots of rich climbers in their gear with Sherpas. It's a lucky thing he only got to 27,600 feet and didn't make it to the Top of the World, 29,028 feet, because his Kodak moment of that accomplishment would be blurry. There were lots of fuzzy slides of bells, snow, blowing snow, ribbons or handkerchiefs on clotheslines in the wind, yellow tents, cairns, goats and yaks. He had one shot he took while walking across an ice ladder over a crevasse.

"I can never look at that picture," said Irene, looking at that picture. "To think it's my boy standing above a chasm he could have fallen into and never been seen from again."

Miles was planning another trip, one last, third attempt.

"This time, I'm going to summit. When I get to the Death Zone, I don't give a toss if they say I've lost the window and they'll have to leave my dead frozen carcass on the mountain if I don't turn back, I won't. I'm returning, in '95 or '96."

"So soon? Weren't you aiming for 1998?" Heidi asked.

"You remember everything, don't you, lass? Aye, I said 1998, but I can't wait that long. I reckon tonight's Jag sale, put towards the Miles to Everest Fund, got me closer."

Everything Miles does is to get to Everest again, he's got that mountain fever insanity Heidi read about. Once you have it, there's no talking you out of it.

"But it's so incredibly expensive, Miles." Heidi said. "For the permit and Sherpas, the guides and oxygen —"

"Yeah, but that's what keeps out the holidaymakers and poseurs. The expense keeps the experience for serious climbers."

"And really rich people," I said. I'd seen enough of the fuzzy equipment they made even the little boy Sherpas cart up the mountain to know it took money to be in this Rich Man's Playground. Everybody seems to be going there now, I thought it was so impossible, there are lineups to get to the top. (He'd bought that slide, one of the clear ones.) I guess I should be more adventurous and have a better attitude, but I just think it's insane to have a death-defying pastime that's like Club Med with ice.

"And who were those climbers they were pushing up the hill in wheelchairs?" Heidi asked him. She was able to make out it was people in those chairs, I thought it was camping equipment.

"That's the trek of people with disabilities who make it to Base Camp, but only that far, we all know there are limits," he said.

"With people pushing and pulling them up? Can that count as climbing?" Heidi said.

"Yeah. Because they're sincere about it and have a good reason to be helped up," he said. "Not like some healthy socialites, who pay Sherpas to carry them to the top."

Heidi knows a lot about Everest but she let him do the talking, after all he'd been there twice and missed. She never brought up the facts she shared with me: Everest is a strong female force with its own name, Chomolungma, Tibetan for "Mother Goddess of the World." The Nepalese call it Sagarmatha, which means "He whose head touches the sky." Climbers burn juniper and say prayers to the mountain so they won't anger the spirit who could cause them to lose their footing or let an avalanche fall on them. It was after two a.m. when Heidi started showing how much she knew. It was like a National Geographic lecture. Miles yawned.

"Stone me, haven't I kept you all up past your bedtimes. I know I'm shattered. No problem, we can all have a lie-in," he said.

"I can't," said Irene, "but I loved it, son. Every time I see it, I see something different." I wondered which blurry new image she made out this viewing.

We were finally shown to our room by Irene. She said Miles christened it Base Camp, I guess because it had all his climbing gear stored in it, even his big boots.

She left us to it. Miles came by and framed our doorway, his hands above the door like he was planning to scale it.

"You're in Base Camp, I'm in Hillary's Step, that's almost as high as I got. Someday I'll be able to call my bedroom Top of the World." He looked at Heidi, and I thought he was going to call her over and whisper, And Heidi, love, I'll be expecting you. Mum and Dad will be dead asleep soon. And then Heidi would have a moral dilemma, because she hardly knew him, but she'd been waiting to see him for over a year. We were only there for five days but rushing into this might not be so smart when he didn't even get home to see her till eleven o'clock, it could make her seem cheap, desperate and easy. And it might scandalize his parents because they didn't seem to think anything was going on between him and Heidi. But no big decision was needed from her because all Miles said was, "I'll use the loo first if that's okay, then it's all yours, my lovely lasses."

It was a good thing Heidi didn't have to go sneaking around the house to find him at Hillary's Step, she could have got lost and wound up in somebody's else's bedroom. The house is so very oddly set up, it looks like one house outside but when you get in you see that they've knocked three council houses together. It's like that place the Beatles have in *Help!* when they all go in different doors but inside it's all one house. Only this wasn't funky like the Beatles', but more like a gamekeeper's cottage, with rooms that led into rooms with hidden cupboards. No wonder the Farnhams find it charming that my garden has so many gnomes, their abode is a home gnomes would live in.

Base Camp was actually what they called a box room, they'd taken all the rucksacks and guide ropes usually piled on the beds and heaped them in a corner. There were two single beds, nicely made up, with crampons and ice axes on hooks hanging above them. Anything that wasn't mountain gear was a mountain poster. Instead of rock stars, Miles had posters of Rob Hall and Scott Fischer, who we guessed were famous Everest climbers of modern times. We knew who Sir Edmund Hillary and Tenzing Norgay were.

"This must be the only room in the house that's not a football shrine," I said to Heidi.

"Oh, I'm sure Miles's room is even more Everest-oriented than this one."

"You'll have to tell me," I said.

"I'm sure we'll both get to see it," Heidi said. "That'll be tomorrow's Everest exhibit."

"Do you think he got his ear pierced in Nepal or Tibet? At one of those mountain villages?"

"I don't know. He didn't have the earring last year, but lots of Englishmen have them. Especially Northerners. They've always had a propensity to be dandified."

"Did you know he still lived at home?"

"The Cobbles is where I sent him letters, I suppose I regarded it as a forwarding address because he can't really have a permanent address yet. He's always away, climbing Everest. Or off adventuring. It's wise anyway. How can he afford his own place if all he can do is use his savings for his next ascent? Lenore, every expedition is at least $65,000 US."

"How can he have that kind of money to throw away? How many Jags does he sell?"

"The Jag dealership is new. Last time he mentioned other work, he said he was a mill foreman. His parents must appreciate him living in and being around. Especially if there are break-ins, being so near the tracks. I'm sure he gives them a feeling of safety and well-being. Oh, I think the bathroom's free. You want to go first?"

"No, you go. Hurry and you'll meet him in the hall, maybe get in a little chat, you never even got to be alone."

"There'll be plenty of time for that."

And not, I hoped, in Hillary's Step. It was his parents'

house for heavens sake, and we were all here. It was not the place for a Dirty Weekend, or a Dirty Mid-Week. I figured he'd get a loan of Mick's Jag or borrow one off the lot and drive her over some hills and dales to some lovely inn.

That of course would mean me stranded in Bickton, where Irene could drag me to panto rehearsal to scare Heather Little Madam Megraines into submission while waving my reviews in her face.

It was morning too soon, Irene arrived at Base Camp and announced, "Heidi, call for you, love. A Phaedra somebody in Bradford. You want to have a lie-in and I'll tell Phaedra you'll ring her back?"

Heidi jumped up, happy to desert her bed, it had not been very comfortable, Heidi was so sarcastic, she said they must have bought the beds off some World War I army hospital. We suspected the pillows and mattresses were stuffed with straw, they crunched so loudly.

"I'll bring you a tea before I'm off to the newsagents, Lenore, lovie," Irene promised.

My first time alone with my thoughts in England gave me the chance to ponder while looking at the all-Everest-all-the-time decor:

1. What if Miles sweeps her away from all this and I am stuck in Bickton-on-Curds for five days?
2. Where will he sweep her off to? Wherever it is, could they give me a lift and leave me in some picturesque nearby village?
3. How can a family decorate their whole knocked-together house in honour of a football team that always loses?

4. Did Heidi tell Miles she was coming here to see him especially? Or does he really think this is just a side trip to see his folks because Irene's friends with Heidi's Mom?
5. I can see how Heidi can overlook the dandy pirate earring, but how about him being thirty-five years old and still living at home?
6. What kind of name is Phaedra for someone who's not in a Greek play?
7. Did Jennie get to do any suturing? I don't think I heard her come home. How long is her shift?
8. I wonder if that ice axe is secure on its hook?
9. When will *Gobsmacked* be on again?

Heidi returned, bringing news from away.

"Phaedra says today's the only time she can really see me, so I've got to get to Bradford by noon, somehow. You can stay here —"

"No! I mean, I'd like to see Bradford," I told her.

"We'll have lunch with her."

"At one of those curry places with the Bollywood videos and Yorkshire's biggest naan bread?"

"I suppose . . . but we've already had a curry take-away . . ." Heidi was obviously not listening to everything Irene said about local famous foods. She was too busy watching the door, hoping Miles would walk through it.

"Is Bradford interesting?"

"I hope so. J.B. Priestly was from Bradford."

I had no idea who J.B. Priestly was, but I would know all about him by the end of the day, I was sure. Phaedra Whistler was an English professor, she was probably going to take us on a tour of his birthplace, writing place and any other place he ever was.

"She has an itinerary planned for us, I'm sure it'll be informative, even though I must admit I'm somewhat dubious," Heidi said. If it was going to be dubious, why were we going? And why would Heidi give up a day she'd rather spend sightseeing with Miles? (And me, too, of course, for as long as she needed me to be the beard.)

"Miles will sleep till very late this afternoon, his Mum says."

"Doesn't he have to go to the Jag dealer's?"

"I suppose not. We'll see him when we get back from Bradford."

Phaedra told us to meet her in front of the Alhambra Theatre, a fabulous Arabian Nights-ish building. The marquee announced the show now playing: *Me and My Girl.* I wanted to see it, that's the British musical where they do the Lambeth Walk, Oy! which was a big hit at our Fundraiser Cabaret. And here it was, being done professionally by British people. I checked to see if the Alhambra had a matinee that day, no luck, if there'd been one I would have pushed for that over anything else Phaedra had planned. She was already forty-five minutes late when I decided to find out who the big statue across the street was. I should have known.

"J.B. Priestly," I shouted across to Heidi. He's very billowy, his tailcoats are flapping in the wind, it looks like he's going to fly away or be knocked over. I returned to Heidi and told her that the library the statue was in front of was also a Film Institute, which boasted a cinematic wonder.

"Like their giant naan bread, no doubt," Heidi said. I guess I did go on about the naan bread being a wonder of Bradford, but I really did want to try it.

A vintage Volkswagen pulled up, driven by a flustered woman all in black.

"Phaedra?" Heidi asked her.

"Yes, do get in or I'll get a ticket! Hurry! I'm not allowed to stop here."

I was thinking, she must have known this was a no-stop area. Why did she tell us to meet her here, in a two-door car, almost an hour ago? She's acting like this is our fault, I don't think I like her attitude; she'd better offer us an apology or reason for being late. But she never did, and the more I got exposed to her, the more I saw she was just a flake, a bona fide Nutty Professor.

Everything Phaedra said was fast, in a big rush, and always in a fit of excitement. She was very eager, like a puppy coaching girls' field hockey by a brook.

"So lovely to meet you finally, is this your friend? Hallo! I had thought I'd give you a tour of the university, but you might regard that as frightfully premature as well as off-putting because it's not a big Canadian one, flash like you're accustomed to, so I thought we'd have a natter at Betty's. Oh, there's David Hockney, hello, David! You know of him, yes? David Hockney?"

"The artist? That was him?"

"He's from Yorkshire. Although I think he's based in America now. He's here painting new works inspired by the countryside — hello, Alan! Yoohoo Allllaaaaan, Alan Ayckbourn! I guess he didn't hear me, I think it was Ayckbourn, he's artistic director of the Stephen Joseph Theatre, in the round, in Scarborough, as well as being Britain's most prolific playwright, perhaps David had a meeting with Alan and is designing a set for him. But why are they meeting here? Could they be planning a nationwide tour that stops at the Alhambra? You wouldn't know it, would you, that Yorkshire has so many world luminaries? Does Betty's of Harrogate suit you?" She swerved in time to avoid a collision with a very large truck full of pipefittings.

"Is Betty's a restaurant?"

"Ahemmmm, yes. You'll have to try a Fat Rascal, I insist, can't go to Betty's and not have a Fat Rascal!" Phaedra said.

Heidi told me later she had the same terror of a Fat Rascal that I did: something very disgusting done in a deep fryer, some great greasy donut with drippings. And who was this Betty?

"Lenore was hoping to sample one of your Bradford curry places?"

"Some of the best ones are on Quebec Street, named after your very own Quebec. General Wolfe had something or other to do with Bradford. There's also a Montreal Street. Bradford is calling to you, Heidi! I had no idea you fancied a curry, wish you'd said so before we set off."

Bradford was behind us and so was my chance for World's Biggest Naan Bread. Betty's of Harrogate turned out to be a fabulous but expensive tea place, and the Fat Rascal was a wondrous thing: a big rock cake scone. I'm glad she insisted on it, as well as picking up the tab, because all we got to do there was listen to her go on and on about the Romantics. She knew everything about Wordsworth and was very envious that we would visit Dove Cottage before she could this spring. She was the world expert on Wordsworth. Dorothy Wordsworth.

"William's sister. They were devoted to one another. She was quite gypsy-like in appearance, and he was very tall, towering above the hedgerows. They must have made quite a picture in Grasmere. And Dorothy's the one who wrote 'Daffodils.'"

"Now, now, Phaedra . . ." Heidi said.

"She saw the field of golden daffodils first, you'll see her extensive journal entry under glass! So what if they also have the couch where 'oft on my couch I lie,' it was Dorothy's poem first. It's the subject of my controversial dissertation, as you well know. Another Fat Rascal?"

"Why don't you have one?" Heidi said.

"Oh no, can't get into that. I'd put on half a stone a week if I did. Have some cake, then. They do lovely cakes!"

We declined, but Phaedra demanded more water for our Darjeeling tea and went into another lecture about her preferred poets. I kept drifting in and out of the conversation, but I jolted back when I heard Phaedra mention Shelley.

"Married to Mary Shelley? She wrote *Frankenstein*."

"Yes, yes, she did."

"A friend of mine in LA wrote a play about Frankenstein when he's in Ireland."

"I don't recall him visiting the Emerald Isle."

"Oh, it's in the book, she told me. The Irish get mad at Doctor Frankenstein and put him in jail, there's a trial and everything."

"I should give it another read, then. Thank you for mentioning it, I think *Frankenstein* might be a good addition to my Canadian curriculum."

"You're coming to Canada?"

"Well, yes, perhaps. But I couldn't possibly start until January of '94, at the earliest," she said and looked at Heidi.

"Of course, myself as well, to start," Heidi said.

"To start where?" I asked.

"Our Trans-Atlantic Academics Exchange Program," Phaedra said.

I just thought we were seeing this Phaedra because she was a colleague or someone Elspeth had forced on us, but she had a master plan and so did my best friend. This was news to me, that's the epitaph they could put on my tombstone: It's News to Me. But I'd be the only one who'd get it and I'd be gone, and anyone looking at my grave would think I was a dead journalist. At this moment, at Betty's, I gave Heidi a you-betrayed-me look.

"You know I had an offer last year from York," she said to me.

"But you turned it down," I said.

"Because Gaëtan died and you and Daniel needed me, but perhaps by next January . . ."

"Sure, sure."

This was so like Heidi, she does this to me quite a lot when I think about it. She doesn't warn me, and I find out as it happens, what does this make her, a Passive Avoidance Person? an Aggressive Avoidance Person? But the deed was done or already in the doing. And who was I to stand in her way? If this romance worked out with Miles, I figured she could move to England for a semester or two, then she could return to Canada, with him. It would be an adventure, a big life change, for a bit. But I wondered: Does it have to be in Bradford? Where will she live? Will she have to get a little car and drive on the wrong side of these English roads through all those roundabouts? And does it mean Canada will get stuck with the Nutty Professor and her Romantics?

Phaedra suggested we do some sightseeing to walk off those Fat Rascals. Harrogate is very pretty and famous for its baths of yore. Betty's was named for the Betty who dispensed the waters at the Pump Room for sixty years. Phaedra urged us, "Do be game and drink the Waters. You can't come to Harrogate and not drink the Waters!" The guide warned us they were potent, we discovered that meant eggy, sulphury, salty, smelly and repeaty! "Horrible, aren't they?"

Phaedra giggled, and then she took us to the Old Swan Hotel, where Agatha Christie wound up when she faked amnesia back in 1926 and had all of England looking for her. Agatha had run away to get back at her husband who was having an affair, she'd even registered at the hotel using his mistress's name and made it look like he'd murdered her, the police were dragging bogs looking for her body. No wonder she was so good at writing such diabolical books.

"We saw *The Mousetrap*," I told Phaedra, who looked at me blankly.

"Is that still playing?"

"Of course, in St. Martin's Lane. It's part of our Show Tour," Heidi told her.

"I never get to London," Phaedra said.

You would, I wanted to say, if there was a show in the West End called *Oft on Wordsworth's Couch I Lie*.

She drove us back to the Cobbles, pointing out where this poem was written or that David Hockney painting was painted and going on and on, then badgering Heidi about when she'd know if they should start the paperwork to make the great TAAEP swap happen. She was already planning which jumpers she would pack for surviving Canada in January. Should she invest in a parka? How fleece lined should her boots be? She seemed to keep missing exits, I thought it was just all those roundabouts, but she was missing turns all right.

I even saw a sign for Sheffield, so I guess the Farnhams are Near it after all, when you get lost on the roads. Heidi was noticing and getting antsy because the afternoon was now pretty much gone, and I knew she realized her man would be awake by now and wondering where we had got to. We finally got home after six, Heidi told Phaedra she'd be in touch.

"Soon, I hope?"

"I'm only here for four more days, I'll let you know before we leave," Heidi said.

"Sooner if you can, we do want to get moving on this. And you'll want to have a look round our university, I should think. Cheerio!" Phaedra sped off.

The telly was on with no one watching it as we came in, I dared to turn it off as we headed back to Base Camp. There were messages pinned under the ice axes over our beds. We each had one from Miles.

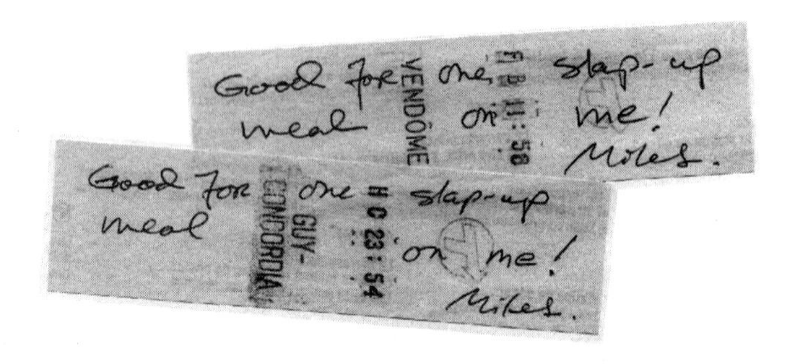

"He saved his Metro transfers!" Heidi said, so happy you'd think it was a bouquet of red roses.

"And they're personalized," I said.

"You got Vendôme for home. And I got Guy-Concordia. What a thoughtful bloke!" she said, so moony eyed it was almost revolting or something you'd want to slap her out of.

But where was he? Would this slap-up meal (hopefully) be tonight?

"You've got something else, Lenore," Heidi said.

And there on my straw pillow was a note from Irene.

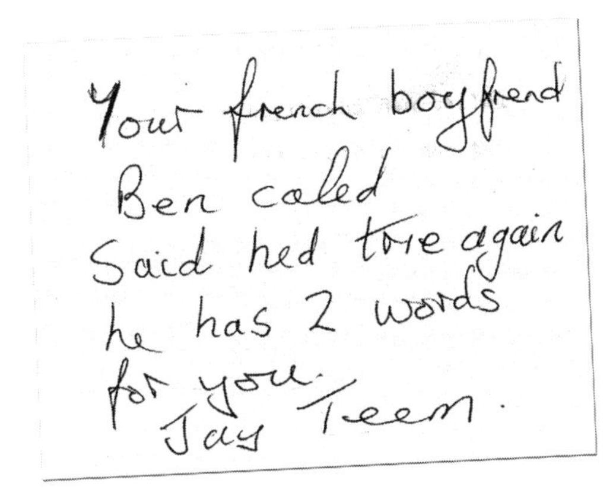

Your french boyfrend
Ben caled
Said hed trie again
he has 2 words
for you.
Jay Teem.

"Jay Teem? Who's Jay Teem?" Heidi wanted to know.

"I have no idea."

"Irene's spelling's not the best. Maybe it sounded that way to her."

Even though the note didn't make sense, it made me realize how much I missed Benoît. The last time I spoke to him was when we got to London and phoned to say we'd arrived safely. He wanted to know if there had been any incidents, I reported no, he told me to watch out for pick-pockets.

"I think they are calling them toots there," he said. "Be careful, eh, chérie, don't assume nothing is what it is, it's a strange country, and this one, it's a sad one with you gone."

I wished I was at the Cobbles when he called instead of out with Phaedra, I thought he was now probably off on some secret CSIS assignment, totally unreachable. I'd have to wait, maybe even days. I fooled myself that maybe this was better:

he'd have even more news of how the Canadiens were doing in the playoffs, and I'd be even closer to going home.

"If we're going out to a slap-up meal, I think I will take a shower, if the inversion's on," Heidi said.

Off she went, and I tried to figure out what JAY TEEM could mean

1. Some contact at New Scotland Yard
2. The Toronto Blue Jays Team, winners of last year's World Series? Maybe one of their players was in Yorkshire. But whywould Benoît care, he's an Expos fan.
3. Jay Walker? Jay Time? Jail Time? Who did I know doing Jail Time? Madame Ducharme? Had all her talk about an appeal got her out? Was she home and wanting her house back from Viola? Or maybe it was a message about Jamie, Cotton's name for him is Jay —

All this strange thinking was stopped by a voice at the door. It was himself, Rip Van Miles.

"Have a cracking day?"

"Interesting, to some people, I guess. We were with a professor from the University of Bradford. She knows an awful lot about poets. And that poem 'Daffodils.'"

"Sounds dead boring. Heidi still with her?"

"No, she's having a shower."

I suddenly felt guilty or shy about mentioning that, like I was suggesting he surprise her there. But he just stood surveying his decorating and then crunched down on Heidi's bed. He was wearing a black t-shirt with a beautiful sunrise coming up over the Himalayas; it said Everest Base Camp Nepal.

"That's a nice shirt," I said.

"It's not authentic. They knock them off on sewing machines, right in their tiny shops. I got it in Kathmandu."

"It's got very nice embroidery," I said.

"You like it?"

"Yeah, it's nice."

"It's yours," he said and stood up, peeled off his shirt and handed it to me.

I could not help but notice that he has a great chest. But still I wondered how he can drink that much lager and not have a beer gut.

"I can't take your shirt," I said.

"Sure you can, lassie. A souvenir of your stay. I want you have the shirt off my back."

I was terrified that Heidi or Irene would walk in on us, it was all very innocent but it might not look that way, him magnificently half-naked and me sitting on a bed. I shoved the t-shirt at him.

"It was very sweet of you, but please put your shirt back on. Now."

"Sure thing, sunshine," he replied and pulled his shirt on slowly and smiled. "Just tell me, you won't ask me to take back me invite on me mum's metro souvenirs, will you?"

"Oh no, we're looking forward to that. Tonight?"

"Yeah. What do you fancy? Italian? Greek? Indian? Thai? Vietnamese? Lebanese? Traditional English?"

"Maybe I'll leave that decision to Heidi," I said.

"Her decision, but if she's too polite to make one, it's my choice." He left Base Camp, and a few seconds later I heard the telly back on.

Heidi looked pretty sensational for our night on the Bickton-town as we made our entrance into the sitting room. Miles jumped up like a gentlemen.

"Ain't you a sight in sapphire!"

He'd been laughing like a maniac, and he was wiping his eyes from laughter when we walked in.

"*Carry On Camping*. That Sid James, he's a bloody master of comedy! We've got almost the whole collection on video."

He was so dazzled by Heidi there was no more Carrying On, he turned the TV off. This was such a romantic gesture, I decided I would say I was waiting for a call from Benoît and let it just be the two of them going for a slap-up meal when Irene and Gordon ran in by the back door.

"Oh, there you are!" Irene said, looking at me wildly.

I thought I knew where this was going.

"Can't go to the panto practice. We were just on our way out," I said.

"Yes, Mum, soon as I get me glad rags on —"

"Oh! Lenore can't go!"

"I'm taking them both out —"

"We need Lenore! It's Heather!"

"Oh Mum, sod that, she won't be scared off by Lenore —"

"How can she be when she's in hospital?"

"Hospital?"

"Emergency. For her wisdom teeth! They've all got to come out, same time. That's what's been giving her the megraines."

"But she'll be okay in a few days . . . ," Heidi said.

"Not always. Our Jennie was laid up for a week and half. And her a nurse! Remember her face, Miles?"

"Oh, yeah, she was black and blue, a real mess, looked like she'd been in a barny," he said.

"Well, can't you do the panto next weekend? Or whenever Heather's better?"

"No. It's the Founding of Bickton-on-Curds panto. It has to be on the day."

"Why, is there some Witch's Curse? The Monarchy Will Crumble? It's the only time the theatre space is free?"

"No! Because it just has to be! It's Tradition. And we've sold all the tickets!" Irene took my hand. "Lenore, lovie, we need a star."

"I can't be in your panto . . ."

"You can. You can, you can. You'll be the little Noddy that could."

They were going to make me play Noddy? He was an elf!

"I'm not British," I told them. "They'll know."

"You don't have to talk that much, just sing, sing, sing," Gordon said.

"Lovely Gershwin bits, Irving Berlin, a Rosemary Clooney, Petula Clark, even some from that *Starlight Express*," Irene said.

"Oh, we just saw that," Heidi said.

"You see, Lenore, they won't even be strange to you, come on, dearie, it ain't more than a dozen songs," Irene cajoled.

"Lenore can learn all of them. They threw about twenty Andrew Lloyd Webber last-minute songs at her for a disastrous marriage ceremony she did last year," Heidi boasted.

"How disastrous?" Irene asked.

"It lasted six weeks."

"The ceremony?"

"No, the marriage," Heidi said.

When Emerson, your nerdy former fiancé that you decided you couldn't marry the day before your wedding, married man-chaser Tess of the d'Urberblondes, another fine mess one of your romances got me into, I wanted to shout, but instead I announced, "I gave up show business."

"When?" Irene asked.

"Right after I did *Bells Are Ringing*. It was not a happy experience."

"But you got them rave reviews. And you do show business for a living, at your Feast-In," Irene said.

"That's show business of necessity. And I don't have to sing so much anymore. We've hired a new headliner. And this is . . . different. This is musical theatre. I made a vow last year, no more." Which was true.

"But you broke it, Lenore," Heidi the Traitor said.

"When?"

"For that Fundraiser Cabaret your group did in April. They talked you into singing that paean from *Working: The Musical*: 'It's An Art to Be a Fine Waitress.'"

"That was one song, for a benefit, this is a whole show."

"This is a benefit, for the sake of Bickton-on-Curds. It's probably even for charity. Isn't it, Irene? Tell her."

"We're always in need of a helping hand. We were bombed in the blitz, lovie."

This got Heidi on a soapbox.

"Until they were shut down and put so many out of work, some of Bickton's finest young men were claimed by the coal mines."

It looked like Miles was about to say they were nowhere Near Coal Mines, but instead he begged: "You must help me mum and dad." They were all looking at me. I was their only hope, I was all they had, poor chaps.

"We've come to you, caps in hands Lenore," Gordon pleaded.

"Oh, the panto cast! All their faces, young and old, lit up when I told them about you. And when they heard you'd been on the Academy Awards, two of them said they saw you, they remembered you were the one praying."

"You can do it, Lenore, you know you can." Heidi, cheerleading.

And here we were, their guests, they needed me to help, and it would be bad form not to agree to do their panto with less than twenty-four hours notice.

As we all headed out the back door, even Heidi in her blue cocktail dress, I called to Irene as she grabbed my reviews from the stuffed drawer. "About my note from Benoît? My French boyfriend?"

"You read it, under the axe?" Irene said.

"What did Ben say the two words were?"

"I'm sorry, love, they were in French and I don't speak it, so I jest put it down the way I heard it."

"He said it in French?"

"All shy, like. But I think it was Je Temm."

I now knew what Benoît had said.

"Je t'aime?"

"That's it! Yeah, that sounds like it. Jee Tim!"

"Mum, you don't know much French, do you? Jee Tim. It's 'I love you,'" Miles said and looked at me.

"How was I to know that? I never got me A levels. I never been to Paris!"

They all smiled at me. My boyfriend had gone international to call and declare his love for me, and I was going to do their panto, all was right with the world.

Chapter Five 

I thought there was nobody I could confess to. It was the kind of terrible secret I'd tell Heidi except she was the reason I needed to tell somebody else. I was so distressed I couldn't call home and tell Benoît, even if I could reach him, because if he found out, I was sure there would be hell to pay, with probably an arrest, his own. He'd have been on the first plane to rescue me. And Heidi. It would have been just as bad if I told Daniel, he'd be so mad he'd tell Heidi's dad and her brothers and well, it would be a Fighting Flynns international incident. It was a terrible, potentially devastating, heart-breaking situation. This was the thanks I got for doing the Bickton panto under duress!

The rehearsal process, as Heidi called it, was one twenty-two-and-a-half-hour blur, kind of like Miles's slides of Everest. I had no chance to think what I was doing, but that'll happen when you have to speed learn twelve songs and what Dot called her "blocking with choro-graphy." In the back of my mind, as we rushed to the church that fateful night, I hoped that when we got to the scene of *Noddy in Love*, Heidi and I would discover, somewhere in the hall, an understudy of some sort, anyone who could do the show instead of me.

And that might have happened if there was even one Eve

Harrington or Shirley MacLaine in the bunch instead of mostly senior citizens or preteens who were "happy with their one little bit of business." We saw why Little Madam Megraines has been the star now and forever.

Heidi did a fantastic job of researching Noddy for me so I'd have some vague idea of what the show was. I didn't want to scare the cast again, especially after I walked in, saw a yellow and red car on the stage and exclaimed, "Oh, who gets to drive the cute little car?" and they gasped, as one person. "Noddy does. He's a taxi cab driver. This is Toy Town."

They had grown up with Noddydom. It was part of their culture. We don't know these things. Imagine if they came to Canada and we suddenly made them do a panto of *The Friendly Giant in Love with Chez Hélène*. They'd be sure to ask, "Oh, what's that great big chair for?" and we'd gasp out, "To curl up in." And they'd say, what's with the giraffe named Jerome and that rooster in the stocking? And the lady who only speaks French to the mouse, who translates it all into English?

It was fortunate Heidi got Des the Librarian, who played Bill or Ben, one of the Flower Pot Men, to open up the library "well after hours" so she could speed read all the Noddy Books. She gave me a quick but thorough lecture. It didn't help when that strange eleven-year-old playing Big-Ears the Brownie rode by on a bicycle, rang its little bell and said, "It's *Noddy for Dummies*."

"Just what you need, a computer twit in costume," Heidi said. By then, she'd provided a rundown of all the characters, especially mine. Dead serious, she said, "Tell me about Noddy." And I answered, "I live in a dear little brick House-For-One, there it is on the stage, next to my car. And I work very hard, and my neighbours are Mr. and Mrs. Tubby Bear, played by Gordon and Irene. And there is a copper named Mr.

Plod, a Katie the Kangaroo and a lazy elephant called Mr. Jumbo."

"Very good. Now, what do you want?"

"What do I want? Not to be doing this!"

"Lenore, I meant, what drives Noddy?"

"His little taxi. This is Toy Town."

"By drive, I mean, what does Noddy want? Need? What's his motivation?"

"Heidi! Are you crazy? He's an elf. There's no time for this kind of talk."

"Did you say that when you played Ella in *Bells*? And Cleo in *Most Happy Fella*? You knew what they wanted as characters."

"Because I had months and months of rehearsal. And you for my acting coach. Heidi, we've got less than a day for me to learn how to be Noddy."

"I know, I know. But for Noddy to be real, to be believable, for you to succeed, Noddy has to be grounded. He's part of Britain's psyche, he's very important to them —"

"Stop it. You're terrifying me, Heidi. I have no idea who Noddy is. I don't know how I am going to pull this off."

"Say he's Northrop."

"Northrop? Our little friend Northrop?"

"Yes. He's a sweet little boy. And that's what Noddy is."

"Okay. I can do that."

"Model him on Northrop and that will get you through this. I know it will."

And that's what did it, I guess, because from that spell of stage-fright panic attack, I was grounded, I pictured Northrop (without Elspeth for his mother), and that's who Noddy was.

As for Noddy's fashion sense, it was already decreed by the books. I wore a blue hat with a bell that always goes jingle-jingle-jing so you hear him coming. Heather Megraines was a skinny Madame because they made a scene about how much they had to alter the red, yellow and blue elf costume.

"You've a good two stone on her," Heloise said, taking it out, adding pieces and pinning me up. I guessed Heather was elf-like.

"You've got the same hair colour as Noddy, we'll give you that, won't have to worry about you fitting into Heather's wig," Heloise said.

Miles pitched in too, building and painting the set, putting out the chairs, even folding programs. He was flirting and laughing it up with Heidi, she looked so happy, I saw this was a good way to get to know each other better, working on a group project under stressful conditions. Heidi stopped him from painting his Jag dealership logo on Noddy's car because it was a taxi.

"I don't act anymore, but I do respect the Method," she told me, "and I've never approved of product placement in the arts."

The musical director twins were marvellous. Cecilia as in the patron saint of music and Sardi — "our real names are Sicily and Sardinia because Mum and Dad always wanted to go to Italy" — are very accomplished and play piano alternating afternoons at a tea house, they also do garden parties and funerals and run the music program for several schools. They loved to play piano, even when not required, boosting team spirit with pub song standards and English airs. But they'd stop playing whenever Miles came around to ask me anything. I assumed it was because they had a crush on him, they did not know that all they had to do was say, "We like your t-shirt," and he'd give them a show.

Dot seemed to be giving hourly reports on Heather's prognosis.

"Crikey! It's like she thinks Heather will pull through and do the panto," said Irene Mrs. Tubby Bear.

Fine by me, bring her on, sang out my inner voice.

Dot conducted four dress rehearsals over twenty-two and a half hours, and any time in between, when she wasn't saying to me, "Lovely, lovie pet, but could you try faster? Spritelier? Bigger? Sadder? Wiser? Flittier? And English please, not northern Saskatchewan?" I was in a costume fitting while being interviewed by the Bickton-on-Curds *Courier*, or rehearsing the songs with Cecilia and Sardi.

Then when we got briefly back to the Cobbles, I was going over the Life of Noddy, with Heidi playing Henry Higgins and trying to make me sound British. I never slept. Everyone else in the house did but me. Then back to the church hall again, and finally, magically, it was opening night, and there I was singing my songs from a big Noddy Storybook. The plot of the panto was this: I, Noddy, am so happy it's spring and everyone's falling in love. That's where all the skits came in, many of them not even featuring Noddy book characters. They threw in songs wherever they felt like it; I sang six in Part One and the cast sang what seemed like fifty, there were so many medleys. The audience had a ball from the minute it began. It was a wise choice to kick it off with "Round Every Corner," we had a Petula Clark love fest as they clapped and sang along. I loved all my songs, even if I had to sing them dressed like Noddy. My favourite of all *was* "I've Got Beginner's Luck," right before the interval.

Heidi came backstage, popped her head into the Sunday school, now moonlighting as a dressing room, and asked was there anything she could do for me. I told her, "Not unless you're Bickton's answer to Edith Head. Look at the bows on my little red shoes. Mr. Jumbo stomped on them." She promised she'd tell Heloise to come see me, she was going to help sell raffle tickets now, she was elated. "Lenore, I just have to say, you are super as Noddy! Hasn't it gone well so far? How can it be half finished already? It's flying by. I must confess, I quite like show business. If you ever return to the stage in Montreal, I'd love to work on your shows." She'd barely rushed out when the door opened again and I thought, "Wow, that was fast." But it wasn't Heloise, it was Miles.

I was alone, he shut the door and gazed at me. Neither of us spoke. I was about to, but he strode across the dressing room, took me in his arms and really kissed me. And it was some kiss, possibly the best one I'd ever had, but what was he thinking? I wanted to shout: I'm dressed like an elf. I'm here because my best friend wants you. I'm dating a cop. I'm not for the taking, especially against a wall painted with scenes from the Old and New Testament!

I managed to pull myself away and snarl, "Are you insane? What was that all about?"

"That song is what it's all about — 'I've Got Beginner's Luck' — 'The first time I'm in love, I'm in love with you.' You were singing it to me, I could tell." He staked his claim.

"I was singing it to the audience."

"But I was your inspiration, like. Admit it."

"My boyfriend Benoît, a police officer, is my inspiration!"

"*Jee Tim*?"

"Yes. Him. Don't think you'll trick me into saying that to you! He's the only one I'd say that to."

"And you're the only one I'd say that to. I mean it. What kind of bloke can Jee Tim be, letting you go off by yourself?"

"I'm not by myself, I'm with Heidi." (And she's the one you should be mauling, not me.)

"If you were my bird, I wouldn't let you go swanning off to foreign lands."

"Well, I'm not your bird. And Benoît doesn't own me, even

if I am his bird. I sure wish he was here because that copper would throw you in jail."

"For what? You didn't seem to mind much."

"Can I help it if you're a good kisser?"

"Oh, so you noticed."

"Of course I noticed. Just get out! I have Part Two of your parents' panto to do!"

"You're not gonna tell on me?"

"No."

"You're not gonna tell Heidi?"

"No. But why kiss me, why not Heidi?"

"Because you're my type, darlin'."

"You've been writing to her for over a year. You sent her postcards and a little Buddha for her birthday . . ."

"Because I like her, yeah, but I know she can only be a friend. All right, so she looked fantastic in that blue getup. But she's so bloody smart, I realize, the more she's around. We've got nothing in common. I want someone I can have a laugh with, like you."

"You've been having laughs with her, I've seen you both."

"Yeah. But she's not what I go for. I'm not what she goes for either."

Oh yes you are, I almost said, and then it hit me: why am I making a case for her to wind up with him? He's a cad, a rat, a louse. I just stared at him. He now had a hurt, angry look.

"She had plenty of chances back in Canada. My last night there, we'd all been out, yeah, it was late, what did Heidi do but go back to her flat alone. She could have invited me up to spend me last night with her."

"But if anything had happened the night before you left, wouldn't it have been what you people call a one-off?"

"A one-off? You are getting the hang of our lingo, lassie."

"Don't lassie me. You would have been using her. A one-night stand."

"No. Not if she meant it too and then came over here sooner to see me. Instead of this pen-pal chase, letting a whole year go by, then bringing her gorgeous bird of a chum along. That's not the way a woman who wants a bloke like me behaves. I never met you much in Montreal because you were working . . ."

"You came to Festin that night, you met me enough," I said.

"Yeah, but you were a different person when you got here. More relaxed, like, not some waitress businesswoman. Still, you caught my eye back there. I asked me Aunt Jemima about you. And okay, yeah, so Heidi was the one I was looking at in Canada . . ."

"She was your date at your cousin's wedding," I reminded him.

"Yeah, yeah. She's a helluva dancer. She knows a lot about Everest. I fancied her, sure, but I dunno, she's too independent. Oh, sod it, why did she send me reviews about her best mate, telling stories of all your adventures? She made me fall for you, Lenore, through her own letters. It's like she was telling me, Miles, this is the bird you've got to know. And I want to know you, I want you, darlin'. I feel like a rotter to Heidi, but can't we both just pretend you're the one I saw first?"

"No. Because it's not true. And I'm taken, Miles!"

"I'm taken with you —"

That's when Heloise came in.

"A problem with your bows? They're not secure, Heidi tells me?"

"And the jingle-jingle-jing hat needs a bell adjustment while you're at it, bloody annoying," Miles said. I was still wearing my Noddy hat, it was probably jingle-jinging the whole time.

Miles winked at me, then strolled out. Heloise gave me a sad look, the same one the cast gave me when they discovered I didn't know Noddy drove a car.

"You'd best touch up your makeup, dearie," Heloise said.

Somehow I got through Part Two, even the reprise of "I've Got Beginner's Luck" and the big closing number, "Come On-A My House-For-One" as the entire cast made their exit into Noddy's little brick house. Just like all the clowns getting into the Volkswagen.

And they all came out again in time for the curtain call and the standing ovation. It was so nice when they presented me and Dot with flowers on stage and Mr. Plod the Copper gave a speech making a big fuss about the girl from Canada saving their panto. It would have been wonderful and triumphant if not for Miles's backstage pass. The big event at the cast party occurred when Dot brought out her Spring Berries Roulade, with much musical fanfare provided by Cecilia and Sardi.

"Oh, the Roulade!" Many cheered.

"It's a big jelly roll," Heidi said.

A biggest-naan-bread-in-Yorkshire-size jelly roll, it was so gigantic you could throw it in the Fraser River and lumberjacks would do a dance on it. There was wild applause for the arrival of the honorary jelly roll slicer: Heather Megraines, in a wheelchair. Miles was smiling proudly at me, and I just wanted to kill him. Townsfolk kept congratulating us all, and, surprise, one of them was Nurse Jennie. She'd been in the audience and even won a raffle prize, which a vicious audience member contested as "a fiddle," just because Jennie's parents and one Canadian guest were in the show and the other Canadian guest sold her the ticket. "Wait till I see her next time she comes to the surgery," she commented to Heidi. Jennie kept the prize too, a basket of three jars of homemade Lemon Curd-on-Bickton. This was the first time we'd seen her since she got us the curry take-away the night we arrived.

I thought Jennie could be the someone I could confide in, perhaps she might not be as totally devoted to Miles as his mum and dad. That conniving, disloyal predator, so smooth, so good-looking, such a bad slide show photographer. Now I knew what the t-shirt Chippendales show at Base Camp was leading to, in his mind. I felt I'd have to find the right time to approach her about my dilemma.

"That must have been some shift," I said to Nurse Jennie.

"You must think I'm a vampire, Jennie Dracula, sleeping by day, out by night," she said. "Tell me, Lenore, are you not sleeping?"

This was a strange question, why bring it up? For sure, she must know about the straw mattresses. As well as the sleepless twenty-two-and-a-half-hour Noddy Marathon. I did not reply.

"Because you look shattered," was her medical opinion.

"I guess I am, doing the panto so fast, and jet lag," I said, which might have been partially true.

"No. It's something else," she said and looked over at Miles.

"Your brother's been helping on the show," I told her.

"So Mum said, that's a first. You Canadians must have some influence on him," she said, suddenly suspicious, as if she thought we were keeping him from some nice local girl.

"So what are your plans for the rest of your stay?" she asked.

"I'm not sure. We were hoping you could do things with us."

"Oh, I will, somehow, before you go, I'll even book off — "

"Better do it soon, then. They've only got three days left," said her mum as she joined us, still in her Mrs. Tubby Bear costume.

"Mum, you know Dot wants you all out of costume for the cast party," Jennie said as Mr. and Mrs. Noah, still in Bible get-ups, walked past.

"Just so nothing upstages her darling roulade. Sod it, I won't get to wear this ever again, so I'm keeping it on long as I can! Unless we do *Goldilocks* again. And Jennie, love, she won't say, but everyone wants to know when Heather's stitches will come out."

"Probably next week, Mum."

"Late or early?"

"Early, I should think."

"Will you get to do them?"

"It's the dentist or her assistant will get that pleasure," she said.

"Oh, too bad," said Irene.

"As I tried to ask our Noddy before, what have you got planned for what's left of your visit?"

Of course I didn't get a chance to answer.

"I was afraid you'd miss out on all them sights Heidi listed off, Woolworth's Land and all," Irene said, "but seems you'll be seeing some."

"Which ones?" I asked.

"Gordon's lending you the motor for tomorrow. I ordered Miles to ask Heidi to pick the spots she wants to visit most, so he'll take you. I heard her tell him she wants to go to the parsonage. Is she a religious girl?"

Lucky for me I'd heard Heidi talk about the Brontë Parsonage enough times. Otherwise I would have been very worried, because what do you do at a parsonage? Post banns and then get married.

Of course Miles had to have a bit of a lie-in the next day, so we couldn't set off right away. I certainly deserved one, but Irene came into Base Camp and chirped, "One of you girls has a call. Guess who?"

"Mon Benoît?" I asked.

"Eh, whot? I don't speak French, my darlin'. The who is . . . Heidi! It's that fast-talking Phaedra from Bradford."

"Tell her I'll ring her back, please," Heidi said with her head under the straw pillow. The roulade had been laced, the Spring Berries had been soaking in Pernod for three days. And Heidi'd done too much celebrating with Dot's Panto Punch, too.

Phaedra was calling again, but it had now been three days since I'd heard from Benoît. I guessed his latest CSIS assignment was too top secret or he'd phoned when we were all at rehearsal, and Jennie Dracula was sleeping in a house with almost every Carry On video but no answering machine.

Eventually Heidi sat up in her crunchy bed and looked at me.

"I should have taken the call, why leave her hanging? I know what I'm going to say," she said.

"No?"

"Yes. I'm going to say yes," Heidi said, smiling.

"No you're not."

"I think I will."

"But nothing has happened yet, with Miles."

"Yes it has."

"When?"

"Ever since we got here. He's magnificent, Lenore. I know all we did together was work on the panto, but that was such fun. We had so much to talk about. He's not only handsome and charming, he's so invigorating, don't you think? And such a guy. A manly man. We'll see how it goes today in Haworth, and anyway what's the hurry? Yes, so we're going home, but he can come visit me over the summer, I can come back before school starts again. I think I could have a very pleasant life here in England, really belong. The northerners are all so friendly, perhaps I'll direct the panto next year. Give Dot a chance to be on stage, maybe do a mother-and-daughter duet with Heather? Something from *Gypsy* maybe. And if Miles can paint and do fix-ups on a set, I'm sure he could build one too. Maybe I could even interest David Hockney in designing it."

She'd caught the theatre bug as well as Miles Fever. Next thing, she'd be financing his expeditions and the Sherpa carrying his bags up Everest for him. My super-smart friend had lost it, she'd gone insane, she was totally out of control! She went back to sleep, but I had to get out of the Cobbles.

I wandered around for two hours trying to figure out what to do. I met many people who'd seen the panto, I tried to enjoy being a local celebrity. But I needed to talk to somebody! Who could that person be? I kept passing call boxes, but you don't phone one of those suicide hotlines because of dating problems. There was a sign above the Butcher Shoppe for a family therapist, but they can't solve the problem all in one session. And there were no children involved, but there could be if I didn't stop this.

But then — I can't believe this now — I wavered. I was a rag on a clothesline, une guenille dans le vent, trying to see the situation from his point of view. I was my own Devil's Advocate. I asked myself, how did Miles get the wrong idea? Could it be because Heidi's too cautious and that scared him off? Even though she's nuts about him and this Show Tour trip for the two of us must have cost her almost three thousand dollars, she never told Miles she was really here because of him. How could he think that when she brought her pal along? I'm everywhere she wants to be, like MasterCard. But how can he not know she wants him, just because she puts up such an intellectual guard and independent front? Men like Miles don't like that, I suppose. They're not manly men enough for a "bloody smart" woman. She could have been more stand-offish with him, cold and snappish, look how well that worked with Lord Peach. She got a marriage proposal out of him. Miles would chase madly after Heidi if she played the Ice Queen, but it's not like she's going to be Your Ladyship if she ends up with him.

And him going after me? Maybe he did it because I got into show business here. Those stage door Johnnies taking actresses out for drinks and all got everybody thinking actresses were all prostitutes. Or pretty loose. Maybe that old fashioned idea still exists in northern England? But I wasn't in the show when he came into Base Camp and made a move on me. Was that because I'm just too friendly, good for a laugh when men meet me, so they think they can really kiss me during intermission, against my will, when I have a devoted boyfriend back home and a best friend selling raffle tickets in the hall? Heidi could never know about that, it would kill her.

I was so mixed up, but then I saw what became my refuge. I didn't expect it would turn out the way it did, I just hoped this pretty church would give me some guidance.

To think it wound up being Catholic, with votive candles for help and confession booths. The light over one of them meant Open for Business. The booth was small inside, woody and brown, like in the movies, when people always had a dramatic reason for being in there: they had slept with the brother of their fiancé like Cher in *Moonstruck*, or they had to confess a crime the priest couldn't reveal and that he'd get blamed for. If it was a comedy, the priest was usually really odd or sexually depraved. But the real-life priest was mumbling to somebody else on the other side when I knelt down. I panicked because what if he'd be like that fuddy-duddy Father Sullivan who did the Flynns' Anniversary Mass?

What would I say when I told some old-timer priest the man my friend made us come all the way to England to find out whether she should sleep with him, wants to sleep with me? I mean, what would old Father Sullivan say to that? I'm not Catholic, so he might dismiss me as an object of desire, but Heidi? She's the Catholic. Sex outside of marriage would be a big sin for her, if she listened to the Pope. And then what if the padre asked, what have you done to make Miles think he can have relations with you? And I replied: Nothing. I have a boyfriend. And then he'd ask personal questions about things that are none of his business. He was taking too long to get back to me, and I was worrying — what am I doing in here anyway, what do they say first as a hello, when the little screen slid across. The priest did a Latin blessing over me. I was shocked. He was not old, he was a Doogie Howser priest. He must have gone to seminary at eight.

"Bless me, Father, I'm not Catholic."

"But you feel like you need to make a good confession?"

That was a good start, so open and understanding.

"Yes. My best friend and I are visiting England . . ."

"Are you having a blast?"

"Well, we were, yes, until what I'm in here for happened."

"I hope you're sightseeing. Don't miss the Dales and — "

"We're supposed to be going to Haworth later today — "

"Oh, can't miss that. Brontëland! Self-guided? Or on a tour?"

"With a guide, of sorts. That's where my problem started,

Father, you see. My friend and I came here because last year in Canada, the British people we're visiting now, well, one of them was . . . very attentive to my friend. And they've had this sort of weird letter writing romance thing going, and she came over here to see if there was anything to it. Now she's so serious about him she wants to accept a university teaching post in Bradford. Even though Miles hasn't even . . . oh, sorry! We're not supposed to use names, eh?"

"Oh, you can. But this isn't a real confession, more of a chat, with the benefits of the secret of the confessional."

"Oh, okay, good, then, I'm Lenore."

"I'm Father Blunt. Rupert Blunt. Might I just say, I loved Canada when I visited Vancouver for Expo '86. Brilliant place. Continue with your story, Lenore."

"My friend Heidi is nuts about this guy Miles because he's rugged and virile and not at all her type. But she can't help herself."

"She's a woman. He's a man. Chemical attraction. Needs. It happens."

"She's so smart and should have known better but any way . . . it hasn't been one-sided. He's been wooing her with cards, sending her things, even a little Buddha from Everest."

"Everest?"

"Yeah, the mountain?"

"The one Miles Farnham has already failed to summit twice?"

"Yes. You know him?"

"He's on my cricket team. He's also my distant cousin."

"I should stop. It's getting too personal.

"No, go on. Has anything happened yet, a get-together so to speak?"

"No. Heidi's not the one he wants, it would seem."

"Oh, they're all the one he wants."

"Pardon?"

"If Miles hasn't made a move on her yet, Heidi's had a lucky escape."

"Really?"

"He's ruined so many, many women. And there will be many, many more. There was a terrible blowout, a public crying scene during a tournament last year. The poor lass came out on to the pitch, baby in tow! He's notorious."

"He made a move on me. A big one. And I feel terrible. It came out of nowhere — "

"You're attractive, you're female, you're under forty, that's all that's required."

"Heidi's very attractive. You should see the sexy blue dress she wore, not that you're allowed to notice that sort of thing, but you would. She's female and she turns thirty-nine in June. But she's too intellectual, he says."

"He doesn't like the smart ones as much. Not that you aren't — "

"No, I know what you mean. But I'm the sort that's good for a laugh. I'm not smart like her."

"There have been a few exceptions, executives mostly, I suspect with access to funding bodies for his climbing, but they're not the norm. Perhaps this Heidi's not as alluring as you are."

The priest said I was alluring. New Priests' School.

"I never tried to be alluring, Father. The time he tried it on, I was dressed like Noddy."

"You're Noddy! That's how I know you, you were cracking! It is you, of course, the Canadian who saved the day. Your English accent was so valiantly convincing. I especially loved what you did with "This is the Moment" from *Jekyll and Hyde*.

Quite a dramatic song for an elf, I wondered if Enid Blyton ever envisioned such emotional range in her jolly character. And everyone piling into your House-For-One at the end, super! I've always wanted to be brave enough to be in the panto — "

I almost said, well, Heidi would certainly encourage you to follow your artistic bent if she directs it next year, when I realized I don't want her to wind up in Bickton-on-Curds, and there's probably a line-up forming for confessions outside the booth by now, so we'd better wind this up.

"She really wants to take that professor job at Bradford, she's going to change her life for him. What can I do to warn her off Miles without her ever knowing how I know?"

"You must discover a way for Heidi to find out but keep her dignity, let her break it off with him, she has to have the upper hand and at the same time perhaps put him in his place so that this never happens again. He's a plague. And seemingly unstoppable, with Canadian girls now crossing the ocean to get at him. You must end his reign."

"How can I do that?"

"I don't know yet. You could enlist Jennie."

"Really?"

"Oh yes, many's the poor lass that has cried on her shoulder. Poor Bunty Gumley, Honey Kewell . . ."

"Have they all confessed to you?"

"No. They're not Catholics. But I've heard it all from other sources. And yes, some of his conquests have been to see me here. I can't tell you what they said. But it was all bad. Let me have a think on this. Here's my card."

And he slipped a business card through the confessional screen.

"If it gets any worse and Heidi's in danger of succumbing,

please call me immediately, even if you have to do so from the Black Bull pub. It's a must-do Branwell Brontë Haunt on the Main Street in Haworth. I don't have a solution right now, but I should, once I have a good think and pray for guidance."

I guess the setting got to me, the confession was over, but I began to spill.

"Father, I should be honest. Maybe I did fancy Miles. If I didn't have a fabulous boyfriend and if Miles wasn't my best friend's intended, I would have been interested. There's something about him, I'd have to be dead not to notice. Maybe he picked up on that, and when he kissed me, I responded to him — "

"Lenore. You must not blame yourself for any of this."

"But I do. I feel so badly about this, and Heidi's going to be heartbroken if she ever finds out."

"She won't, if we do our best. Have faith. God bless you. Go in peace."

There was a lineup when I got out of the confessional. I think they would have glared at me or judged me for taking so long in there, but they'd all seen me in the panto.

"Loved 'You've Got to Have Heart,' duck!"

"Gave me goose bumps what you did with 'A Piece of Sky' from *Yentl*."

Why was Miles suddenly interested in being our tour guide, especially to the home of the Brontë sisters? This time, if Miles had hinted that maybe he'd like the day to himself and Heidi alone, I'd have said, "You're dreamin'! Not without me. I've always longed to see where the Brontës wrote all their books." Heidi really wanted to go there, she'd been before on her first trip to England, after college, now it was "something of a personal pilgrimage." She felt it was important that I see it, even if I'd only read some of *Jane Eyre* in high school and finished it with Coles Notes. I'd seen both versions of the movie. I suggested Brontëland could just be Heidi and me. I was willing to drive on the wrong side of the road, without an International Driver's license, if they let me. Or we could take a train or a bus, we found our way to Bradford, didn't we?

"Miles wants to go."

"His mother made him ask us. He'll think it's dead boring."

"Not if it's a day out with us."

"He'll probably desert us and wind up at the Black Bull."

"Lenore! You know about the pub where Branwell Brontë drank? Have you been reading the guidebooks?"

"Some, not all. A little bit." I lied. I'd never looked, not once. I left all that to her.

"Well, he's a sweetie to take us if he's not interested. And if he wants to lift a pint or two while we trek all over the moors, that's fine by me."

She was besotted, but if it got too bad I had my priest's calling card.

So we found ourselves on the way to Brontëland with a man who'd never read any of the Brontë books but would have made a move on all three Brontë sisters given any chance.

Just after Keighley and before Haworth, after many green hills with lovely sheep and cows, Miles stopped at Ben Shaw's chippie. It was time for us to sample a true Yorkshire delicacy: "fish and chips with scraps to eat now." Scraps sounded like they'd be horrible, somebody's leftovers that weren't chucked in the bin, but they were crunchy side bits. And they came with a huge piece of fish with chips, served up in paper. So evil and delicious and not something you'd want to eat more than once every five years because they could kill you. Miles also ordered us three teas, and the lady brought them to us as we sat there on her concrete stoop by some poppies eating our fish from newspaper. I was so cynical, I thought, ha, this is probably our slap-up meal on him. In any case, it was in keeping with the Cobbles dining: everything had been take-away, fry ups, or beans on toast, and always with tea.

Haworth was otherworldly, stuck in time, on a narrow, cobbled road winding up a hill. There was the Parsonage set in the graveyard, so grim and sad looking. What a depressing place to grow up, even if they did get famous and write so many books there. Heidi sort of sighed.

Miles smirked and said, "Ah, Brontësauruses."

If anyone else had ever said that about her beloved writing sisters, she'd have wanted to smack him, she'd be so hurt. Instead she gazed at him.

"Brontësauruses?" he repeated.

"I got it the first time."

"Ah, come on, lass, you don't think that's funny?"

Heidi didn't say anything, and I thought, Hallelujah, she's seeing some light. That's when he ruined everything, he gathered her into his arms and said playfully, "I'm sorry! Forgive me!"

"You're forgiven," she said, and he gave her a quick smacker of a kiss on the lips, and I knew she was a goner. What will he try to get up to if the weather stays nice like this and we have to walk to Wuthering Heights? Where's my card from the priest? Are there any call boxes on the moors? Will I have to perform an exorcism myself?

"Shall we go into the Parsonage Museum?" Heidi asked, and we both said sure. Miles was pretending but I really was interested, it proved way more fascinating that I ever thought it would be. It was so good, I decided I would read their novels now. This was really their house, where they wrote all those books; it had little tiny rooms, but they were little tiny women. I always thought they were poor as church mice, but they had nice furniture and a servant. We saw the parlour where they'd meet at night and share their writing, walking round and round the table, arm in arm. They still had the couch where Emily breathed her last. And in a case the collar of Keeper, the faithful dog she ran with on the moors, who followed her coffin to the church and attended her funeral. Being surrounded by their stuff made Heidi deliriously happy.

"This is the armoire Charlotte described in Mr. Rochester's bedroom," Heidi said, pointing out a old cabinet with apostles painted all over it.

She got very excited about the strange little Gondal books they created when they were kids. "Juvenilia," she explained to me. And there were the pamphlets their parents wrote too, the father's about a bog and their mother's about the joys of being poor. Heidi then took us across the graveyard to the church, where "the girls but not Anne" were entombed under the floor, up near the altar and the pulpit where Charlotte's minister husband-to-be (only she did not know that) broke down in front of the whole congregation because he was so in love with her.

They had a prayer tree at the back, and we clothes-pinned our wishes to it. I saw that Heidi's wish wasn't for herself, it was for Daniel: that his grief for Gaëtan be lifted. Miles scrawled one asking that his football team win a game. Mine was that I hoped everyone in my life would continue to be healthy and happy. And then I wrote a second wish, when Heidi wasn't looking, it said, Please don't let H. be hurt by M. Or wind up staying here.

That's when Heidi asked were we ready to walk on the

moors to Top Withins, it would be a threc-hour trek at least, there and back.

"Not if you're with me," Miles said. "Let's go, lassies."

This was not a pleasant walk along the Public Footpath, then a saunter across the moors. This was a major hike with a man who climbed Everest, almost. He was quick-stepped, deadly as fish and chips with scraps to eat now, leading us on a merciless galloping hike. We stopped to pet some friendly sheep and goats that would have followed us, but Miles was faster than a border collie.

"Keep up, keep up! Eh, you ever see that film *An American Werewolf in London*?" he yelled back at us.

"Yes. With the mist of the moors closing in," Heidi called.

"And then that Yank bloke getting attacked by the werewolf? It's true about the mists. Coming up on you all of a sudden."

Oh great, I thought, the two of us lost on the moors with this lecher. He stopped in his tracks and stared at us.

"Don't be afeared, but the Patfoot, Yorkshire's own fiendish hell-hound of the moors, may be about," he said.

"Isn't that the werewolf?" I said, unimpressed.

"No, the Patfoot's different altogether, with blazing eyes and snarling teeth. He can be big as a donkey. Awoooooo," he began howling. Heidi howled back. And then they both started hee-hawing. It was a truly horrible occurrence.

"And the wuthering, the wind . . . ," he whispered and started making haunted wind sounds as he began hiking too fast again.

"Are you trying to scare us?" Heidi called, laughing.

Are you trying to kill us, you maniac? I wanted to scream but didn't, and then, thank goodness, there was this old ruin in sight at the top of a hill.

"There it is, Top Withins. The inspiration for Wuthering Heights," said Heidi.

It was the stone remains of a derelict farmhouse, with sheep hanging out in it. There was a great old gnarly tree too, battered by too much wind. While Heidi strolled around inside, I looked out what was once a window, and that's how I saw Miles with his back to us, out on the moor, peeing. He was relieving himself at Catherine Earnshaw's homestead! Not even camouflaged by a bush, using the stark but beautiful landscape as his toilet. What a pig! But then he probably did that all over Everest, the Top of the World one great big pee station! Why did I get to see him defile the sacred Brontë Country grounds and not Heidi? I mean, this would be the nail in the coffin for sure. But no, it was only me as witness, Heidi was taking a picture of a sheep. I got away from the window, I didn't want him to know I saw him. Why do men do this? Because they can. But really, why can't they find a restroom like the rest of us? Soon we heard him shout, "Better head back soon, or we won't get any pints in at the Black Bull."

After seeing so many of the Brontë sisters' bad brother Branwell's things at the Parsonage, I realized how appropriate it was that Miles wanted to drink at Branwell's Black Bull haunt. They were fellow ne'er-do-wells. Losers! Poor Anne Brontë, losing her job as a governess because her brother was sleeping with her charges' mother. Poor Emily Brontë, having to cross that graveyard in the pitch dark to drag Branwell out of the pub so their father wouldn't find out. Poor Charlotte, having to write for a living to support them all because he was absolutely useless. And now Heidi, about to change her life and stay here because of a lazy git ladies' man just like him!

"Why are you scowling?" Heidi asked me.

"Because they let Top Withins go to ruins like this," I lied.

"But that's part of its charm and literary significance. Oh, I can hardly wait to be part of all this."

She ran ahead of me, raised her arms to embrace it all, and I blurted, "Heidi, are you out of your mind? For him?"

"Pardon?" And she smiled at me so euphorically I knew she hadn't heard what I said, thanks to some wuthering.

Miles saw us flagging and offered a lift. When Heidi said no, no, he backed into her, picked her up and carried her piggyback for at least a mile until she said, "Thank you, Miles." He put her down, stroked her face with the back of his hand and gazed into her eyes, and I thought, I am going to have a nervous breakdown.

He strode on ahead of us, and Heidi said, "I can't believe we're leaving in two days."

I did not say, And I'm counting every second, girlfriend.

"Village is in sight!" Miles rubbed his hands together. "First round's on me."

How many rounds could there be, he was driving.

The Black Bull is a charming old pub. Miles ordered us each a pint of Black Sheep, a fine English ale. Heidi excused herself.

"Be back in a tic, I have to use the loo," she said.

"You don't need to go to the loo too?" Miles asked me.

"No. And I know you don't." I was telling him off, but Miles — being Miles — took it to mean that I wanted the chance to be alone with him. He brushed the back of his hand across my cheek now.

"Hey!"

"Whooaa, lassie. I was wiping the dust of the moors off you," he said.

"How dare you make a pass at me in Branwell Brontë's local, or anywhere, for that matter?"

"Oh, now you sound all upmarket, like someone I know."

"Heidi does not sound upmarket. She is upmarket, and you, mister, are downwind."

"And over the bloody moon for you," he said.

"You're horrible. Heidi's not gone two seconds and you're trying it on. Why were you so flirty with her all day?"

"She didn't mind, why did you?"

That's when Heidi came back from the loo. I figured the good thing about him pursuing me meant he wasn't going to make a move on Heidi, as long as this never happened in front of her and I could fight him off.

"Miles, thank you so much for bringing us here and being such a good sport," Heidi said.

"A pleasure, me darling, what finer way can a Yorkshire lad spend his day, ayup?" he said and looked from Heidi to me.

"And all the time you've taken off from the Jag dealership to be with us," Heidi said.

"Yes, I may have lost a commission or two, but I'll make up for it."

"For the Miles to Everest Fund. Aren't there other means of getting there besides self-financing? It's so much work for you," Heidi said.

"Well, lass, there are five categories of expedition: there's your national, your individual, your commercial, your guided and your expedited."

"I suppose you'd love one that's national or commercial, because it would be sponsored?"

"Who wouldn't, yeah?"

"Does England have a national team? Or Yorkshire even?"

"I'm not what they want," he said.

"I'm sure you're what a lot of people would want," I was horrified to hear Heidi say.

"Not as many as you'd think," he replied, looking at me.

She looked over at me too.

"Isn't that strange, Lenore? That it would be difficult for him to find a sponsor?"

"There are so many climbers now, Heidi," I managed to say.

"I know, but not all of them are of Miles's calibre."

Miles had pushed his empty pint forward and signalled to the bartender.

"Again for you two?"

"I haven't even started mine," Heidi said. "And this will be my shout," she said as she paid for his second pint that could lead us all over some dale into a ditch.

"I would think Canada would have government-sponsored expeditions, even some provincial ones," Heidi mused. "Weren't there some climbers in Quebec talking about trying it without oxygen?"

"No," I snapped, "no one would ever say that. How else could they breathe way up there? And if they did, all the spots must be spoken for by our own Québécois," I said.

"When are they planning this?" Miles, of course, wanted to know.

"I'm not sure. It could only be hearsay, who knows? But I think I did read about it. I'll research it when I get home, shall I?"

"If you would, oh yeah, I'm very interested. I've never tried it without oxygen."

And that's all they talked about the whole way back to Bickton-on-Curds. I even heard Heidi tell him very few Canadians had ever summitted Everest and our country would probably welcome an accomplished climber on their team. "Someone who'd made it to the top," I called from the back seat, and they both ignored me. Heidi showed no concern when I pointed out the sign to Heptonstall, where Sylvia Plath was buried. This was not like her, not to want to visit the gravesite of her favourite suicidal poetess and maybe even have her picture taken next to it. I'm sure it was on her Must See List before Elspeth gave her command. I'd seen this splendid scenery already; I didn't even find the "Humps for 45 yards" road signs all that funny anymore, so my mind could wander to:

REASONS WHY HEIDI SHOULD NOT BE STUCK ON MILES

1. He has an earring.
2. He's slept around and around and around, with everyone from Near Sheffield and Beyond, he's a plague.
3. He has no steady job.
4. He still lives at home and always will.
5. He peed on the moors.
6. He drinks like a fish.
7. He went all the way to Everest twice, never made it to the Top of the World and took bad slides.
8. He kissed me while I was in my Noddy costume.
9. He started to striptease for me at Base Camp when she was in the shower.
10. He made moves on me in the snug when she was in the loo.
11. He is a lazy slob. He doesn't wash a dish, pick up his own clothes, a spoiled-rotten Mum's Boy.
12. He's a danger on the roads in his dad's clunker.

13. He called the Brontës Brontësauruses.
14. There's no future with him. Okay, so there could be quite a fling with him in the present, but it'll quickly become a bad past.
15. He loves *Carry On* movies.
16. He watches telly too much.
17. His out-of-wedlock offspring are introduced to him at cricket matches. During the game.
18. He knows how good he looks in those hiking shorts.

I knew I had to stop this. We seemed headed for that slap-up meal tonight.

Like some miracle, there was a folded message waiting for me on my straw pillow when we got back to the Cobbles.

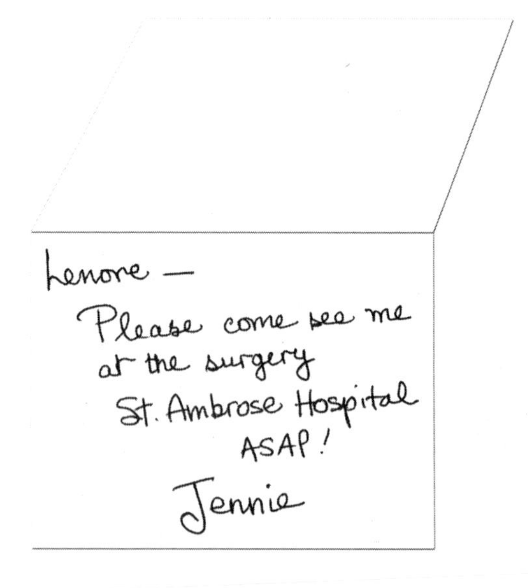
Lenore —
Please come see me
at the surgery
St. Ambrose Hospital
ASAP!
Jennie

Chapter Six

It all came together quite magnificently, as if God or some Mother Goddess had orchestrated it.

I didn't let Heidi see what my note said, I let her think it was something very personal from Benoît.

"Oh, Lenore, he must miss you. He can't wait to see you again."

"Yes, that's the gist of it," I said. I had to get to the surgery, but I was afraid to leave her alone with Miles. Lucky for me his mum and dad were home for the evening, and the telly was on. It was quite clear Heidi was what he wanted now. Too up-market, too smart or not, he was coming up for no oxygen. He brokered the deal.

"About that slap-up meal I promised ye?"

"Yes?"

"I don't want you to think it was the fish and chips at the chippie," he said.

"I didn't." She laughed nervously.

"I was hoping it could be tomorrow."

"Our last night?"

"It can't be tonight. I have to make up for lost time at the dealership," he said.

"I could go with you, we could talk, I'm quite good at paperwork," she said.

"You'd be dead bored, no, you have a night in. Hey Mum, Rita from Corrie's on this chat show," he called to Irene in the kitchen.

"Rita from *Coronation Street*!" Heidi said, all excited. "Her accent is so different."

"All posh," said Irene. "Takes a fine actress like her to talk like us and sound like she means it."

Irene and Heidi settled in, listening to Rita. Miles gave them maybe three minutes with her.

"Ah, you'll see her on Corrie later tonight anyway," he said and switched channels.

"Miles! We was interested in what she had to say," Irene moaned.

"Not when me favourite program's on other channel," he announced, and suddenly there was *Gobsmacked*. We hadn't been there a week, how could it be on again?

Special Edition! Viewers' Favourites! *Gobsmacked* was so popular it could be on three or four times a week. With everyone glued to the telly, I could make my escape to the surgery. The show started off with the winners in "The Most Humiliating" Romantic Category. It was so horrifying I couldn't stop watching. It's also what convinced me later that a Greater Power was running the fateful events of this evening, sending Heidi a message. A woman named Esme Subcastle had been in love with her best friend Nigel Saltminster since they both read maths together at Oxford.

Now Nigel had never in any way showed he was interested in her in a romantic way, but today, in front of the studio audience, she was going to let him know. And when she did he was, yes, gobsmacked! And she was gobsmacked right back when Nigel said he could never regard her as anything but a friend. "Are you . . . gay?" Esme asked. "No, just not interested," was his reply. That's when Miles started his obnoxious hooting Carry On laugh.

"Oh, that is too cruel, now they can't even be friends," Irene said. "Stop laughing, Miles."

"Stupid berk! What did she expect?"

There was a brief glimmer of disgust from Heidi, and then she said, "Well, Nigel's no prize."

"He's not interested, darlin'!" Miles yelled at the TV.

When I couldn't take Esme's humiliation anymore, I told them I was going to take a little walk.

"But we walked six miles over the moors today," Heidi piped up.

"Yeah, but I'm going to find a call box and see if I can ring Benoît. In private." Off I went, leaving them all there, gobsmacked.

As an only child, I used to think I'd like to live in a big old house filled with family, like the Waltons. After life at the Cobbles, I wasn't so sure. It's shocking when people you thought were so much fun aren't so much fun when you get to know them too well. People on holiday are different from people in their own homes, or in your home for too long. But then, the Farnhams of Near Sheffield are nothing like the Waltons.

I knew the Brits call the hospital the surgery, but I was still surprised when I walked into a hallway waiting area, not an operating room. They paged Jennie for me, and I also heard them call another name: Bunty Gumley.

Bunty Gumley? Wasn't she on Father Blunt's list? One of

the fallen women who had cried on Jennie's shoulder? When Jennie arrived she was not alone, she was with her cousin Rupert. Father Blunt.

"Hallo, Lenore," Jennie greeted me. Father Blunt gave me a half wave.

"They just paged Bunty Gumley," I said.

"She'll be joining us."

"She works here too?"

"She's a doctor. Obstetrics."

"Did she deliver the Miles baby the mother brought to the cricket pitch?"

"No. She . . ."

"Oh no. She wasn't the mother of the baby — "

"She's the aunt."

"Oh my God, he's an epidemic. Sorry, I know he's your brother."

"You're right, he's diabolical. Miles wasn't always like this. He was shy, gormless, and then, well, he blossomed into the irresistible specimen he is today. If he wasn't my brother, I would have fallen victim to him. But not to worry, Rupie has a plan."

"You said you would, given a prayer and a think, Father."

"Please, call me Rupert out here, Lenore. Would you be at all acquainted with the Greek classics? Like the works of Euripides?"

"Eh?"

"You're an entertainer. I thought being in the arts . . ."

"Just Broadway show tunes. And whatever drama Heidi makes me see. Sorry."

"Well, there's a classic anti-war play I think we can take some measures from . . ."

"*Lysistrata*?" Jennie said.

"Ahuh . . ." I said. I knew then what "it's all Greek to me" means.

"And in this play, the women are so fed up with their men always going off to war that they refuse to sleep with them."

"Like the prostitutes with the fishermen in *Never on Sunday*. Hey, that was Greek. Melina Mercouri's character got the idea from going to Greek plays."

"Really? I never saw that film," Rupert said.

"Myself as well," Jennie said.

So I was up on something Greek over them. When we started comparing plots, they seemed to coincide, the best part of it was that the women won in the end.

Dr. Bunty Gumley arrived and Rupert shared his plan; it sounded excellent to me if we could pull it off. Jennie and Bunty said they had to make some calls, and I could watch.

Less than two hours later, Jennie and I marched into the Cobbles and got a shock.

Heidi was sitting there in Miles's Everest Base Camp Nepal t-shirt.

"Heidi, that shirt . . ."

"Miles wanted me to have it. He said I slept in Base Camp. It's sort of a been-there-got-the-t-shirt present."

"Where . . . why . . . how did you get it?"

"I was folding it after it had been out on line," Irene said. "Miles grabbed it off me, give it to Heidi and said, 'Here lass, I want you to have this!'"

"Oh, great, so it happened here, you never left this room?"

"Well, yes. To put it on."

I was like some psycho trying to guard her honour.

"Where is Miles now?"

"At the Jag dealership. I got to see *Coronation Street*, my mother will be so happy, I can let her in on — "

"Super!" said Jennie. "Well, get your glad rags on, Heidi, we're having a girls night out."

"Are we?"

"At the White Hart. I was too busy working. I've been a horrible host, but I shall make up for it. I do so want you to meet some of my mates. They want to know all about Canada."

"Oh, that's great. I'd like to know more women here. Do I need to change? Can't I keep this t-shirt on? It's kind of fun and pub-like, isn't it?"

"Yes, but the fact that Miles has never made it up Everest, well, it's a legend and a local joke, it gets rather tiresome for me, actually, they do go on."

"Oh, okay. I'll change then. Be right back." And off Heidi went to Base Camp to remove her Base Camp shirt.

"What are you two up to? It's not some hen night, is it?" Irene asked.

"No, Mum."

"I'll come too, shall I?"

"No, Mum, you can't. You've got to be under forty."

"Oh. I'd have a laugh, they all know me."

"Some of them don't."

Jennie was being a good daughter and protecting her mother from finding out the evils that sons do. But a part of me wanted Irene with us at the White Hart because if she knew, she'd give Miles a clip around the ear, maybe even kick him out. Especially if she found out she was a granny, at least once, by now.

The sign over the pub door said "Duck or Grouse." It was a warning for low beams ahead, if you didn't duck, you'd wind up grousing. How fitting, I thought, low beams to avoid because of a low-life.

All the women Jennie and Bunty called were gathered at the White Hart, already finishing their second round, when we got inside. Jennie introduced us.

"These are our friends from Canada. Some of you may have seen Lenore brighten our Bickton stage?"

"We certainly have," said Sardi.

"Sit down, star," said Cecilia.

I was definitely gobsmacked to see them in the crowd. Now I'd find out why they stopped the music whenever Miles came around.

"Me mum did your costume," said Jessie Kildare, the daughter of Heloise.

"Your Noddy was bloody brilliant," said someone who turned out to be the Honey Kewell who had also cried on Jennie's shoulder.

"And this is Heidi, her friend and mine. Give her a great big Yorkshire welcome!" said Jennie, and they all did. They gave her an even bigger one when Heidi announced, "What are you all having? This round's on me!"

This was clearly not a crowd that usually hung around together, you could tell they were all trying to figure out why they had all been called here tonight, as if this were an Agatha Christie story where strangers are gathered together only to get murdered one by one.

Dr. Gumley started: the Blunt approach. She looked at Jennie.

"All these lasses here, Jennie girl, and your brother Miles not about?"

"He's at the Jag dealership," said Heidi.

Honey Kewell snorted. "He's working on the Jag dealership!"

"Owning it?" asked Heidi.

"Michaela doesn't own it yet, does she?" Honey asked Jessie.

"Mick will when her father passes on."

"That won't be for ages. He's too fit."

"That family. My Eric says they're too upmarket. He'd never buy a Jaguar from them, even if we had the dosh."

Heidi whispered to me, "Mick with the Jag at the pub the night we got here is a woman?"

I acted surprised. "I guess so. Not Mick as in Jagger, it's Mick short for Michaela. But if her Dad owns all the cars, why would she buy a Jag off Miles?"

Now Heidi might have found some way to excuse this if everyone else hadn't started talking. And boy did they talk! Heidi just listened, her eyes getting bigger and bigger. At one point, I had to tell her to close her mouth. Cecilia and Sardi revealed that Miles dated them both secretly at the same time.

"He was two-timing twins?" Heidi said.

"And we only found out — "

"When he suggested a threesome!"

Daisy turned out to be the Cricket Mum and Bunty's sister. Sydney turned out to be someone from the mill.

"Where he was a foreman?" Heidi asked.

"Farnham the foreman? Not bloody likely!" Sydney laughed even though she had so many reasons to cry. He'd convinced her to withdraw all her savings from the building society to help the Miles to Everest Fund. "And he didn't even make it to the top."

"Again!" Everybody screamed and pounded the table. Women from all over the White Hart that Jennie hadn't called because she didn't know about them joined us, even Lulu and Saffron the barmaids. The stories kept on coming.

By the end, the tally was three women who invested in the Miles to Everest Fund, two broken marriages, one restored (with "my Eric and two kiddies"), one severe drinking problem almost in check until tonight, a house full of broken dishes and furniture due to uncontrolled rages, a factory worker given her cards because Miles broke up with her at her place of business and it got very ugly, and two other illegitimate children who could have been trotted out to the cricket pitch. And this was just the Near Sheffield crowd.

The one thing they all had to admit, though, was that Miles not only looked good, he was fantastic in one department.

"But where has it got any of us?" Bunty Gumley asked the wronged women who answered her.

"Heartbroken! Devastated! Divorced! With a Social Disease! Used! Bankrupt! In traction! Fired! Two-timed! Knocked up!"

Saffron was philosophical: "Why do we go for the bad boys when there are decent blokes about?"

"Because we're weak. We can't help ourselves," replied Lulu.

"But we can. We must," declared Dr. Gumley.

"How many of you got involved with Miles because it was just for a laugh?" Jennie asked.

Jessie and Bunty put up their hands.

"I knew he was dead wrong for me. All I wanted, at first, was something purely physical and meaningless. I thought I was in control, but I wasn't. By the end, I wanted to die, I crashed my car into a tree." And this was a doctor speaking, she wound up at her own surgery.

Miles actually told Jessie he liked being with her because she was good for a laugh.

"But me big mistake was needing to be good for more than

that. I'm a nice girl. I believed I was the one could change him."

"We all think that, love. We hope it will lead to the altar or even a cosy love nest, a bed-sit for two, and not still livin' with yer mum and dad," said Sydney.

Dr. Gumley declared that Miles needed a sign in the window of any car he drives stating: Satyr on Board.

"You two Canadians are so quiet. Has Miles tried it on with you?" Sydney asked.

Cecilia, Sardi and Jessie exchanged looks but said nothing. Sydney, of course, noticed.

"Ah, hah, I spy something happened. Must have been at the panto."

"No, nothing," Heidi said.

"Lenore?"

"Of course not. I had to learn twelve songs."

Jessie, Cecilia and Sardi didn't believe me, they gave me a group oh-you-can't-admit-it look. Sydney pointed at Heidi.

"It was you then, Heidi. Admit it, my girl."

"No, never, I've been his pen pal for a year. Only because I was his date at a wedding in Canada. We're friends of his parents and Jennie. We didn't even know he'd be here when we visited."

Thank you heaven, she had denied him three times!

"We're going home to Canada safe from his clutches, but you all should put an end to his goings on," I said.

"What do you suggest? What do people in your country call this sort of meeting of like minds?" Sydney asked.

"A colloque?"

"No, your Indian people. A wigwam?"

"A powwow?" I said.

"Yes, a powwow. That's what this is. So let's decide how we'll fix him good and proper."

"Send him to Coventry!" yelled Daisy.

"None of us except Jennie is speaking to him or having anything to with him already, he is in Coventry," Jessie said.

"No one else will speak to him! We tell every woman and child who will soon be a woman that he's no good, a rotter, and any one of them who doesn't listen, we send to Coventry too! And boycott their places of business," Honey Kewell declared.

I saw why this country was so effective with their suffragettes.

"Let's tell Michaela first!" said Lulu.

"Yes. Oh, let me do it! We'll tell Mick he had two Canadian birds under his roof this whole time he was seeing her!" Daisy whooped.

"There'll still be birds after Michaela."

"Not if we tell everyone he caught something from the Canadian girls."

"Hey, please," Heidi said.

"All right. Say it's some new VD from Nepal," Jessie said.

"Let's put posters of him up on poles: Dangerous Sex Offender. Serial Dater. Heartbreaker Home wrecker," Honey suggested.

That's when Heidi, after an evening of mostly stunned silence, offered a suggestion. "Why not show Miles up good and proper on his favourite program on telly? Get him good and *Gobsmacked*?"

"Oh yes, yes!" they screamed.

"What'll our bait be?" Jessie put it to the throng.

"He likes threesomes," Sardi said.

"So why not suggest a sixsome?" her twin suggested.

"Or a moresome! But it can't be any of us. He's had the lot of us, well, except for his own sister. You Canucks, when are you leaving?"

"Tomorrow," Heidi said.

"Ohh, too bad, can't be helped, you'll miss out. But no prob. We won't have trouble finding six willing non-participants. Especially for *Gobsmacked*," concluded Daisy.

"Oh yeah, nobody wants to be on the receiving end but everybody likes to be on the giving end," Saffron said.

"Then we'll give till it hurts!" Lulu hooted.

If they pulled it off, it would be a ratings smash. "You'd think one of the Royals was getting wed," Jennie might report. Miles would be given his cards by his mum and made homeless, womanless and, unless he got some kind of job, Everest-less. This was my wishful thinking. Right now we were just a pub full of angry, vengeful victims of a scoundrel.

After last orders two of us had to grouse when we smacked our heads on the low beams as we all spilled out of the White Hart onto the streets. Had we given off an aura as we marched away, the entire Bickton town would have caught fire. Jennie walked a crooked line ahead of us with Bunty. If all tonight's manoeuvres somehow didn't work out, Jennie promised Operation Goodnight Irene as a final straw, she'd tell her mother all about Miles's Evil Ways. That would truly finish him. "Enough of playing Happy Families. Mum's got to find out, it's no fair she's the only woman in Northern England not to know the truth about him."

"Just like my mum and my brother," Heidi told her.

"Your brother's a shameless womanizer?"

"No, quite the opposite, actually. It's time my mother knew about Daniel."

"Your Daniel's gay then?"

"Yes."

"I wish Miles was."

"I wish he was too."

"You'd not say that if you'd ever been with him, love," Jessie said as she hooked arms with Jennie and marched on.

"I have been such a fool," Heidi said to me.

"No, you haven't. How were we to know?"

"I've made a lucky escape."

"That's what Rupert said."

"Who's Rupert?"

"I mean . . . Rapunzel."

"There was someone at our powwow tonight named Rapunzel?"

"Yes. She's from Leeds? Her husband Eric took her back?"

"Oh yes. She was the one who said, You made a lucky escape, my girl. It always ends in tears with him."

Heidi was even making up my lies for me. She was slightly perplexed, three pints of lager can do that to a sadder but wiser girl.

"They were all so friendly, eh, those English women?" she said.

"Yes, they were."

"The White Hart was supposed to be a way for them to meet us, wasn't it? But they didn't make that much of a fuss about Canada, did they? It didn't seem to be about us for very long," Heidi said.

"We were no big deal once they all got talking about Miles . . ."

"It's quite frightening that every single woman there had been involved with him."

"Yes, what a coincidence. He's some wolf. It was, like, a hundred percent, if you don't count his sister and you and me. What a ladykiller."

"I thought it was strange from the minute we got to Bickton-on-Curds. Miles not being on the train platform? And then not coming home till after eleven because he was selling cars at night? But he was so nice afterwards, showing us his slides. And then being so sweet the next day, leaving us those metro transfers good for a slap-up meal."

"That wound up being at the chippie."

"They were good fish and chips, Lenore. He was taking us out, you know that."

"And you had on the great blue dress."

"But then the panto crisis happened. I was happy to pitch in, but part of me desperately wanted to be disloyal for even a couple of hours and leave you at that rehearsal so I could have some time with him. But he was loyal to the panto and his folks."

"And because you were so involved, Heidi."

"All the time we could have spent, but he was always having a lie-in."

"Because he'd had so many lie-downs."

"Who did he go after at the panto, for all we know?"

"He kept pretty busy with the show. When would even he find an opportunity?"

"The piano-playing twins know something. Oh well. Our day on the moors was nice."

"He peed on them, Heidi."

"He didn't!"

"When we were at Top Withins."

"Oh my God."

"He's a class act, is Miles."

"Oh, thank goodness I couldn't reach Phaedra today. She'd be so disappointed had I told her yes, then changed my mind."

"Never mind the mess of your life if we hadn't gone to the White Hart. What dumb luck, eh? Who knew a night out with the birds could reveal so much?"

"I could have been his final conquest before he left Canada, you know? That last night he was there, it felt like something could happen. But I was afraid I'd wind up feeling cheap or too involved. From all the reports, I missed quite the farewell performance — but wait, how many women did he fool around with when he was in Montreal?"

"Who knows? Do any of them know about Quebec's no-oxygen Everest team?"

"I did bring that up, didn't I. Oh, we're leaving as soon as we can. If that's okay with you."

"Yes. Sure. Is there enough time for Scotland?"

"No. We've only got two days left. You saw how long it took us to get to Haworth."

"I know. But Scotland's up there, and we'd pass highland cows grazing, and we could get gorgeous sweaters."

"But let's see if Jennie and Bunty are trainspotters to London Town. We're taking the first Thomas the Tank Engine outta here!"

"We pass Wales on our way back down, couldn't we drop in there?"

It was a shame not to be able to add another country to my list when Wales was in the vicinity.

The next morning we had our bags all packed and were ready to go. We'd rung for a taxi and said our thank-yous and goodbyes to Gordon and Irene. She went into Hillary's Step and told Miles. Again. This time she shouted at him.

"Shift yourself, you sleepy boy. The girls are leaving."

He came out looking tousled, unshaven and messy but still, unfortunately, quite attractive. Heidi also looked pretty damn good, one could almost say she looked hot. She was letting him see what he would be missing.

"Heidi, love. You can't go!"

"We can."

"Don't leave me. I was taking you out tonight. Like I promised."

"It can't be helped."

"Aw, stay. Is it Lenore who has to go? Because of her frog fella?"

"His name is Benoît."

"Yeah, Jee Tim. You can stay longer, can't you? A couple more days? Change your plane for me?"

"Nope."

"It won't be the same once you're gone."

"You can believe that one, mister."

"Umm, we'll keep in touch? And yeah, maybe get me that info on the Quebec team, eh?"

"And then maybe if they're desperate and looking, you can contact them, maybe come over and stay with me?" Heidi asked.

"Yeah, I'd like that. Sure."

"Maybe even woo me, marry me for your Canadian citizenship?"

Gordon really liked this. "Oh, mother, the girl's proposing to him now. Just what we need, the lad gets his feet under her table, and we all immigrate to Canada. You played a blinder there, my son! With a professional lass, too!"

"Marry you, Heidi?" said Miles.

"Only, of course, if necessary, for accreditation for my national- or provincial-funded team."

"Well, who knows, yeah?"

"And then you could sponge off me and then off my country or my province so you could traipse up Everest yet again using baby Sherpa boys to carry your load."

"Sweetheart, love, I don't get what you're on about."

"And you never will. Bye bye, Miles. And this, my darling, is only the beginning." And she rubbed the back of her hand across his face, and off we went.

When we got out to the street, the taxi driver turned out to be the same one who'd brought us here when we arrived at the nowhere-Near-Sheffield train station.

"You found them, at home, then, ayup?" he asked.

"Ayup, they were home," Heidi said, and then she sighed.

Chapter Seven

Some people find the trip home longer, but not me, the way home was shorter. It was a pretty good flight, too, with not one bit of turbulence, and the movie was *My Cousin Vinny*. The Air Canada theme Salute to the Oscars let me see why Marisa Tomei deserved to win.

"She's very good in this movie, quite believable, people underestimate how difficult comedic acting is," Heidi commented.

I agreed. "Especially with her speech about the little deer getting its head blown off by a hunter because it wanted a drink of water in the brook."

"And she was very convincing as the star witness about the tire tracks."

"Poor her though, eh? People will always think Marisa didn't deserve to win because Jack Palance was confused."

"No matter what, there will always be the naysayers who contend that an American in a comedy did not deserve to win out over British thespians."

"Until *Vinny*, the only nominated performance I saw was Cotton's. If I'd had a vote and didn't have to vote for Cotton, I'd have voted for Marisa."

"How do you think Cotton is doing at Betty Ford?"

"She's in week six by now. I'm sure Jamie will give me a full report when I get home."

Heidi knew there'd be a big lineup for the bathroom when the movie ended, but she said it would be worth it, she badly needed something to make her laugh, poor broken-hearted girl, even though she'd been very brave and philosophical.

"Miles wrote to me first, you know? Last year. After they'd all been in Canada."

"A card? A letter?"

"A thank you card the whole family signed, with photos. And he added "Keep in touch, yeah? Thanks for making my stay so fun. Miles."

"Oh. How romantic."

"I know, not much. But that week the *Gazette* had a little piece about Everest, so I sent it to Miles with a good-luck card saying 'To the Brave Summitteer.'"

Overall, I'd had a good time on my holiday so I worried that I'd really pay for it if Heidi's Travel Karma held true. Heidi would not have to pay for it, that was certain, because of all the bad things that happened to her while she was away, that could be some consolation. To think two people can go away on the same holiday together and have a totally different experience. My holiday vs. Heidi's.

GOOD THINGS:

1. I discovered a new country, I got to Europe. I saw London. I saw Yorkshire. Tasted many new things. Saw shows in the West End. Learned many new words and expressions. Now appreciate the Brontës.

2. Got to sing a lot of wonderful songs, even if I had to dress like an elf and learn them in a panic. I'll have them or the rest of my life.
3. Went to confession.
4. Met lots of great English people.

BAD THINGS:

1. Got hit on by best friend's intended.
2. Bad day with Jemima, except for the exceptional English tea, if I don't count that it cost us fifty bucks.

WHAT HEIDI GOT ABROAD:

1. A broken heart and a merry chase with Miles.
2. Saved from ruining her life.
3. A romantic time in Brontëland because she didn't know any better.

When Heidi got back from the restroom, she had someone with her.

"Lenore, this is Woodham St. Antoine."

He looked familiar, I thought he must be one of her professor pals from Concordia, I'd seen him before.

"Woodham is coming to live in Montreal."

"Welcome. Bienvenue."

Had she ever met him before? Why did I know this face?

"He's got a sublet in NDG."

"On Coffee Street, if you can imagine that," he said. "Do you know it?"

"No."

"I quite like the fact that I can say I'm living on Coffee.

Well, must get back to my seat, I'm blocking the aisle. See you in town, Heidi."

"Yes, call me," she said.

Call her? She'd just met him. She was working fast on mending her broken heart. But he was cute, with tufty red hair and a moustache. And about her age.

"Did you just meet him?"

"Yes, in the lineup for the bathroom."

"I thought you knew him from before."

"Me too. I looked at him as if I did and that's what got him talking to me, I apologized, and he said, 'That happens every so often.'"

"He didn't tell you why? Is he some royal?"

"I thought he might be an actor. Or a politician. But he's not, he's a biochemist. He cleans up toxic sites."

"Do we have any?"

"Oh yes. Across Canada. He's here for two years, and then he'll see and they'll see how it goes."

"He told you all this already?"

"Yes, it was quite a lineup."

"You were gone a long time."

"He was waiting for me when I came out."

"Waiting to go in?"

"No, he was finished, I suppose. He wanted to get my card. And take me out."

"He picked you up?"

"No. I suppose I picked him up. Or maybe it was mutual."

"Another British guy? Will you never learn?"

"It's not like that. He's new to Montreal, he wants to meet people."

"He seems nice."

"Yes. He does. And maybe this way I'll find out who he is. Why he's so familiar. It's strange, but every so often when I looked at him I could see this little boy or see him as a teenager."

"That's odd."

"Sort of like out-of-body experience flashes, I guess."

Of course Benoît was at Mirabel when we arrived, waving at me from the visitors' deck above. Woodham had managed to manoeuvre his luggage trolley behind ours, he and Heidi were having a great chat. So I'd look up and there mon gars always was. Benoît put his hands over his heart and smiled, I almost cried. When we got out he gave me a sizzler of a did-I-ever-miss-you kiss that had bystanders whistling. This was not like him at all, not in public.

When he'd brought us to the airport, he'd been in uniform and driving the paddy wagon. This time he was in his Canadiens windbreaker with his own car. We got to see where Coffee Street is in NDG. When Heidi introduced Woodham, Benoît asked, "Where are you going, new man in town?" and that was it. Benoît told him about St. Antoine Street — "Hey, Woody, they like you so much, they name a street already after you."

When we got home, all my plants were alive, my mail was neatly stacked and the house was full of improvements.

"Everything work here now, Lenny. Nothing is not working. You will find many surprises, but the most important one . . ." he said as he led me into the kitchen. He opened the new back door, a screened door with gingerbread trim, and said, "Voila! Let there be lights!"

He flipped on the porch light, a lantern that now came with a bonus, floodlights over my yard.

"Now, walk outside, chérie."

And I walked out onto my new porch, a deck even nicer than Madame Ducharme's.

"The other one was no good, like your car, all rotten," he said.

"I know, but this . . . this is all brand new. It's a masterpiece."

"We can't paint it for one year. It's pressure-treated lumber."

"I like it natural like this. I can't believe you built it for me."

"Not all alone. I had some help, les gars came by. And Daniel, he give me his days off. He worked so hard, but he's so sad, Lenny."

"I know."

"We got to fix him up with some nice guy."

"I don't know if he's ready for a relationship yet."

"Better that than le sauna."

"He's not going to bathhouses, is he?"

"Voyons! Like he would tell me? But if he's with someone, maybe he won't do that."

"I'll keep my eye out for a good catch," I promised.

"But not one of your theatre guys, hein? They are too much the queen, I think, for him," said Benoît le Matchmaker.

"We owe him, he matchmaked for us."

"He did a good job, I think. Okay now! Another thing, you can have musique out here now any time you want." He flipped another switch, and suddenly I heard the band Tower of Power. Benoît sang along with them to me — "wonderful, marvellous, girl you're everything to me, you're super fine, so glad you're mine . . ." He placed his hands over his heart again and said, "This song, it says so much how I feel about you."

He danced me across my new porch, down the steps into the garden I'd need to plant, and then back up the stairs into the house, and well, that was just the beginning. It was great to be home, and to be home with him. Was I ever going to pay Good Travel Bad Karma for this!

At first, I thought the Bad Karma had missed me and landed on other people. Heidi called me the next afternoon from upstairs and said, "Have you looked in Madame's garden?"

"Why?"

"Well, Elspeth's children are playing in it."

"That's nice. Elspeth probably dragged them along while she leads Viola astray through more steps of *The Artist's Way*."

"Maybe, but they look quite established. Northrop's brought his hockey net. And lots more, well, look."

And I did. These kids had brought a lot of toys for an afternoon visit. Along with garden furniture I recognized from Elspeth's massive Baie D'Urfé cottage.

I went out again on my spanky new deck and called over to Elspeth's kids, "Hey, Frieda. Hi, Northrop."

"Lenore! We saw your *Titanic Dogs* movie!"

"We saw you in the lifeboat! You had a close-up and everything."

"And they used your scene in the commercial. For the Hallmark special. And there was lots of Brioche et Montcalm too!"

I had forgotten that our Movie of the Week could be on when I was away.

"We taped it. Was your England trip nice?" Frieda asked. "Did you get to Madame Tussaud's?"

"Yes, we did. And when I get my pictures developed, you'll see how many celebrities we met there."

Tussaud's was fun, I posed with anyone I thought someone else would want to meet. I'd already met Liza in person, but I had a shot of me with her in wax, too.

"Did you see any shows?" Northrop wanted to know.

"Yes. And I was in a play when I was there. Have you ever heard of Noddy?"

"No. Does he fall asleep a lot?"

"He doesn't have the time to nod off, he's too busy helping others. He's an elf. There are dozens of children's books in England about him."

"We don't read children's books."

"Anymore?"

"Never."

"In the school library sometimes I do," Northrop confessed.

"Or when the teacher would read some to us. My mother doesn't let us, unless they have mythology in them," Frieda said.

"Is your mom here?"

"Yeah, in the house."

"Is she helping Viola become an artist?"

"They stopped that. Viola got stymied."

"She got too frustrated."

"Oh, that's . . . oh."

Another prayer answered. Viola had realized there were other creative outlets besides the arts.

"Viola's at her lab."

"And your mom is waiting for her?"

"Yeah. I guess. We live here now," Northrop said.

"Oh, you do? That's nice."

Heidi'd heard it all and decided we should pay a visit to Viola's right away.

We went by the garden, past the kids, into Madame's cuisine. Elspeth was sitting at the big teak table with a cup of herbal tea.

"Welcome back, wandering ones. How was it?" she asked, bored already.

"Very nice," answered Heidi defensively.

Elspeth stared at Heidi the empty-handed. "You didn't do my Tesco's shopping?"

"We didn't get near the grocery stores."

"My camomile shampoo was at Boots. Don't tell me you never got near a chemist's either? I can live without my necessities, I suppose. How was the University of Bradford?"

Betrayed again, even Elspeth knew about the Bradford offer before me, but then they were fellow academics.

"I'm not taking it."

"So is he following you here then?"

"No. We're through. I knew there was no point. I got him out of my system."

"Nice for some people, poor Lenore must have been bored."

"No, she wound up starring in a panto. She was a smash hit."

"In the West End?" Elspeth asked.

"No. Bickton-on-Curds. In Yorkshire."

"So you got to Heptonstall? Did you deface Hughes's name on her tombstone?" Elspeth demanded.

"We didn't get there."

"I gave you directives!"

"It was our holiday, not yours, Elspeth."

"Oh, you are a disappointment, Heidi. Don't tell me you let all literary pursuits be foregone."

"We went to Haworth," I said.

"But Plath's right near there. A stone's throw."

"Have you driven on any of those roads in England? Do you know how far anything is from everything else?" Heidi asked.

"I haven't driven anything lately."

"And why not?"

"Because Douglas drove off in For Womyn Only."

"But it's your van."

"I know she's my van, but Douglas didn't see it that way. And he got out with her just in time, they were coming to seize her."

"Seize your car?" I asked.

"Why not, they came to seize everything else. My travails, you have no idea. I hope Viola's got some gin left. You two want one?"

"Uh, no, I'm returning to work soon," I said.

Heidi, who wasn't, said yes, she'd have one. So Elspeth made them gin and tonics. They looked very nice, with limes in them, too, she could really mix drinks. Elspeth continued with her saga.

"I suppose it was fortuitous because For Womyn Only would have been evidence."

"Of what?" I always ask the probing questions.

"My participation in what turned out to be a pyramid scheme."

"Last year's For Womyn Only, send two dollars to the first six names on the list chain letter?"

"Which provided me with the windfall that bought my SUV. And was under investigation by the USFDA. And the RCMP. How was I to know?"

Luckily, Heidi and I had broken the chain on principle, they'd have been coming for us next.

"And then, well, the rest of my never-ending spiral downward is your doing, Lenore."

"Mine? Why?"

"Because you introduced Douglas to that odious Dr. Kitchell, who invested in his stage blood patent."

It's so creepy. Just because Paul played Dr. Kitchell the show-tunes-writing dentist in *Bells Are Ringing* and was first introduced to Douglas, inventor, after one of the shows, they always called him Dr. Kitchell.

"Dr. Kitchell waved ten thousand dollars in front of Douglas and bought him out. Now Dr. Kitchell's sold it to some theatrical makeup conglomerate and it's going to be the Ben & Jerry's of stage blood. Cornered the entire Halloween market share. That devastated Douglas. He wanted a lawsuit, he was talking to lawyers, many lawyers. Then he dragged out every patent and every invention that never worked and invested everything we owned!"

"Is that why he wanted to charge Viola for his services?"

"And me too! As if I was interested, hah! When I have Elijah! But Douglas needed money. And, well, they were coming for the car."

"Even though it's yours?"

"I had in essence signed it over to him."

"Why?"

"I thought to keep the house and our open marriage. And in lieu of a divorce."

"Divorce?"

"You can't ignore how Elijah and I feel about one another," she said.

We'd tried to, we'd been shocked they were so flagrant, to use Heidi's word, but we thought it would pass over. Now knowing they had an open affair, with Douglas almost going to father Viola's child, it seemed like Bloomsbury in Baie D'Urfé.

"They came for the car, but Douglas took off in her."

"For where?" I asked.

"Who knows? Maybe to Florida to join your former paramour Fergie."

Fergie, who'd dumped me on Boxing Day and run off to Florida to get into the Tourist Industry and everything else.

"Now that's unfair! And we don't talk about him anymore, Elspeth," Heidi said.

"I suppose not. Now that Constable Archambault is around all the time."

"He's not here that much."

"Darling, he was at your house every day. He had it totally under police surveillance. I know! And then, all that sawing and hammering!"

I knew she was right. My new deck had taken a while to build. As well as all those new shelves in the cellar. Benoît had transformed Lenore's Folk Art World, my vast assortment of collectible treasures that got my basement declared a folk museum. I'm even in a guidebook. Except for all the taxidermied animals Fergie left behind, I like everything else that's down there. I got a big surprise when I went to do my holiday laundry. Benoît was about to leave, but I called upstairs to him.

"Benoît? C'est différent down here."

He came down to meet me. "You like it? Everything is off the floor now."

"Lots of stuff is gone."

"The best of your collection is still on display. What's gone was ugly and was of that Fergie. Les animaux of le taxidermy? I put them all away."

"Where?"

"In storage behind the shelf."

I could see he'd built the new shelves with one of my big cupboards behind them, that was odd, but it wasn't as if I ever wanted to look at what Heidi had christened Fergie's Salute to Taxidermy.

"They always bothered me, Benoît, those poor stuffed dead creatures, but I couldn't throw them away. Heidi even contacted

Redpath Museum at McGill, but they already had enough stuffed wildlife."

"I know, chérie, now they won't make you feel sad no more. Or make you think of that Fergie. See you soon, eh?" he said, gave me a goodbye kiss and headed off up the stairs, two at a time. My cellar certainly looked better, more efficient. He even had a better system for the empty beer bottles, but, I wondered, when did Benoît start drinking Labatt Blue? That was a grim reminder of my past with Fergie. Maybe one of the guys from the force who helped him build the deck had brought Blue, Benoît is a St. Ambroise or Boréal man.

"So then they came and took our house," Elspeth said, now on her second G&T.

"Not your beautiful house in Baie D'Urfé?" Heidi said.

"It is mine no more. We were out on the streets."

"You and the kids?"

"Until Viola said we could stay with her, pending your approval."

"For how long?"

"I guess, until, well, I'm not sure, as long as Madame Ducharme lets us."

She wanted me to make their case on my next visiting day.

"My children are very clean, tell her. Take them with you to the prison if you have to, she'd probably appreciate a visit from some wee folk, now that you aren't carting those monstres chiens with you for les petites visites."

We'd managed to ship the dogs to Hollywood, but now we had Elspeth next door. Life had gotten worse.

"So thanks to the kindness of Viola and her willingness and need to share this massive row house and its incredibly reasonable rent with myself and my offspring until we resettle, I am now living in Lower Westmount with the likes of you."

"And Viola is okay about all this?" Heidi asked.

"Of course. But she's at the lab more and more, she works so hard, even most evenings now. I don't see her all that much. She's a very good roommate, but I think she feels I push too much. She's aware that she has deeply disappointed me. She abandoned her Artist's Way exercises. She even took her little song off the answering machine, which was probably for the best. Because people do need to know that I'm in residence here now. It's quite lovely what the children and I came up with, you'll enjoy it next time you call and no one's here. I must say I am very happy to see you both home. Are you too jet-lagged, either of you, for tonight?"

"For dinner?" Heidi asked.

"Yes, dinner would be involved, I'm sure."

"I'm off to Festin," I was able to say.

"I'm not," said Heidi.

Elspeth pounced.

"Good, then you could child-sit for me."

"What?"

"You said you weren't busy."

"Elspeth, I just got back."

"It's not as if you have to go back to work right away. Elijah needs me to help him sort pieces."

"Why aren't you living at Elijah's?"

"I think his wife would mind."

"He's married?"

"I was married. It was an open arrangement. And don't tell me you don't think Douglas didn't have someone, I could never prove it but . . ."

"I am not babysitting so you can go off with your married lover."

"It's the only time he has free this week, she's at some benefit, we need to sort his pieces for the Pot Party."

"The Pot Party?" I asked.

"I told you both about it months ago, we had to keep postponing it, and then we were going to have it at our house when the garden was in bloom, but Madame D's will do nicely enough. And with this being Westmount, we should fetch really good prices."

"Elspeth, no — "

"Don't tell me Westmount has some law about commercial trading on private property? We'll charge tax if they insist. Who do I see about that, anyway? Do I have to get a permit? Is that at Victoria Hall?"

And that's when her darling changelings came in from playing. Even today, I still think they can't be hers and Douglas's, they're so not like them. Once again she proved why I was right not to like her: Elspeth is Evil. She ensnared a friend and set her own children up for possible disappointment.

"Frieda and Northrup, how would you like an evening with Aunt Heidi?"

You'd think she'd said they were going to Dairy Queen, La Ronde and Parc Safari Africain, they got so excited.

"Yes! At your house, Heidi?"

"You can order in Chalet Bar-B-Q and watch her videos, she has all kinds," Elspeth said.

"Sure, Come On-A My House," said Heidi, so kind to these little children from a broken home. Of course, Heidi had a great evening.

"They are the sweetest kids. I kept expecting them to turn on me. Or get whiny and demanding, but no. Frieda saw my *Diary of Anne Frank* book and asked to borrow it. And Northrop still says he wants to be a stagehand. And work on one of your shows. I'll let you tell him you based your performance as Noddy on him, he'll be so pleased."

After *Dr. Quinn, Medicine Woman*, they watched *Titanic Dogs*. I got some screen time, but Heidi warned me, "The movie's quite, quite remarkably awful." Northrop knew every fact about the *Titanic*, but of course these children are very smart.

"But it's disconcerting to hear children use words like bondsmen, foreclosure and bankruptcy."

"Elspeth says they have sophisticated minds."

"They sure do, but I mean, really, little kids with that much information?"

"It must have been a nice change for them, being at your house."

"They asked me, do you and Lenore ever fight?"

"Why would they ask that?"

"Because fighting's all they got in Baie D'Urfé and at Viola's too, I would imagine, only passive-aggressively understated," Heidi reasoned.

"Poor little kids."

"They cheered like mad when you got into the lifeboat. We replayed it seven times. Do they ever love you."

During Cotton's big comeuppance scene on the *Carpathia*, Heidi got a call from Woodham, settling into his new house on Coffee. He asked her to recommend a nice place where he could take her for dinner. So she got some kind of reward. She wondered who Elspeth would sucker into babysitting next time.

Heidi's evening went way better than mine, Festin was in almost total disarray. Daniel kept dropping in while I was away, but Marie-France told me they fooled him by putting on "Le Big Show pour l'autre patron." (I wonder if she got early parole by being a prison stoolie, still it was good to be informed.) Marguerite Vichy had conniptions on the hour and what Marie-France called Les Didos du Chef. The Quebec vineyard we bought our house wine from got mad that we let Festin also be a BYOB restaurant because that cut down their sales. Their rep came and threatened Jocelyne they'd charge us more if we didn't cut out BYOB. And Tyler John Biddiscombe's latest theme restaurant, Prom Night, would open right across the street, very, very soon.

I'd only been gone two weeks! The only good news: my Yellow Door discovery had made a difference. Our very own "La Bolduc" was immensely popular and bringing in a big new crowd. Marie-France was not pleased. And I was worried.

"Pas les bikers? Pas des Hells!"

"Non, non. Les fogies. Les oldsters. L'age d'or! Ma tante! Grand-mère et grand-père."

The mostly senior citizens love singing along but leave early and aren't the best tippers, so the staff's pourboires pickings were slim. Marie-France figured any chance we had of keeping les jeunes et les Baby Boomers would vanish with the opening of Prom Night.

Daniel had been working a strange split shift, so I had to wait a week before I could see him to discuss Festin strategies. The condo was so gorgeous but lonely, I kept expecting Gaëtan to walk in, and Daniel was thinking that, too.

"I have to sell it. He's everywhere, Lenore. We're everywhere. What am I doing here alone anyway? I'll never get over him or us if I stay here."

"You'll get a fabulous price, I'm sure."

"That's what the agent promises. She says it will go fast, but they probably all say that."

"Have you told your parents?"

"That I'm selling or that I'm gay?"

"That you're selling."

"I'll tell them the condo's up for sale. The gay matter will have to wait, even if Heidi Knows Best. She said something at Mirabel that had la mama asking questions."

"Don't you think she should know?"

"Not yet. I'm dealing with enough right now, don't either of you push me."

"Sorry. Thank you for helping build my new porch."

"Beautiful, isn't it?"

"Oh, yeah. I love it!"

"Benoît was desperate to get it done by the time you got back. It's too bad about him, eh?"

"What's too bad about him?"

"He didn't tell you? Come on. You must have seen him quite a lot since you're home?"

"A lot more than usual, yes."

"That is so like Benoît not to tell you."

"Why?"

"Because, he thinks, it will make ma blonde sad."

"Will it?"

"Yeah. But it will make it easier for him if you know. Right after you left, he got suspended, Lenore. And any chance of working for CSIS is finished for him. That's over."

"Why?"

"Because he's a man in love. He did it all for you. You better get the details from him."

We were sitting out on my new deck having lunch when Benoît told me the truth, as soon as I asked him, right out in a roundabout way.

"You did a lot at my house, mon gars."

"I miss ma blonde."

"You were practically living here, Elspeth said."

"I was here a lot, yeah, to do this much work."

"I spoke to Daniel. I know they made you take time off."

"It's no big deal, but if they give me time off I like it to be with you around. If I know before I can get this time, I could go with you to England and passer les vacances. Instead I'm here, and I say a way not to miss Lenny so much is to be where she live and make everything better for her."

"Why did they suspend you, Benoît?"

"Because they don't agree with my methods, là! But what I do, I had to do!"

"What did you do? Tell me."

"Okay. Okay, you want to know. It turns out me, I make la surveillance on some people, but somebody make la surveillance on me too. That Bad Restaurant Man —"

"Tyler Garrow John Biddiscombe?"

"It start with him. Not all gay people are nice, Lenny. They got a network, too."

"What happened?"

"He make a complaint that I spy on him."

"Which you did, to help me!"

"It's not your fault, pense pas à ça!"

"But he's a criminal. He was trying to ruin Festin so he could buy it for nothing. Insider trading, whatever, it was illegal."

"And you stop his sabotage avec l'information I get for you. He don't like that. Then you save Festin again from Gaëtan's old boyfriend Edward who wants to blackmail you . . ."

"Because you presented the confidential documents to prove he knowingly gave Gaëtan HIV."

"Franchement! But I'm not allowed to do that, c'est pas juste! Who's the bad guy here? Me! Because I am using connections I have with CSIS to find these things, but hey, they do this all the time. But me, now I have two big strikes."

"Was the third one for all the spying you did for me on Fergie in the States?"

"No, they don't know about la surveillance on your bad boyfriend. Fergie never report me. And the Americans were happy to know about a bad guy like that in their country."

"Then that was a good thing you did, don't they take that into account? Helping another nation deal with criminals? How can they forget you made that big bust, you were the one who caught Madame Ducharme way back, she confessed to you."

"And she's now your good friend, you rent her house for her, they make two movie avec ses chiens, and you're in one and the other one is about you. That doesn't look so good, non, that's not the big selling point no more, ma blonde, ma criminelle, they could put it in *Allo Police!*"

I was ruining his career.

"En tous cas, that's not the final straw for the camel, hein? You won't believe it. What do me in the best? What is my Strike Three? It's Liza Minnelli."

Not Liza!

"Taking the police van to bring her to Festin. Because when I get her back to the set, there is someone who take her picture and it end up a headline in the paper. Your Tax Dollars at Work. They love Liza, but they don't love for me to be Cop Car to the Stars. Tyler Garrow and the old boyfriend of Gaëtan have already made the report on me. So the Boss say I am a rogue cop, a loose cannon, they have a hearing, they suspend me, and CSIS is no more. Fini! Bye Bye là! I will never be an intelligence officer because I am not so intelligent in my decisions.

But that's okay because Lenny, I tell you there are so many people who are doing so many bad things all over the world, planning bad things you can't imagine, and you can't catch them all. And I want to catch them all, and I can't. I will never be able to do that. So no CSIS, but me, I'm still a cop, and if I can keep the people near me and ma ville safe, that's fine by me."

He'd been suspended for six weeks, so he was around a lot, especially once I knew the truth and he didn't have to leave to pretend he was going to work. I didn't mind because he was home with me during the day too, we were having a very good and spontaneous time, it was like a honeymoon with a handyman. I figured it would stop when he was a working police officer again, but it had me thinking: does he want to move in here? Is he trying to show me how invaluable he can be? He paints, he fixes, he cooks, he buys groceries, he's crazy about me!

We're a great couple, together all the time. And it was my fault he was on suspension. But after England and being stuck in that Cobbles hovel, I'd been looking forward to being at my house on my own, with extended visits from Benoît. But him living here all the time, I wasn't so sure. I'd got used to being on my own and never relying on a man. But, I told myself, he's only on suspension for a few more weeks, enjoy him while this lasts.

Madame Ducharme was so happy to see me and very pleased with her biscuits and canister of tea leaves from Harrods. She would treat some of her buddies in lock-up. She'd decided that her autobiography would be a self-help book as well.

"Mes crimes sont une éducation pour le monde."

And what lessons would her crimes provide: Don't Kill Off People You Share Jury Duty With. And if you do, don't use herbs from your own garden they can trace. It is sad, she's such a classy lady and she's stuck in Joliette for a long, long time. But the people she murdered are dead for a long, long time, too — forever. What a terrible waste. Her loser admirer in Utah wrote to find out her date of execution. She decided not to tell him there's no death penalty in Canada.

It would disappoint him, he'd stop writing, he only writes to women on death row, and he was the only one of her pen pal admirers who was consistent. Randall Kingfisher wanted her bio that he was helping "shape" to include letters she received, as well as far too many that he wrote to her. That was so stupid she'd fired him and decided to write the book solo. Who knew how Kingfisher would have misconstrued her words? And twisted them en anglais.

Heidi and I never liked Randall one bit. What a user. But Madame did seem to attract them, even there in the pokey.

She was thrilled when I brought her the copy of *Titanic Dogs* Daniel videotaped for me. I could easily part with the tape, it's quite possibly the worst made-for-TV movie ever made. I couldn't believe they let it go to air, Benoît watched it with me and was shocked at how bad it was. "Ça c'est le iceberg?" was his remark when he watched the cheesy scene with everyone on deck looking up in horror at something the ship is about to hit. I commented to Heidi that it was strange they waited for May and didn't put it on in April for the *Titanic* anniversary. "But it's not really about the *Titanic*, is it, Lenore?" was her assessment. Les girls de Joliette would watch *Titanic Dogs* in le salon de culture et de loisirs (Reine's name for the common room) over her Harrods tea. She expected this was the French language version?

"No, Reine. Il n'y en a pas."

But there has to be, c'est la loi!

No, I said not the language law for TV, and not for Hallmark Hall of Fame in the USA.

"Les Américans. Pas de respect!"

She said she should have written "version française" into the dogs' contract or release form. Still, les girls could tell what's going on, you'd be surprised how many people locked up in here are very good at English. Did I like my part in it, she asked, I told her it's quite brief, but she'd see a lot of the dogs. She'd had a postcard from les Chiens de Californie. It had such good news, they would get their own stars in the Hollywood Walk if this keeps up! They're going to be in a new show.

"Mais c'est seulement un pilote," I warned her.

A pilot often leads to a series, oui? Yes, I said, and knowing Hollywood, this could happen. I'd had a postcard from Casey and a breathless phone call from Jamie, who said as soon as Cotton got out of Betty Ford, they were shooting the pilot.

"The numbers for *Titanic Dogs* were extraordinary, Len! And all because of the shaggy dog cholera tale Casey came up with. Cotton is Patron Saint of the Dogs in this town. She's bigger than Doris Day."

"No one is, Jamie."

"Sorry to be sacrilegious, but sorry, Dodo no longer has the monopoly on being Number One Celebrity Friend of the Dog."

"People didn't really believe that tale?"

"I guess they did, because Cotton's got so many requests to do public service announcements for the Humane Society and anything else that barks, meows, swims or flies. She's still waiting on film offers, but then the pilot got the green light. That Casey McCordick!"

Casey pitched a show to star Cotton and Valerie titled *Silver & Gold*.

"It's about two former child stars who are now storefront lawyers."

"What?"

"This is the town that gave us *Flashdance* the welder-dancer! Unlikely dual careers work. Child stars grown up is so Hollywood, so *Whatever Happened to Baby June*, so *What's the Matter with Helen*? Oh no, in that they run a school for child stars, I think. Debbie Reynolds, Shelley Winters?"

"I missed that one. Well good for Casey. And she's writing a role for you too?"

"Yes, can you believe it? I play a repeat offender they take under their wing. I start clerking for them, then I'm a paralegal, then I'm investigating, and I guess by season three I'll be a judge. We think it'll fly."

Cotton as the Academy Award® nominee is Stella Silver, first billing and Valerie is Gloria Gold (non Academy Award ® nominee). One of the running gags is Gold looking forever young when she's not.

"Val's very centred, she's okay with that too, oh she's just so happy to be working. And so am I. Bless you for bringing our lovely Casey to us."

"You were the ones who hired her to walk the dogs."

"Wasn't that a smart move? And she's still seeing that Calhoun. He's the one who got her the meeting to pitch some suits he was driving. Who knows, they could prove to be a Hollywood power couple. How's your Benoît doing off work?"

"You know?"

"Well, I called one day with this news, but you were still in England and Heidi's brother Daniel answered the phone. How is Danny Boy by the way? Still alone?"

Jamie for Daniel? I didn't think so.

"He's still grieving. So you called when they were building the deck. Did you talk to Benoît?"

"Yes. Does he do voice work? He should. Quelle voix."

Benoît left me the message that Jamie had called, he never told me they'd had a chat.

"Anyway, Cotton gets sprung in one week, and then, well, we go into overdrive. They are talking one of the *Cheers* directors for us, honestly. Valerie wants some ancient *Salt and Pepper* director, but he's at the Equity Seniors Home, he certainly looks his ages of man, dear."

Jamie seemed even more flyé since I'd left.

"Anyway, the pooches are gonna star too, of course, so I postcarded Madame to ask la permission, le blessing. When are you coming back this way, chickepen? I miss you!"

So Jamie was not coming our way, or home, soon. And why would he, he was in a pilot. He could wind up with an Emmy for Best Supporting Actor in a comedy. He sublet his condo before he left, but I wondered about his sailboat in Pointe Claire. I figured it would stay in dry dock or wherever they put left-behind boats.

Madame was delighted her petits chiens had settled in so well in Hollywood, making a name for themselves. Perhaps she could use their salaries to fund an appeal or do improvements on her house. I asked her about the additional tenants, and even though she thought she had reason to despise their maman Elspeth (she did) but couldn't remember why (Elspeth was very vocal about Madame being a vendu sellout for feminists), she did welcome l'espirit de jeunesse. Please bring les petits on my next visit, I could tell the authorities she was their grand-mère. Or their God-Mère. Joliette would be a life lesson for them: never go astray from the law. Certainement, they could live in her Westmont house. "Les pauvres enfants" surely deserved any little bit of happiness possible after being thrown out of their broken belle maison. How did Elspeth let things get so bad?

And things were just about to get worse, much worse.

Chapter Eight

Elspeth pronounced that Wednesday night, June 9, would be the Pot Party. I told her to please stop calling it that, even if she found it funny or naughty.

"Just what Benoît needs on his record: a Pot Party at the house next door."

"Are you bringing him?"

"I think there's some hockey game on. Like . . . the play-offs?"

"Oh, you and your Montreal Canadiens. You better not keep running out from my party to check the score. Heidi, who will you be bringing?"

"I was thinking Woodham might want to come."

"And who is Woodham?"

"A friend from England."

"Is he the reason the other Brit didn't work out?"

"No, I met him afterwards."

"In London?"

"No, en route home."

"Waiting to board?"

"On the plane."

"Was he in your row?"

"No. I met him in line for the washroom."

Elspeth's dirty Mile High Club laugh made my skin crawl. "Say no more. Heidi, Heidi, Heidi."

"Stop that, Elspeth. He wants to know more people, this way he'll meet some of my academic circle. And who knows, he might even buy a few things. He has very eclectic taste."

The week before she had driven him to Ikea, where he bought some stylish furniture to replace the ugly stuff the subletters had left on Coffee. She'd been seeing him at least twice a week. She'd also solved the puzzle of where we'd both seen him before.

"At Cinema V. In *35 Up*."

That's why we kept seeing him grow up when we looked at him, he's one of those kids who began at seven and kept being interviewed every seven years for the BBC documentary. I'd seen *28 Up* on Vermont ETV, and then Heidi made us go see it when it was *35 Up*, one of the swan song films of Cinema V before they closed it. We remembered Woodham because of his tufty hair that never changed from 7 *Up*, they even did one of those montages and the audience laughed because his hair stayed Up and the same.

"Was Woodham very interesting?"

"I can't remember. I know he wasn't that snobby one. Or the Cockney one who wanted to be a jockey."

"Or the homeless one who wound up living in a caravan on the moor? He was a scientist, wasn't he?"

"I don't think so. I could rent *35 Up*, but then it might make me examine him too much, and that would put him off."

And it would be difficult to date someone you watched grow up, it would be like someone you babysat, somehow. Just weird. She was better off not reviewing it.

Viola was not pleased about the Pot Party at her home in Madame's jardin. Never mind that it was the same night as the

Stanley Cup final game. Proof that Elspeth was also a psychopath.

"Then tell her no," Heidi counselled.

"Who can say no to Elspeth? Who?"

"Douglas."

"Douglas! No word from him. Not a penny of child support."

"They're such wonderful kids."

"Oh, yes, but . . ."

Yes but what? She could have been carrying their half sister or brother by now if we hadn't intervened.

"Elspeth's such a force, and I have no idea how long she's staying here. I hang out downtown, I only close the lab when the security guard comes by and says it's time to go. Otherwise she'd have me doing writing exercises or babysitting so she can go off with that Elijah."

"Give her an ultimatum, Viola. Say it's a strain on your artistic way."

"Yes, it's blocking your path to creativity."

"I already have! She said it was my U-Turn and referred me to Chapter Nine of *The Artist's Way*, Facing the Internal Blocks to Creativity."

I was freed from the shackles of the Pot Party because my boyfriend might have been suspended, but he was still policia très grata with some people. He scored two tickets in the Reds to a Les Canadiens final against the L.A. Kings. I'd never been to a Stanley Cup play-off at the Forum, but I got to be at the one where we won back the Stanley Cup! After seven years it was ours again.

Patrick Roy was fantastic, all those overtime saves in the other games and then coming through on this night of nights. He was such a hero, I was so happy they gave him the Conn

Smythe Trophy. The Canadiens are now the most successful franchise of the twentieth century! History Magic in the making, and I was there. It was so fabulous. But not so fabulous when we got outside. St. Catherine Street's worst nightmare was in progress, again.

"Pas encore!" Benoît said.

Fans on the rampage, Montreal had another riot to celebrate our hockey victory, complete with breaking glass, shouts and sirens. A bunch of kids on top of a bus rocked it back and forth with people still inside it. Two teenagers tried to run past us with their coats filled with stuff they'd looted. Benoît grabbed them both and shook them, and they dropped new running shoes on the sidewalk. Another guy was trying to break a depanneur window with a brick when Benoît stopped him. He aimed for Benoît's head, but he dodged that and threw the thug face up against a wall, it all happened so fast. Benoît would have handcuffed him but he didn't have any bracelets on him. He was in full-throttle cop mode, he's really good at his job, but quite scary too.

Benoît ordered, "You go home, Lenny. It's not safe here."

I yelled, "It's not safe for you either!"

"I know what I got to do here. Go home, be safe."

A store owner came out of his store, crying, "Où est la police?"

"Ici!" Benoît shouted.

I couldn't see any police anywhere, was Benoît going to do this alone?

"They call out the riot squad for this, they know, they're prepared, but they don't have one cop for every person who makes the riot," Benoît said. "Please, chérie, va-t'en!"

I hated to leave him, but I was a burden. I knew he was going to get some gear from the riot squad and join them, even though he was suspended and it was probably against the rules. He's such a hothead, but it's his duty to protect us. My brave and handsome hero. As I trudged home, I was so worried for Benoît and so upset, every time we win the Stanley Cup is there going to be a riot? What kind of fine tradition is this? A Higher Order will punish and curse us and never let Les Canadiens win it again.

I walked into Madame's jardin to find another riot in progress. I heard it as I came up the street.

Viola was screeching at Elspeth in front of quite a few entrapped Pot Party guests.

"I know what you were doing! Fixing me up! Don't think I don't know."

"I thought you'd become fast friends. You and Rhea have so much in common."

"Just because we're both lesbians?"

"It's where you start, isn't it? You do go to the movies sometimes? She's a professor of film studies, you can appreciate her landmark thesis — "

"I did not wish to hear about Lesbian Servants in the Cinema all evening," Viola said.

"Why wouldn't you?"

"Because some of us don't care about the movies! Or all things academic. Some of us have other interests."

"Dr. Rhea Van Priesen was the first woman to see *Rebecca* and ask, Mrs. Danvers, was there ever a Mr. Danvers?"

"If she told me Madame Curie was gay then I'd be interested."

"Madame Curie gay? What about Pierre?"

"Professor Van Priesen was shocked because I've never seen something called *The Children's Hour*."

"You haven't?"

"No. And I don't want to go to her film lecture series at the F.C. Smith Auditorium, either."

"How can you connect with anyone new if you don't explore your horizons?"

"Because I don't want new horizons! I want Charlotte back! Do you know how many years we had together? How happy I thought we were? Now I'm stuck playing house with you!"

"You asked us to move in with you."

"I had no choice."

"And neither did we!"

Heidi told me she could see it coming all evening, Viola was slowly seething. Rhea Van Priesen did go on and on. She was intently focused on Viola and looked like a praying mantis if it was a professor of film studies. "Or that Gorey woman who moans on the pillar on PBS *Mystery*!" And there had been a great deal of wine flowing all night.

"As soon as Rhea left, Viola erupted. Our lovely, calm girl turned into a banshee."

The battle raged on.

"I want you out!" Viola screamed.

"Where are my children supposed to live?"

"Your children are not the problem! I would gladly keep them if I had to, you're the one who has to go. Get out, get out, get out, you crone!"

And even though I knew that being called a crone is supposed to be a compliment to feminists because it means you're respected and wise, Elspeth grabbed Viola by the hair.

I had seen the best in action already tonight, so I knew what to do, and I pulled them apart pretty fast.

"Stop it. There are children . . . somewhere around here."

"They're asleep," Heidi said, taking hold of Viola. "I made them go to bed right after *Hockey Night in Canada* went off."

"Before the riot?"

Elijah spoke up. "Another riot? That is revolting, and typical of sports hooligans. I'll bet the police have done nothing again." He had remained silent through the fight and done nothing himself, not even help me pull his lover off Viola.

"The police are doing plenty, okay? You try handling that mess!" I yelled at him.

"I was just expressing —"Elijah said, his tender ego bruised.

"Benoît almost had his head smashed in with a brick, so you just shut up about a riot you weren't in," I said.

"I hope those little kiddies didn't hear any of this," Woodham said, looking at Viola and Elspeth, accusing them, not me.

"They hear everything," Elspeth said. "Frieda will make a fine journalist one day."

She stared at Viola and said, "Well, I hope you're happy, you've made my little family feel so welcome."

"You're not welcome! I want you out by the end of the month. July first, find a new place to live, and move like everyone else does in Montreal."

"I'll be out of your hair before then," Elspeth said, looking at Elijah.

"And get all this soi-disant pottery out of my garden! What a load of crap!"

People went up to collect and pay for their pieces of Elijah Pottery. A very distinguished much older woman, in a gorgeous shawl and great dangling earrings, was wrapping them in newspaper. There were some pretty ugly pots, a couple had so many holes in them he should have called them colanders. The biggest and ugliest of them all was being bought by Tess Hardy, I couldn't believe it when I saw her, Elspeth had invited

Tess of the d'Urberblondes to the Pot Party. On another occasion I would have been breaking up a fight between Tess and Heidi. Tess was as blonde and man-chasing as ever.

"Can I give you a lift, Woodham?" she cooed.

"You live in the Plateau, Tess," Heidi said.

"I could go out of my way to the outskirts of NDG for our foreign guest," she said.

"No, I've already rung a taxi, thank you," he said.

"When did you do that?"

"Earlier, when I used the loo. He's coming in about ten minutes," Woodham said.

"Cancel it, I'm driving you home."

"No. You've had a great deal to drink, I'm afraid."

"Everybody has."

"And that's why they're not driving. Perhaps you should hire a taxi too, or take mine, I can ring for another one — "

"Goodnight!" she said and walked off crookedly.

Woodham took Heidi's hand and kissed it, quite gallantly.

"Thank you for a most interesting evening," he said.

"Parties at this house have traditionally ended with Elspeth fighting with someone. The parties at Lenore's are much more pleasant, I assure you," Heidi said.

"I expect I shall get to see if that's true at your birthday celebration. I'm quite looking forward to that."

He was a man of his word, he had rung a taxi, which was honking its horn.

"Better dash. I'll call you this week, Heidi. Bye now." And indeed, off he dashed.

It was so strange, our Canadiens had won the Stanley Cup for the twenty-fourth time and nobody cared. Even a riot on St. Catherine Street was overshadowed by the pottery fiasco in the jardin. Heidi asked me all about it but no one else, this made me wonder, what kind of Montrealers were they? Were they all insane? Were they even earthlings?

Finally everyone had left except Elspeth, Elijah and the older lady. I noticed that Elspeth and Elijah weren't all over each other, So in Love the way they usually act. I figured it was because he was with his mother or his aunt. They left together. Elspeth never introduced us.

"Who was that woman, Elspeth? His mom?"

"No, his patron."

"Like, his agent?"

"No. She's his wife," Heidi said.

"His wife? Elijah brought his wife?"

"Yes. She's very supportive of his work," Elspeth said.

"And everything else, I guess."

Elspeth turned so nasty, I thought she was going to go for my hair too. "You just try being the Other Woman sometime, Lenore! The Mistress, the Woman in the Shadows. Try loving someone so ultimately and so forbiddenly. You have no idea how painful it is!"

Yes I do, I've heard enough of those Reba McEntire hurting songs to know never to get involved with a married man. I looked at Heidi, I'd had a bad thought.

"Hey, wait a minute, Woodham's not married, is he?"

"Of course not. He was. But they divorced by the time he did *35 Up*."

"Good thing. And there's nobody back in England?"

"No. Not that he's mentioned. I'm sure of him that way, Lenore."

"And he's coming to your fête on the twenty-first, eh?"

"Oh yes, if we're still seeing each other then."

"Your fête will be held on the Day?" Elspeth asked.

"Yes, you know we always mark the Solstice with my birthday."

"Ah yes, the Solstice. It's your big four-o, isn't it?"

"No, not yet, it's the three-nine. The Big Jack Benny."

"Don't be afraid, sister. Three and nine are power numbers, it should be a very good year for you."

We planned to try our best to make sure Heidi's birthday party, held as always in my garden, would not be "fraught." The guest list was:

Lenore & Benoît
Heidi & Woodham
Elspeth but NOT Elijah
Northrop & Frieda
Viola
Daniel
Sheila and Hugh Flynn, the parents

Heidi told Elspeth while we were cleaning up after the Pot Party that she and her kids were invited but not Elijah.

"But he's my life partner."

"How can he be, when he's married to another?"

"He's my soul mate."

"My mother won't approve. You're an adulteress."

"Your mama doesn't have to know."

"I told her already. She thinks it's disgraceful, the same way I do. It won't be pleasant. Don't bring him."

So Elspeth was not coming, in protest, but the kids were. And they were scarily well behaved and wonderful, as always.

Heidi had even asked Viola if she thought they were on Ritalin, Viola said they were not medicated to her knowledge. Northrop got along really well with Heidi's dad and Benoît because they're all hockey fanatics. They had quite a discussion about the Stanley Cup and the riot. Northrop had even been to the parade, his teacher had taken her class. A boys side, girls side thing was happening, all the menfolk were by the BBQ.

"Northrop's a pretty big name for a little fellow like you," Mr. Flynn said.

"Yeah, it's a big name."

"You have a nickname?" Benoît asked.

"No. I have a middle name."

"And what's that?" Daniel wanted to know.

"Andrew."

"Would you prefer to be called Andrew?" Woodham queried.

"I'd like to be Andy."

Hugh Flynn liked this. "Andy! That's a great name. Like Andy Bathgate."

"Who's that?" Northrop Andy asked.

"A hockey player. And there's Andy Hardy. And Andy Griffith. Amos and Andy. Andy Williams. Raggedy Andy. All nice guys."

"And Andy Warhol, a very strange guy," Daniel added.

"If you like Andy, that's what we call you," decided Benoît.

"I'd like everybody to call me Andy. And they can call me Northrop more when I'm older."

"To Andy," said Woodham, raising a toast.

That's how he became Andy to all of us.

"They tried to call Prince Andrew Andy but it never took," Sheila Flynn said.

"Yet she had a lovely name, Sarah, and they called her Fergie," said Viola.

"Too bad about their marriage, the Duke and Duchess," Sheila called to Woodham.

"Yes," he said.

"And their lovely little girls, Beatrice and Eugenie," she said.

"I'm afraid I don't follow the Royals much," he said.

"Do they have much trouble with e-coli in England?" asked Hugh Flynn as he barbecued.

"Not more than anywhere else, I should imagine," Woodham replied.

"E-coli wouldn't be one of the toxic problems you'd look after?"

"No. Mine are limited to refinery sites."

Heidi's dad always brings up inappropriate things. She told me that when they were in Washington for her cousin's wedding, they also took a tour of the Kennedy Centre. "We had this very preppy guide who looked like Meryl Streep. And in the middle of the tour, next to a sculpture of JFK with a view of a bridge on the Potomac, my father asked her, 'Is that the bridge the plane crashed into?'"

Heidi was horrified at the time, but now she thinks it's pretty funny. And so like him. Of course he would bring up food poisoning at a party.

Everybody kept admiring the new deck.

"I had a lot of help," Benoît said.

"How much work did that tanned guy do?" Viola asked him.

"What tanned guy?"

"The *Miami Vice* wannabe? The day-old beard and no socks with his shoes?"

"Who was that?" Benoît asked.

"You tell me, he was over here, he didn't look like a cop."

"Oh him, he was at the wrong house," Benoît said.

He didn't sound very convincing to me. I wondered if Benoît had unsavoury types helping him out, ex-cons on a work program. But he said the guy didn't stick around, so I suspected one of Fergie's creepy buddies.

"Cheechio?" I said out loud.

"Who's Cheechio?" Northrop-Andy asked.

"A . . . business associate of Auntie Lenore's ex-boyfriend," Heidi said, trying to protect these young sophisticated minds.

"What kind of business?" Frieda asked.

"Bad business," I told her.

"How bad?" wondered Andy.

Frieda looked at me and said, "Come on, tell. We've heard it all, we won't be shocked."

"Cheechio and Fergie disappeared cars into the Lachine Canal," I confessed.

"For the mob?" Frieda wanted to know.

"I don't know. Really, I don't. But Cheechio was a bad man, and he came looking for Fergie when he took off two years ago, I thought it was him again."

"No, this guy wasn't Italian, he looked more like one of your people, but not Irish," Viola said to Heidi.

"Celtic?" Heidi said.

"Yes, Celtic. And even more tanned than Elijah after his trips to Salon de Bronzage," Viola reported.

A Celtic tanned type had been at my house when I was in England, and Benoît wasn't telling the whole truth about him. There would be a quiz later.

The minute we finally had everything out ready to eat, Sheila turned to her children and said, "Daddy has something to say."

I figured it would be grace, because he always says it when we eat together.

"I thought it could wait till later," Hugh said.

"No, now is a good time," Sheila commanded.

So it wasn't going to be grace yet. It looked like an announcement.

"After all these years . . ." he began solemnly.

Heidi and Daniel looked worried. I was too, I was afraid he was going to say they were getting a divorce, but instead Sheila Flynn burst out, "He's going to be in *My Fair Lady*!"

"Oh, Daddy, that's wonderful!" said Heidi the Show Business Maven.

"When?" asked Daniel, also pretty pleased.

"In November, with Light the Lights in Ottawa. You know I've always wanted to be a song and dance man," Hugh said.

Hugh Flynn could have been one, he has a lovely singing voice, he sings a lot, whenever he's up fixing things at Heidi's I can hear him singing Irish songs. And he loves to tell jokes. He's a great guy.

"And the Old Timers' Hockey is getting a bit too rough and active for him . . ." Sheila Flynn said.

She thinks going on stage is easier than being on an ice rink? Anyway, come the fall we'd all be heading to the Nation's Capitol to see him play Eliza Doolittle's Dad in *My Fair Lady*. I vowed I would not go anywhere near Ottawa till that curtain went up. Otherwise, with my track record, Eliza would break something and I'd wind up singing "Wouldn't It Be Loverly?" Daniel said he had an important announcement too.

"I'm selling the condo."

"You are, son? You haven't been there that long, and it's got a great view over the river. It's so close to your Festin restaurant," said his dad.

"And it's the nicest apartment you ever lived in," said his mom.

"Yeah, but I was about to renegotiate the mortgage, and I realized just because I inherited this place, it's not really me."

"So it's not all paid up?" his mom asked.

"Oh no, quite a bit, of course, but not completely."

"Oh. I thought Gaëtan owned it all."

"Almost. In seven more years he would have."

"It's so different to be the owner and not the roommate, isn't it? So many more costs and all the responsibility," Sheila said.

It was killing me, listening to this.

"Yes, but . . ."

You could feel Heidi's spirit saying TELL THEM, TELL THEM, TELL THEM, and maybe he would have, who knows, but Mrs. Flynn changed the subject to Heidi's new romantic interest.

"We rented your movie, Woodham."

"Did you?" he said, charmed, when I could tell he was thinking, Oh no.

"It must be hard growing up in public like that, but you did very well for yourself."

"You think so? I find myself quite dull, actually. I thought they should cut me from the film."

"You weren't angry or disappointed like most of them. And you never said anything mean about other races or were too posh, even when you were a little boy. You're a success, except for your divorce, but that happens to many people when they don't meet the right person the first time."

"I'm determined to be more interesting when Michael Apted comes round for *42 Up*. If I haven't made any significant life changes, I'm not participating."

He actually admitted his life had been unaccomplished. I wondered how I'd feel if they'd Up-ed me every seven years. I was with Fergie for nearly eight years, they could have filmed me at the beginning of being with him and when it was over. I'm in a far different phase now, I'd like them to interview me, these could be my Up seven years.

Woodham thought he was boring, but he knew how to give presents.

"Salsa lessons?" Heidi said when she got past all the coloured tissue in the gift bag and found a certificate.

"We start next Monday. For twelve weeks. It will take us right into the fall."

"Wow."

"Of course we'll have to miss if you go away on holiday or I'm posted away on sites. We'll get what we can out of them."

"Well, thank you."

"You said you like to dance."

"And can she dance! Come on, Birthday Girl, show us your stuff!" Benoît said and cranked up my music system.

Heidi started first with Woodham, pretty soon we were all dancing fools in the garden. It was terrific, with so much swapping everyone had a chance to dance with everybody. We all danced with Frieda and Andy, Benoît even had him up on his shoulders. I could see Sheila Flynn having thoughts of oh she could be a nice girl for him when Daniel danced with Viola.

When I got a chance to dance with Benoît, I asked him to tell me who Viola's tanned mystery man was because it was driving me crazy. He whispered, "A guy who used to be on the force I thought would be nice for Daniel." From Viola's description, I was worried my boyfriend had no taste in men for other men. "But he had gone to seeds, this guy, he's a bum, so I told him I didn't need him to help me with the deck."

Céline Dion and Clive Griffin were singing "When I Fall in Love" when my back gate opened and in walked a surprise of surprises visitor.

"Charlotte!"

"Is it too late to come to the party?"

"No, not at all, come on in," I said.

"Happy Birthday, Heidi," Charlotte said and handed her a Roots shopping bag.

"Did you just get back?" Heidi asked.

"Just this second. I drove."

Charlotte and Viola looked at each other.

"Hey, sweetie," Charlotte said, "Can I come home?"

And Viola said, "Yes, oh yes."

And they both cried and held on to each other.

Sheila said, "Where has Charlotte been?"

And Heidi said, "Toronto."

"Just there?"

"She's been gone a while."

"Why? What was she doing away?" Sheila asked.

Heidi blazed the frontier and told her, "They broke up."

"They're a couple? The two women?"

"Yes, Mama, they are."

"Oh, now all that Judy Garland business makes sense. I asked your father if he thought that was strange, them both liking her so much."

"And what did Daddy say?"

"He said No, Judy Garland was a wonderful entertainer. You know how many times Heidi watched *The Wizard of Oz*. But I've heard that all the gay people really love Judy."

"Not all of them," said Daniel.

"We call them the Judys," Heidi said.

Charlotte and Viola went home to Madame's pretty soon after that. I kept Elspeth's kids and left notes on the front and back door that she should stay on my couch for tonight and left my back door unlocked. But in the morning, Elspeth wasn't there . . . and she wasn't there the next day either, or on her kids' last day at school. We made sure they got on their bus and that one of us was always home for them when school was done. It was fortunate that Elspeth had her kids at the artsy FACE school downtown. Otherwise getting them back and forth to Baie D'Urfé would have been a trial at such short notice.

Viola combed Elspeth's bedroom and found signs that she had packed a bag and had gone off somewhere. She felt really bad.

"It's my fault, ordering her to get out."

"But not without her kids!" I said.

Who knows how long it would have been before we knew where Elspeth was if I hadn't found the little clue she left us. And where I found it made such perfect bad sense, really. It would be another move Elspeth would blame me for if it didn't work out, since it all came to her because of something on my fridge.

"Ooh, what's this?" she'd asked.

"A business card a nice Greek man gave me in the British Museum."

"He has a taverna on Santorini?"

"Yes, sounds magical, eh?"

"It would be, I was on Santorini . . . many, many years ago."

"The last time you were truly happy," I said, but she missed my sarcasm.

"Yes! Yes, beautiful Greece. Is his place a jewel on the Aegean?"

"I'd like to find out someday. It's up there because it's my goal for my next holiday."

"You'll never want to leave. I should never, never have left. I wasn't destined to be with Douglas or to have children. They're strangers to me. What a disastrous life-churning mistake!"

She'd put the card back, and now she'd left me a note under it, probably the afternoon of Heidi's party when she dropped off the kids.

[illegible] and I choose the siesta to make our escape.
I have returned to Greece.

Elspeth

Fergie and now Elspeth. Why do people always leave me goodbye notes on my fridge, why don't they say it to me in person? Elspeth knows why not, because I would say *What kind of mother are you? You're not a mother, you're a monster! What are we supposed to tell these poor kids, you psycho?*

She'd left her own children, we had no idea for how long. Viola said Elspeth had signed them both up for different summer camps for three weeks. We got all their things packed and sent them off, hoping to God their mother or father got back when camp was done. We tried to contact relatives. Heidi told the kids a big, fat lie: Elspeth received a fellowship and had to leave immediately to do research. Andy went for it but not Frieda, but then nothing much gets past her.

Chapter Nine

Sheila Flynn called Heidi after Canada Day to rave about how beautifully Ottawa had celebrated. "It was so Canadian, it made us all so proud, and there was a wonderful show." Daniel joined them for a picnic at noon on Parliament Hill, then they all went back in the evening with her brothers and their families for the fireworks. "You were the only Flynn who wasn't there with us, Heidi." La Mama's guilt trip. Heidi had wanted to go, the Flynns had even invited Woodham to join them. "You can take him up in the Peace Tower and go see those Group of Sevens you like so much at the National Gallery," Mrs. Flynn had planned. Woodham, however, preferred to see Ottawa for the first time "without throngs of revellers." He asked if they could attend the Canada Day activities in the Old Port instead, so she'd stayed in Montreal. She figured it was for the best, it was much too soon for Woodham to meet the rest of her family. Especially her nieces Siobhan and Meaghan — "they'll start planning on being flower girls."

Heidi knew it was probably too much for her to wish her brother would choose our Nation's Birthday to break the news of his sexual orientation to the folks. Daniel told them something else instead: he had a buyer for his condo.

"But those people are very aggressive and demanding, eh?" Sheila Flynn complained to Heidi.

"Well yes, they want immediate occupancy," Heidi said.

"They're giving him the asking price, but where is he supposed to live? How can he find a new place that fast? In the middle of summer?"

"I don't know, Mummy — "

"Well if those two Judys aren't going to stay at Madame Ducharme's, maybe Daniel could move in there? That would be nice for you, if he lives next door?" It was a really good solution, actually, because we'd just had a little shock when Viola told us she and Charlotte were moving.

"They've accepted our offer," they both squealed.

So the Judys were moving to a "mini-mansion" in Montreal West and very, very soon.

"We need a fresh start," Viola said.

"And what you can get here for the price versus Toronto!" said Charlotte.

A place to live had been one of the reasons she and the Child Model, formerly twenty-two-now-twenty-three, had split.

"Chloé wouldn't settle for a beautiful bungalow in Mississauga or Burlington, one even had an in-ground pool, no, no, it had to be Cabbagetown. Have you any idea what the prices are like?" Charlotte asked me. I had no idea.

Chloé the Model was an eye-opener, a selfish, tantrum-throwing divette who drank and did recreational drugs too much and kept late hours. One morning Charlotte woke up in their "soulless furnished Cabbagetown rental" and Chloé wasn't home, yet again.

"I said to myself, what are you doing, Charlotte? You had it all in Montreal, Viola was the very best. Beg her to take you back. So I got in my Volvo and drove right here, the entire way chanting and praying that she didn't have someone new. And if there was a new girl, I was prepared to scratch her eyes out."

"Oh you, you're such a romantic," Viola giggled, forgetting how much pain Charlotte inflicted when she left her.

"I wonder if Viola will sing any of her Yellow Door Songs of Charlotte's Web should they decide to have a Reconciliation Ceremony," Heidi said to me after they left.

As for Viola's baby issue, they would adopt, they decided on a baby girl from China.

"But won't that take at least two years?" said Heidi.

"Yes, so it will give us time to read all the parenting guides and get our new house in order."

Their other house was so magnificent, this new one will have to outdo it. This, of course, would leave Reine Ducharme's house empty except for the children Charlotte nicknamed Hansel and Gretel. Viola felt no responsibility for them at all, she and Charlotte did their best "providing a roof over their little heads" till they went off to camp. When they got home, they'd be mine and Heidi's to look after. I'm still appalled by how blasé Viola the Mother-to-Be was about those kids. And how easily she let Heart-Breaker Charlotte back into her life. I expected way more of her. Daniel liked his mom's plan, so he would become the new man about the house at Reine Ducharme's.

Heidi considered taking Madame's for herself so she'd have more room and let Daniel have her place upstairs. But we never really knew with Madame's, it had been under the radar for a while, and we worried that someday authorities would say Madame can't have a house and be in Joliette Prison too. If Daniel hadn't gone for it, Heidi would have offered it to Woodham so he wouldn't have to live on Coffee anymore. Even if he did have a park right across the street.

"We've sat in Coffee Park of an evening," Heidi said, "well, one, actually. And we watched the train go by, through the children's swings. It makes him think of England."

Sheila Flynn had wanted to know what Woodham's reaction was to some Royal matters.

"Mummy, he told you he doesn't follow them . . ."

"Yes, but he must have an opinion on Andrew and Fergie announcing their formal separation? And her saying now she's going to be a roving goodwill ambassador for the UN? Is she nuts? Is the UN nuts?"

"I'll ask him, next salsa lesson," Heidi promised.

The salsa dancing was interesting but not in the most exotic of settings.

"Somehow I didn't envision us doing the salsa in an old factory overlooking Décarie Boulevard," she said.

We'd both expected it to be in some Cuban supper club on the Main.

"Without a functioning air conditioning system, it was so hot last time I thought it was trying to kill me," Heidi said.

Besides all the near-death-by-salsa lessons, they'd gone out for dinner a lot and seen most of the sights of Montreal. And oh yes, she helped him buy a car. That took up quite a few evenings and a weekend till he settled on just the right one.

Frieda and Northrop-Andy had been at camp for over two weeks with still not a word from their mom or dad. Benoît threatened to do all he could to track them down. I was afraid he was going to use CSIS intelligence means somehow and get in trouble. "No, by the police method, Lenny. Abandoning your kids is a criminal offence." I asked him to please hold off on arresting them till we'd tried other means. Meanwhile, I called Santorini. I had quite a chat with my friend Costas and gave him Elspeth and Elijah's names with a really good description, then I FedExed him a picture of Elspeth for posting. Wanted: For Abandoning Her Children.

"I think they may come to your taverna," I told him.

"They are very bad peoples?"

"The worst. She abandoned her kids!"

If she turned up, he would force her to call me so I could say, get the hell back here or I report you to my police. Costas promised that he and his friends would run them out of Santorini.

"Peoples like them are bad for the island," he said.

Daniel did not say so, but I figured he was behind the surprise fire precautions raid on Prom Night: The New Theme Restaurant the day before they were to open so splashily. Quelle surprise, they were not up to code, especially with all the streamers and fireworks they wished to use. The place really was a fire hazard, it was no fiddle, it was legit, they had nine violations. "Sometimes you must fight with fire," was all Daniel would say.

They wouldn't be able to open for quite a while, especially after our darling Jocelyne wandered over during the raid and pointed out another glaring infraction. This really gave us more time to get our Festin Ça Roule! bus going. Benoît was the one who reminded me I'd had an idea once for a van that picked up hotel guests looking for a fun place to eat.

"You told me they have that in Rochester, they take you to Mount Etna, le restaurant Italien?"

Lots of movies being shot in town, and didn't he know it, he got suspended because of the Midnight Ride of Miss Liza

Minnelli. He figured some celebs would like to be driven to Festin if they "have time between les shoots. Festin can be known as a place to see les Stars." Being the driver for Festin Ça Roule! made Marie-France happy, she had her chauffeur's license, she got it while at Tanguay Prison, well, it is next to the Driver's Bureau, at least she put her incarceration to good use. She loved ferrying customers to us, she'd been pretty disgruntled playing sous-chef to Marguerite Vichy, this was a good career move. Daniel and I decided not to pay extra to the Quebec vineyard for our house wine, so it was salut to them! We went BYOB all the way. If that wasn't enough, Benoît came up with another great suggestion, then Heidi improved on it.

"Maybe you can make Festin more kid friendly?"

"If only I could get Andy and Frieda into the act, it would make child-minding easier," I said, thinking I was joking.

"Our colour-coded chart will certainly be put to the test once they get back from camp," Heidi said. "By kid friendly, Ben, you don't mean more like McDonald's, do you?"

"Non, jamais! But maybe with a mascot? Something big the kids like? Hey, an ours!"

"A bear? Like A&W's?"

"Or like Youppi! des Expos."

"I don't think Youppi! is a bear."

"Mais comme ça."

"We tried animals of the forest last year," I reminded them. "The talking moose, the exploding beavers in the canoe?"

"Voyons, les idées folles of that Tyler. We won't have no wires in this bear, Lenny, it will be somebody en costume. Le vrai deal."

"A bear would be so Canadian, Lenore. And you know what's missing?"

"What?"

"You. And les Filles du Roi. You don't sing as much as you did."

"We have La Bolduc."

"But not forever. She's already been asked to sing the national anthems for an Expos game. She'll move on."

Benoît agreed. "You can maybe shake up the things a bit avec Les Filles."

"Have some of them be other strong Québécoise figures. Like . . . Jeanne Mance. And Mother Marguerite Bourgeoys!"

"They're nuns, Heidi."

"I know. They did so much for New France. Marguerite Bourgeoys was a great educator, she taught the French and Indian girls. She could play games with the customers' kids? And people love singing nuns, Lenore."

Everyone at Festin was energized with our new plans, it was great for team spirit and morale. Jocelyne proclaimed, "Les nonnes, c'est le fun!" We were pretty happy. Tyler John Biddiscombe sure wasn't. He stormed in the day after the fire department raided his Prom Night.

"Who pulled the fire alarm?" he yelled at me.

"Whose restaurant isn't up to code?"

"We were up to code till your partner called in the firedogs!"

"Ever heard of the Bluebird Café? Montreal has a terrible history of disastrous fires. If you have a firetrap, you've got a firetrap."

"And who came up with the handicapped ramp?"

"You sure didn't, or you wouldn't be cited for not having any."

"We're a heritage building, it's not necessary."

"Oui, mon chum, c'est nécessaire!" Jocelyne launched into an impassioned speech about what it's like for people with wheelchairs and walkers whose needs are overlooked, then she went back to setting the tables. Tyler John had hardly any idea what she said, but he got her point and he glared at me.

"Is reporting Prom Night some little act of revenge?"

"It's a big act of avenge. You and your scummy friend Edward! He infects then kills Gaëtan and blackmails us, you try to steal Festin, then squeal on Benoît and get him suspended and make him lose his dream job with CSIS. You're the criminals! But you're not getting away with it again. You open all the theme restaurants you want, Biddiscombe. You can even finally open up across the street from us, which is mean and evil. You don't want to play fair, so I'm going to do everything I can to fight you and compete. I know what I'm doing now, and this place is going to do so well your head will spin faster than Carrie's on Prom Night."

"And just how are you going to compete, with your Wal-Mart Ginette Reno?"

"La Bolduc is bringing in a whole new crowd. And they won't like it if you make things nasty for her or us. You get me?"

"What kind of new crowd?" I was silent, just gave him a look, I have had dramatic training. It worked. "Not the Hell's Angels? Not Rock Machine?"

"I can't say. You don't want to cross them, is all I can tell you. I give them what they want."

He was doing his best not to but he looked kind of worried. I'd bought us more time even though he didn't know I'd threatened him with the Grey Brigade.

Finally it was Frieda's last day at ballet camp. Heidi and I were so happy to rescue her from there, even though we feared being full-time foster co-moms. I thought the place was strange and nasty when we were allowed to go for visiting day. Some of those ballet kids were hateful, especially the little girls who pranced by us and said, "Where's Weirdo? Oh, there she is." And we realized they meant our Frieda.

"Who are those mean little girls?"

"Stupid kids in my cabin," she said.

If Frieda was her mother's daughter she'd have pulled their hair out of their little bunheads. (I know I felt like it.)

"I hope you ignore them," Heidi said.

"Oh yes," she said, all mature, but we knew they probably hurt her feelings every chance they got.

When Frieda led on ahead of us, Heidi turned to me and said, "Did I ever get you to read *Cat's Eye*, by Margaret Atwood?"

"No," I said.

"It's so enlightening about how cunning, vindictive and vicious little girls can be, I think it will be insightful for us to read it, seeing as we're going into a whole new area."

Cat's Eye for summer reading? If we had to read girlhood books to understand Frieda, she should have suggested *Anne of Green Gables* and *Angelina the Ballerina*, some Judy Blumes even. But then it was early days for us.

"Given the intense nature of the Camp de Ballet program, we discourage all visitors until days we've designated," their brochure said. Frieda gave us a tour around the camp, she took us to her cabin, "Fonteyn," next to the younger girls' cabin, "Kain." We saw the barre in front of a big mirror they had to practice at for three hours every morning, in the afternoon they had to do more pliés, arabesques and tour jetés in a big hall and go for lessons in ballet history. We went into a classroom with just "Nijinsky Diagilev" written across the blackboard. Heidi was worried.

"You do get to swim and go out in canoes, don't you?"

"Oh yes, sometimes. We walked in the woods once, there was poison ivy but I didn't get it," Frieda said.

We had the salad bar lunch with her in the marquee and she told us why the girls who called her Weirdo were really stressed.

"They all think they're going to Winnipeg," she said.

"Why?"

"To the Royal Winnipeg Ballet School? You go there to train. Like in Russia. People send their children away to boarding school to become ballerinas."

"When they're only ten years old?"

"When they're eleven and get their toe shoes. That's why I never wanted to be really good — my mother would send me away there."

"Oh no she wouldn't," we both said.

Oh yes she would, we knew we could say.

"Madame says the RWB scouts are coming to the final presentation. Lots of the girls in Fonteyn and Kain are really driven. Ever since I was three, my mother challenged me to be the best ballerina, but I didn't want to be a ballet dancer."

"What did you want to be?"

"A Brownie."

"Would you still like to do that?" Heidi asked.

Sure. Northrop could be called Andy, why couldn't she be in Brownies?

"I think I'm too old now. I think it will have to be Girl Guides."

"Heidi and I were Girl Guides, it was so much fun."

"Would you like that in September, maybe?" Heidi asked her.

"Oh yes," Frieda said.

"You won't have to take ballet ever again," said Heidi, who has never taken to the ballet. Her family has a problem with ballet, they all think it's sissy.

"Oh, but I couldn't give up ballet and never see it again," Frieda said.

"Well no, after all your training," Heidi conceded.

"I don't want to dance, but I'd like to make my own ballets."

"Choreograph, you mean?"

"Yes. I would like to make a ballet of Anne Frank."

"Anne Frank?"

"Yes. I love that book, Aunt Heidi. When Anne wrote in her diary how she had to pack only one suitcase, it made me think of us in Baie D'Urfé. Only we could take a lot more stuff. And we didn't walk through the streets with our clothes under our coats, we drove to the safe house in a taxi. And we weren't in hiding in the Annex, but we were on the run from creditors and weren't in our home anymore."

"Anne Frank was a brave little girl, like you," Heidi told her.

"Am I Jewish?" Frieda asked.

"No. Would you like to be?"

"I don't think so. They get taken away and put in camps, people are so mean to Jewish people."

"Not anymore."

"No? I thought maybe that's what we are, in secret. And they're coming for us and that's why my parents ran away."

"That's not why they're gone. They're both a little mixed up," I told her.

"One of the other Fonteyns said my name is Jewish."

"It can be. But I think you were named after Sylvia Plath's daughter Frieda," Heidi told her.

"We never went to church."

"But did you ever go to temple? To a synagogue?"

"Yes. One time with my teacher. It's her religion, she got the rabbi to show us the Torah."

"Are any of your relatives Jewish?" I asked, hoping we'd find out if there were any aunts or uncles.

"I don't think I have any. It was always just us," she said.

It broke my heart to leave her, but we knew when we were allowed to come back the next time we'd take her home. She waved bravely as we drove away, and we were the ones crying. We didn't get very far when Heidi turned the car around.

"We can't leave her there, Lenore."

"You said it. Let's spring her outta there!"

"Stalag 17 was more child-friendly!"

We found Frieda still in the same spot we'd left her.

"Do you want to come home with us today, sweetie?" Heidi asked.

"I can't. My mother paid for three weeks," she answered.

"That doesn't mean you have to stay," I said.

"Yes it does. And I have to be in the presentation at the end. I can't let the corps de ballet down. I'll be okay."

We never cried when we went to Andy's camp, we didn't want to leave! Douglas must have been the one who chose it because it was frivolous and inventive. It was run by Gus in a Smokey the Bear hat. I thought he'd be a catch for Heidi if Woodham didn't work out until I saw that he had his eye on the counsellor named Mimi. Our visiting day there was so great, Benoît and Andy went out for Father and Son in the Woods Paintball War and came back messy and paint splattered, while Heidi and I got to go swimming in the clear, black lake. Then, in a big tent after a hot dog lunch and banana boat dessert, Gus gave each table an empty Tide box, an egg carton, some crayons and bits and bobs. "Now, campers, make something that could save your lives if you were stuck in the woods." We were all going to die, our lifesaver was such a disaster. That didn't keep Gus and Mimi from extending the ultimate invitation, and we accepted. That's how we got to be part of Family Camp Out when it was time to bring Andy home. I hadn't slept in a tent since Guide camp. And did I imagine a cookout with ghost stories and a sing-a-long by the campfire would be such a mystical experience? Why was that? Was it the stars? And the other crickety sounds from the woods? What was that sense of well-being that came over me? I felt so content, it was like Benoît and Andy really were father and son and they were my husband and child and Heidi was my sister. I wasn't alone, I had family. And all these wonders are mine because Elspeth is so selfish.

And then at long last we went to bring Frieda home. We could hardly wait for the rescue, but she had the presentation to get through.

It was a bizarre sight: these kids sleep in cabins, which is normal for a summer camp, and there were some tents up, but the kids were all flouncing around wearing tutus and costumes, some were walking on their hands and doing acrobatics even though the temperature was three thousand degrees. "If most of them weren't so cute, this would be Felliniesque," Heidi said.

Frieda wrote to tell us what the Presentation would be.

"They're doing *The Nutcracker*?" Heidi was perplexed.

"Sort of Christmas in July?"

"I've never taken to ballet," Heidi said.

"And I've never been to one, I win."

"Never?"

"Never. Not even Les Ballets Trocadero," I said.

"How can you never have seen ballet?"

"Just lucky, I guess."

Now here we were, two ballet snob foster moms sitting on plastic folding chairs in a big tent, swatting bloodthirsty mosquitoes, at 110 degrees Celsius. "Toto, I don't think we're in Place des Arts anymore," Heidi said to me.

I wanted to know where these dreaded Royal Ballet scouts from Winnipeg were. I looked around for people in Ukrainian dance costumes or cowboy hats.

"Those two look suspect," Heidi said and pointed to the front row at some unisex pencil-thin people with combed back hair.

A few seconds later, we found out we were wrong: two little unisex children ran over and hugged them, their parents, whose endearment for them was, "Oh! Nos mignons! Les petits rats de l'opéra!"

"I think if I have to experience ballet, I'd like it to have a story I can relate to. Like Agnes de Mille's *Fall River Legend*," Heidi said.

"What's that?"

"The Lizzie Borden ballet."

"Oh, Heidi. The only ballet you like is about your axe-murderess?"

"No, I can like some other ones. But I always hate it when they have those ballet sequences in the middle of Rodgers and Hammerstein musicals."

Finally it started. My first ballet: The Summer Camp Nutcracker.

Well! These kids had been through an intensive program for three weeks only to end up dancing backup for the teachers. They gave the role of Clara to the meanest kid in Cabin Fonteyn, but Madame who ran the camp took the lead ballerina part. And the camp counsellors had the other prima roles. They somehow got a grant to bring in two guest artists from Russia to play principals like the Nutcracker Prince and some grandpa character. The visiting Russians were much younger than Madame and way more agile.

"She's quite past it as the Sugar Plum Fairy, don't you think?" Heidi whispered to me.

"And she keeps looking at the Russian Nutcracker boy like he's the one missing the jetés or whatever they're supposed to be doing," I said.

Frieda was terrific, she danced a number of different parts: a mouse, a Chinese girl, a Spanish gypsy, an Arabian princess, a doll. She twirled very fast around the artificial Christmas tree and was a very convincing swan when they threw in a bit from *Swan Lake* so Madame could play the one who dies.

Then, thank God, it was over. Most of it had been so pathetic and awful that Heidi pronounced, "There was no scout from the Royal Winnipeg Ballet here." A voice behind us said, "Oh yes there was." We turned to meet an incredibly elegant woman in sunglasses who seemed to have just arrived from the Riviera.

"I'm Ellice Portage, Royal Winnipeg Ballet. Are you mothers?"

"Yes, and we don't care how wonderful you think our little dancer was, she's not going with you!" Heidi said.

"Even if she is the best one," I said, "she's just a child."

Ellice smiled, then walked off to have a word with Madame, and a few minutes later, Frieda came running over and we hugged her.

"You did so well, honey, we were so proud of you!" Heidi told her.

"You were fabulous!" I gushed sincerely.

Frieda looked at us in surprise, I guess she never heard reviews this good from her mother.

We'd packed up her things and were taking her out of her cabin when we heard a lot of sobbing as a corps de girls rushed into Fonteyn and threw themselves across their cots, tear-streaked bunhead faces buried in their skinny pillows.

"None of them made the cut," Frieda said.

"No Winnipeg for any of them?"

"Nope, Madame said they didn't have Eet."

We walked ahead of Frieda to the car, luckily she didn't hear us. "Too bad. I'd love to see them all banished to boarding school," said Heidi.

"Not if it's what they want. If those driven little ballet-climbers ever end up in Manitoba like they wish, I hope they all wind up where the buffalo roam, grand jetéing across the prairie so they won't get trampled."

"I've never heard you so vindictive."

"I prefer to think of it as protective."

"They were mean and rotten to our little girl, anyway. Bad cess to all of them. My God, Lenore, she's not even our child and we're like this."

We drove her away from ballet camp and hope she'll never, never go there ever again. Unless she insists.

Benoît said he had a surprise for me, so Heidi took the kids. He'd been going off somewhere secretly quite a bit, and I thought maybe his heroics at the Stanley Cup riot got him back in the CSIS good books, but that wasn't it at all. He drove us out to the West Island along the Lakeshore until we got to Pointe Claire and a marina.

Benoît said, "Follow me." Down to a dock we went past an array of magnificent boats, until we stopped at the sailboat called *Hello, Gorgeous!* I knew this name.

"*Hello, Gorgeous!*, that's the name of Jamie's boat."

"Oui. C'est son bateau!"

Jamie hadn't been back and I thought *Hello, Gorgeous!* was dry docked, but she looked as if she'd been out, she was in the water at least and well swabbed.

"Is Jamie home? Is this the big surprise?" I asked, expecting him to pop out on deck.

"Non. He's too busy with his pilot for the TV."

"So whose been using his sailboat?"

"Voyons, climb aboard."

"We're going out? Sailing?"

"Mais oui."

"Is someone going to sail this thing for us?"

"Oui, chérie."

As I looked up the dock to see who that would be, Benoît started untying ropes.

"Hey . . ."

"You got to put on the life jacket, ma chouette," he said as he adjusted it on me, then he got to work.

"What are you doing with the sails and those jibs or whatever they're called? Do you know what you're doing?"

"Pas de problème, chérie. Moi, je suis le capitaine."

"You? You never told me you were a sailor."

"Because I wasn't before. But I have been taking des leçons. I know what to do."

The day Jamie had called and flirted over the phone with

Daniel and Benoît, he'd told them he had to make a decision about his sailboat and were we interested in using it?

Benoît said he didn't know anything about the sea, and Jamie said, "Oh, you can learn!" Jamie set Benoît up with lessons, and today he was taking me out for a sail.

"The first time it can be just us."

"To be romantic?"

"Yeah, and because if I make a mistake it's only you and me who capsize, not the kids."

Benoît must have been first in his class because he was really good at sailing, I couldn't see any mistakes. We had a great day, wind-wise, and the waves weren't big and choppy. He'd even brought a picnic and champagne. But he could only have one glass of Moët.

"I'm driving."

Benoît taught me as we sailed, so by the end of the summer maybe I'd deserve to be the first mate. I'd know all about knots in nautical miles as well as the ones on the ropes.

"Sailing's not something I ever thought of, but it's great, eh?" I said.

"Jamie told me this can sail all over the place, maybe even on a big trip someday."

"Who knows, eh?"

He looked just like he belonged at the helm. With the sun beginning to set, the light made him look even more handsome. I wasn't driving so I'd had most of the champagne, and it made me so happy to think of how nice my life had been since we got together. Benoît had done so much for me, things I never asked him to do, he was always ten jumps ahead. Just the day before Heidi pointed out another one.

"Have you noticed how quiet it is, late at night?"

"Yeah."

"The Surfboard Boys ride no more."

"Blake must be gone."

"I'll bet Benoît had something to do with making our streets safe."

I figured now was a good time to congratulate him on a job well done.

"Did you have words with Blake Farnham?"

"Why you ask me that?"

"Because our neighbourhood's been so peaceful since we got back from England. We tried to convince his mother Jemima to come home and deal with him, he was so bad. Blake and his late night rowdies were really out of control before we left. And that Trans Am's no longer peeling up the street. I haven't even seen Blake since we got back."

"Yeah, okay, I say a few things to him. That's it, that's all."

"Well . . . thank you."

He didn't smile, a dark cloud crossed his face. He'd always been shy about praise, but now he seemed to have a problem with it too.

That was the only weird thing in our perfect, perfect day. The sky was magnificently red and purple as we sailed back to shore.

Chapter Ten

Reine Ducharme was happy to approve her latest new tenant but hoped "pauvre Daniel" was not moving in all alone.

I told her he hadn't met anyone who could replace Gaëtan. But, she said, there were "plus des poissons dans la mer pour les homosexuels, oui?" I told her there may be more fish, but Daniel isn't swimming in the sea, he's still very sad. She recommended he try les personnels. If only he was on Death Row in the United States, he'd be fighting them off. I figured Daniel didn't need to kill anybody for that, all he'd need was to be in prison.

Her nutcase admirer in Utah gave up on her because Reine finally confessed she's not going to the chair, but she'd been corresponding with a "très gentil homme" from Denmark.

"Herr Lars Sprüngli," she told me and blushed.

Herr Sprüngli is a Danish-Swiss and speaks and writes seven languages, he sends her beautiful letters. He read about her in an article on Canada's Serial Killers. He's such a dedicated foe of the death penalty that he often travels to the USA and protests outside prisons where people are about to be executed. Lars felt that perhaps it was time he corresponded with someone he's not destined to lose as a correspondent.

Obviously Reine was truly, madly, deeply in love with him. It was nice for her to have a preoccupation, I thought.

September arrived so fast because August flew, we were so crazy busy in a good way with the kids. Heidi worked some magic and got a family recreation pass, way past the deadline, so we took them to Westmount Pool and enrolled them in all the children's programs. I've never been to that library so much before, either. We took out a lot of children's books and videos, but Heidi decided we better go easy on the Disney ones.

"Why? They're beloved childhood classics," I said.

"Where they kill off all the mothers. Bambi? Ariel the Little Mermaid? Snow White, Belle. Pinocchio never even had one. Sleeping Beauty's the only one with two parents."

Heidi's the only person in the world who would analyze Disney cartoons.

"Pollyanna. They're all . . . orphans," she said, lowering her voice and not because we were in a library.

"I'm an orphan," I told her.

"Yes, but . . ." she whispered and gestured toward the kids.

"They're not orphans," I said.

"Their parents have abandoned them."

"They're not orphans, and they've got us. They have two doting mothers and two father figures who show them off at the cop shop and the fire hall. It's kids' heaven," I said.

"You know what I mean, Lenore."

She saw that I had put down *Pinocchio* but picked up *Dumbo*.

"Not *Dumbo*!"

"Dumbo has a mother."

"Who gets separated from Dumbo because she defends him. That terribly sad scene where she enfolds him in her trunk and rocks him from her cage?" And Heidi started to cry in the children's section of the Westmount Library.

"Okay, okay, I'll put *Dumbo* back. And *Old Yeller* too, I guess?"

"*Old Yeller* I approve of, sure," Heidi said, wiping away her tears.

"They shoot the dog."

"But only at the end and he's rabid. Old Yeller is a hero, he saves their lives, and the boys have a strong mother. It even has Moochie, I loved him, let's watch it tonight!" So we all sobbed and sobbed, and from then on Andy really, really wanted a dog.

We had so many great days of sailing on *Hello, Gorgeous!*, all hands on deck learning the ropes. The kids enjoyed helping with Daniel's big move, and they were at Festin whenever they wanted to be there, which was often. Heidi wasn't teaching at Concordia during the summer, so she took them to every Eco Museum or Insectarium within reach, she even got them all on an archaeological dig for a day. We wanted them to have a lot to write in their What I Did on My Summer Vacation compositions. Fall brought a big change, going back to school created more of a routine but with all new activities for everyone to experience. Heidi talked to the Girl Guide people and got Frieda into a local company, but she had to promise to "pitch in" as some sort of leader. "I wouldn't call it blackmail but it was close, and they really could use me, since I am a veteran," Heidi figured.

Benoît registered Andy for an Atom Division hockey team, so they spent lots of time at the arena. We're afraid we'll become those people in the stands who scream like maniacs when their kids are playing. Daniel got them into a children's hands-on Les Impressionistes et Plus series at the Museum of Fine Arts. We had a crackerjack Parenting Team going on, it may have been a strange set-up to some people, but it seemed to be working. I loved it. The children were no burden, they were a gift.

First it was days, then it was weeks, finally it was the whole summer and into September with not one word from either of their parents. No news at all, until the great ferry disaster in Greece.

It was just a little story in the *Gazette*:

> **Greek Ferry Sinks**
> **234 rescued, 2 missing**
> Two tourists are missing after a Greek ferry sank when it hit an uncharted reef two miles out of Kythnos. "They were last seen in the vicinity of the one toilet on the ferry," said another English-speaking tourist.

This sounded to me just like Elspeth and Elijah deciding to try Mile High Club on a Greek ferry, and they could have gone down with the ship. Death by Sex at Sea.

Was that wicked wishful thinking? It was too fitting, but it meant these darling children would be motherless, which could be a blessing. Oh, Elspeth had made me so cynical and cold and insensitive, I knew these kids would want their mom back, no matter what. Poor little souls.

Costas of Santorini called me before I called him.

"The bad womans you are looking for, she was nympho on ferry."

"Is she dead?"

"Oh no, they think so first time but she wash up on the shore. With the tanned mans. Both alive. They are in all the papers. Everyone know what they doing in toilet when ferry sink!"

"Good!"

"I tell them all she is woman who abandon her childrens."

Elspeth called me from Greece three days later. I finally heard from the Mother of the Year.

"Lenore! Our names, they weren't in the paper?"

"No. There was only a little mention. When are you coming home?"

"Don't ask me that. I'm still apoplectic, we almost died, you know. Thank goodness the tide was with us, we washed up on the beach. Is Viola treating my children well?"

"No. Viola's back with Charlotte. They bought a colossal new home. They're going to adopt from China. They have nothing to do with your kids anymore."

"I was wondering who the male voice on the answering machine was at Madame Ducharme's."

"It's Daniel, Heidi's brother. Viola has left the building. And your kids."

"But Viola so wanted to be a mother. I thought she'd welcome the chance to have my two."

"You were wrong. We have them."

"Who's we? Not you and Heidi?"

"Yes, and Benoît and Daniel."

"Four parental figures? And not one of you is married. That might be confusing, so much for stability, they might get overstimulated. Oh well, it can't be helped. They've always admired you and Heidi."

"And I'm sure you're giving them lots to admire in their mother," I said.

"At least I left the children in good hands. Has Douglas contacted you?"

"How would he know to contact me? Have you spoken to him?"

"No. Why don't you find out the license plate number of For Womyn Only and track him down?"

"Why don't you? Elspeth, you get back here right away or I'm reporting you to the police. Benoît will call out the dogs. And the Greek cops will come after you and then Interpol. You are too bad a mother to get to stay in Greece."

"This is the land that gave us *Medea*, you think they'll condemn me?"

"Yes! They'll run you off every island you hit."

"I've been run off smaller islands than this. We are the stuff of legend. Our tale is epic! We're like the gods of their mythology, we should be dead, but instead we belong on Mount Olympus! We swam up out of the sea like Poseidon, Neptune and — "

"You are insane! You're not Greek gods, you're disgusting sex-maniacs who got a lucky break."

"Don't you be judgemental with me, my dear!"

"Don't you my dear me, you selfish monster. You get on the first plane out of Kythnos or whatever island you're rediscovering now. Come home. Your children are so confused, poor Frieda and Andy."

"Who's Andy?"

"Northrop."

"You changed his name?"

"No, he did. And we let him, okay? But the poor little kid needs his mom. You get back here or I'm turning your crime over to the police."

"Don't do that, Lenore. My children can't be a burden yet, they're in the golden years when they love you, and you can't say they're demanding, can you, what's the matter, don't you like my kids?"

"We love your kids!"

"Good. They're yours."

And then she hung up.

"'They're yours?'" Heidi repeated to me, for the tenth time.

"Yes. That's what she said. That's it, that's all."

Daniel, Heidi, Benoît and I were deep in conference on my new deck. The kids were up at Heidi's watching *101 Dalmatians*.

"From such long distance, maybe Elspeth didn't actually say that," Daniel speculated.

"What else could she have said besides 'They're yours'?"

Daniel came up with, after too many days on *Hello, Gorgeous*!, "Their oars."

"They're whores, m'excuse but it's possible," offered Benoît.

"There's Horst," said Heidi.

This one made us all agree that Elspeth had indeed said, "They're yours."

"Which means they're ours," I said.

"Unless you want to give it to the police, chérie, we get them both back here that way," Benoît said.

"And for what, Ben? The kids are better off with us."

"Their parents are bankrupt narcissistic sociopaths," Heidi declared. Then she informed us that Elspeth wasn't coming back to teach. Ever.

"She called Concordia before she called you, Lenore."

"Her job came before finding out about her kids?"

"Yes. She's unbelievable."

We figured even with all the mistakes we'd make, we'd have to be better for them than Elspeth and Douglas.

"We can do a good job, we're doing okay I think?" said Benoît, we all nodded, then our kids screamed.

As we all ran upstairs, Heidi said, "Cruella De Vil isn't that scary."

"What's wrong?" Heidi asked and looked at the TV.

Audrey Hepburn was hiding behind a fridge and a man was dragging himself across the floor with a butcher knife.

They weren't watching *101 Dalmatians*.

"*Wait Until Dark*?"

"It's so scary. She's blind and she broke all the lights so the killer can't see too!" Andy yelled.

"But he had matches and was scaring her but Suzie found gasoline and threw it all over him!" Frieda screamed.

"The fridge had a light in it! Suzie stabbed him but he wasn't dead cause he leaped out at her!" Andy added.

"What about *101 Dalmatians*?" Heidi asked.

"We've seen it before," Frieda said. "My mother says Cruella is a female power figure."

"You didn't have to watch it again, Frieda."

"Yes we did because it has dogs in it." She glared at Andy.

"I didn't like seeing the puppies so sad and cold, and the silly guys going to skin them for coats," Andy said.

I thought it was a strange movie for them to be watching, I'd said so to Heidi.

"But don't all the puppies get separated from their parents?"

"They get rescued, Andy chose it," Heidi said.

Wait Until Dark had continued through all the commotion.

"Shall we rewind it back to where Alan Arkin leaps out at Audrey Hepburn and see the rest?"

"Yes, please," said Andy.

"I always scream at the leaping part, too," Heidi told them, and then we all sat and watched the end of *Wait Until Dark*.

When we returned to my place, Benoît said, "C'est trop sadistique, hein? The blind woman against the psychopath? What will we tell Youth Protection if they come, eh? We got the kids watching scary movies where they stash drugs in dolls?"

"Heidi Flynn, lock up your videos," I said.

The ferry disaster wasn't the only Water Damage we had. Everything sank for one of us on *Hello, Gorgeous*! We watched *Silver & Gold* when CBS aired it as a late summer pilot. It got really big ratings because nothing else new was on and great reviews because, wonder of wonders, it's really good. Casey is such a clever comedy writer she made them all into interesting characters. Jamie's a riot, Casey even worked it in that he sings in community musicals. That's the bonus when the writer knows who she's writing for, she can use all the actor's strengths and talents and make her work look good too. It's very funny how Casey has Jamie doing most of the singing while Cotton and Val as the former child stars, now storefront lawyers, back him up. Jamie called us with the best news:

"CBS bought six episodes! We'll be in the January replacements lineup! *Silver & Gold's* a big hit!"

"We sure enjoyed it, you were hysterical — "

"It's all because of you, Lenore!"

"No, you believed and you stuck it out in Hollywood, Jamie."

"You started this, you gave me Casey, you gave me Cotton, so I am giving you . . . *Hello, Gorgeous!*"

"No!"

"Yes. She's yours, as long as you let me sail her whenever I get back to Montreal."

"You're not really giving me your sailboat."

"I owe you, chickepen. Somebody gave you a restaurant last year, let me give you a boat."

So that's how I own a sailboat. Who knows, someday I may be

in a regatta. The first ones to officially celebrate my acquisition of the Queen of the Seas were Heidi and Woodham.

She'd already asked if they could take her out because it turns out he's a sailor.

"Remember there was a brief clip of him on Lake Windermere with a little skiff in *35 Up*?"

I hadn't seen the movie again as recently as Heidi, so I just agreed, and then the Owl and the Pussycat went to sea in my beautiful blue-green boat. But without the fairy-tale ending.

Heidi returned in tears. I was glad Daniel had taken the kids to the Dog Trials at Westmount Arena. I thought Heidi must have sunk the ship because the first thing she said was, "It's all over, Lenore. It's finished."

It started off badly because Woodham St. Antoine doesn't know as much about the art of sailing as he let on.

"He blamed it on being rusty, so things were a little tense," Heidi said, "but eventually he found his sea legs again and we were sailing along . . . and . . . and . . ."

And what? what?

"He remarked on how very much he's appreciated me being his friend since he arrived, how he's come to rely on me," she said, and I didn't want to know but I knew where this was going.

"He was breaking it off?"

"It was never on, Lenore. He wants us to be friends, but that's all it's ever going to be."

"Is he gay?"

"No, just not interested. Oh my God, I'm Esme Subcastle! I'm that pathetic wretch on *Gobsmacked*!"

"Are you absolutely sure all he wants is friendship?"

"Oh, he really, really values that. He doesn't know how he

would cope without my kindness and generosity of spirit. And all I've done for him."

"But all the salsa dancing?"

"That is so him, all dancing but no action. At least not with me."

"Never?"

"Not once."

"Oh, Heidi, no. So, it's just been dinners and helping him buy furniture and cars . . ."

"And watching the train go by through the children's swings. I never made a move on him because I was waiting for him to make the overtures."

"Has there been anyone else since he got here?"

"Oh yes. A number of women, he revealed them all to me today! The first was a female colleague in the toxic waste field."

"Not in the field?"

"Oh, who knows? And next was . . . someone else," she said like I should know who she meant. Who had he met besides us and her mom and the Judys? And . . .

"Not Elspeth?"

"Worse! Think blonde. Very, very blonde."

"Not Tess!"

"Yes, Tess! And you'll never guess when!"

"Not right after the Pot Party?"

"No. On Canada Day!"

"No! The day your folks invited you to go to Ottawa?"

"Hmm, yes. Oh, she is diabolical, that one, he was sitting out in Coffee Park, watching the train go by . . . when who gets off and walks by but her."

"Why was she on the train? She lives in the Plateau."

"Loyola campus is just up the street. We teach there sometimes."

"But it's summer. It was a holiday, nobody was working."

"Oh, she was working — the streets! Tess told him she was going in to give the bookstore her course book order list . . ."

"Isn't the bookstore downtown?"

"There's a little one at Loyola, but it's more for supplies. And she wasn't bringing in any book list."

"Did she know he'd be in the park?"

"If he hadn't been, she would have subtly banged down his door. Anyway, she says, why don't they go for a drink to celebrate Canada's birthday, and she suggests Lasso's," Heidi said.

"That Western bar near McDonald's on St. Jacques?"

"And he says, but it's not even ten in the morning. Would you settle for a coffee?"

"But she didn't settle for that, did she?"

"Well, it started with coffee on Coffee . . . and then, well . . ."

"At his house?"

"Probably on one of the new pieces of furniture I helped him buy at Ikea."

"Just like that?"

"Barkus is willing, to quote Mr. Dickens. He's a man, she's a tart . . ."

"But Heidi, you were willing, weren't you?"

"Of course I was. What is it about me, Lenore? I needed to be more than his platonic pal. I really liked him."

"But he's kind of boring, Heidi. He even admitted it."

"I know. But he so wants to change his life, remember? I asked him if Michael Apted would be impressed next time he comes for *42 Up* if his dramatic significant life change meant being taken in by the likes of Tess of the d'Urberblondes!"

"Oh, he's such a worm weakling. Idiot man, how could he not want to sleep with you?"

"I told Woodham to turn *Hello, Gorgeous!* around and get us back to shore. He said he didn't think I'd be like that, that I was being rude, he was all set for a nice day's sail."

"Just like you were all set for a nice day on the Hill with your family."

"I stood up my own kin because he wanted to see in Canada Day at the Old Port. No wonder he was so out of it when he finally met me, he was like a zombie, he'd been drinking and fooling around with her till he met up with me."

"Rotten bum. Loser."

"And he only told me because he wanted my advice as a woman and a friend. 'How can I give a woman the message that I'm no longer interested?' he said. 'I have quite a dilemma, Heidi. A colleague of yours, well, she's always been a sexpot. But it seems she's something of a stalker as well. Perhaps you could intervene? Say something to her?'"

"You must have wanted to kill him."

"No, I wanted to kill myself. What's wrong with me? If I'm perceived as huffy and standoffish, men can't wait to ask me out, once. But if I like them and give any kind of chase, I don't even get one date."

"You're just not very lucky with English guys. And Woodham was rebound for Miles. This has not been a good year for you, Heidi."

"It hasn't been a good year for me for a long time, Lenore. I've wanted something to happen to me, and nothing has."

"Things have happened, you almost got married."

"Yes, and I almost had a baby. And I almost wound up with a job in Yorkshire. I thought my Travel Karma could be bad, but my life karma is even worse. I'm always on the brink of change, but nothing happens. And I'm thirty-nine years old. My life is all almosts! While you, Lenore, look at your life. You've got a great boyfriend, a successful restaurant, a beautiful sailboat, you've starred in two musicals and a panto, you've been an overnight sensation on a TV talk show, you got a marriage proposal from an Arizona rancher millionaire, you've been to the Academy Awards and seen by a billion people wearing a maharanee's jewels, feminists call you from Greece and give you their children, what have I accomplished?"

"You're a doctor of English, and now you've also got two kids who need you."

"Two children that Elspeth could come back and take from us anytime. My life, Lenore! It's like I'm stuck inside Joni Mitchell's 'Both Sides Now'!"

"Heidi, Heidi, that's too sad and horrible, please don't say your life is that song."

"But it is. I'm so . . . not going anywhere, with no one. I don't want to envy your life, Lenore, but yours now is so rich and — "

"Before it could be any of that, I suffered, Heidi. And don't forget I had a real rotten rat of a boyfriend for eight years, if that makes you feel better."

"Yes, Fergie was pretty awful but — "

And as if the Powers Above wanted to prove that point to Heidi, there was a knock at the door: the police, both female, both stunning, a blonde and a brunette, with fabulous makeup too, it was like two Charlie's Angels had arrived. I suspected maybe it was a joke, they were some female version of Chippendales and were here as a surprise for Benoît from the boys in blue. But it's not his birthday, he's at work, and he's doesn't live here. They showed me their badges, they were real cops all right, Constables Malone and Pradesh, so then I was worried that they had bad news about Benoît. But they weren't here about my current boyfriend.

"Did a John Ferguson come here?"

"He used to live here until a couple of years ago, but he took off," I said.

"To Florida?"

"Yes. He left me a goodbye note on the fridge with his forwarding address."

"You haven't seen him since?"

"No, I never saw him again."

"That's true, I can vouch for that, officers," Heidi said.

"What kind of vehicle was he driving when you last saw him?"

"A really beat-up, ugly Ford pickup, with new tires he charged to my card without asking me," I answered.

"Why do you need to know about it, please, officers?" Heidi asked.

"Because it was dragged out of the Lachine Canal."

"*What*? Was he in it?"

"Not anymore. The driver's side door had come off. There was a lot of damage to the vehicle. His body could have floated away," Brunette Cop said.

"He never wore a seat belt."

"How long has his truck been down there?" Heidi asked.

My mind was racing, maybe Fergie never got out of town that Boxing Day after all. But then who sent me the FedEx bundles of cash the first year he was gone and those postcards the second?

"The truck's been submerged about four months," Blonde Cop said. "Was he a taxidermist?"

"No."

"There were a lot of animals under a tarp in the truck. All stuffed and mounted."

More of them? A whole bunch of his Salute to Taxidermy were in my cellar in a cupboard behind the new shelves. Had Fergie brought new ones to sell to people in Montreal? Or did he want to store them with me? What was he doing back here?

They questioned me about the state of our relationship before Fergie took off.

"Excuse me, is she a suspect?" Heidi finally asked.

"We need to question anyone who knew him," Blonde Cop Malone informed us.

"Should she have a lawyer present?"

"No. This is simply a preliminary inquiry."

I knew Heidi was trying to protect me, but she was making it worse, then she made herself look like a suspect, too.

"Four months ago, officers, we were in England. On holiday."

Why did she offer up this alibi, we didn't need one. I knew we weren't guilty. That's when I sang a little like a canary.

"You might want to talk to Fergie's pal Cheechio. They disappeared cars into the Lachine Canal as a public service."

"Would you have this Cheechio's coordinates?"

"No, I'm sorry, I don't. Really. He was this acquaintance colleague slimy pal of my ex. I found out they even sold marijuana they were growing in my garden. There was a bar they hung out at."

"On the Main?"

"Fergie on the Main? Never." Heidi looked suspicious again.

"Can you remember the name of the bar?"

"Brigadier's."

"That dive?" Blonde Cop Malone said.

"Maybe you'll find Cheechio there."

"That could help us, thank you. If you think of anything else, please call us." Brunette Cop Pradesh said. She gave me her card, and they left. Heidi and I looked at each other. The Bad Luck with Men Sweepstakes was over.

"Okay, you win," Heidi said.

Chapter Eleven

My ex-boyfriend could have been floating up or down the St. Lawrence Seaway while Both Sides Now suddenly improved for Heidi. It began when she was a guest at the best fortieth birthday party Toronto had ever hosted.

"Jane has such connections. It was at Casa Loma."

I've only been to Toronto once, so I've missed this wonder of Ontario. Heidi says it's known as the Castle-on-the Hill and even has secret passageways and turrets; a man ran out of money building it so lavishly, but a society took it over, now it's used for big weddings and functions. And big birthday parties.

"If you have to turn forty, this is the way to do it, beyond fantastic."

There was a dance orchestra, a fountain spouting champagne, and ice sculptures depicting different phases of Jane's life on every table. I didn't even know that Heidi had a super rich friend until she got invited to this bash. But it's all part of the life Heidi had in her "Toronto dark-period years" when she was at U of T getting her PhD.

Jane's family has numerous homes, just one of them is a cottage on an island in B.C. you can only get to by seaplane. "And when you get there, it's so affectedly rustic, it has no electricity. It's all operated by a generator. And servants." Heidi was flown in there for Jane's thirtieth birthday blowout. Jane's always been very generous to her friends in circumstances that involve anything that celebrates herself.

Jane is so wealthy she doesn't have to work for a living, "so of course she has a job that pays in the six figures." She's very big in advertising, a workaholic who "knows everybody." That's how come one of the people at the party happened to be a former Montrealer and part of Heidi's old Loyola College gang.

"James Murphy."

"A nice Irish boy?"

"A good Catholic even. My mother loved him."

"Was he your boyfriend?"

"He should have been, but he was dating my friend Joanne, it was very serious, he was crazy about her, but they broke up. And I was dating you-know-who."

"The big rat of your life?"

"Yes, him."

"Oh, too bad."

"Yeah. And then James took up almost right away with Molly of McGill, and before we knew it they were engaged and then married. We all went to the wedding, even Joanne, but I didn't see much of him after that."

"Was Molly there?"

"Not likely. They divorced years ago, very messily, no kids. Good thing, she was kind of strange. I had such a great time with him, we were laughing at everything, you know how it is? We had such fun when we were all at Loyola, which became Concordia while we were there. The party was so incredible, and then in the middle of it, Jane led us outside to buses that drove us to . . . the Sky Dome!"

"You didn't!" I sure knew what happened next.

"Yes, and there we were in all our finery at the Blue Jays World Series game!"

"Oh my gosh . . ."

"Yes, yes. Heidi Flynn was there when Joe Carter hit that three-run homer, bottom of the ninth! Fantastic! We were all screaming and hugging each other. Can you believe it, the Blue Jays did it two years in a row."

James didn't feel it was disloyal to cheer for the Blue Jays because he lives in Toronto now. And he gave her dispensation to cheer for a team that wasn't the Expos when she was a visitor and owed some of her higher education to Hogtown. It made sense to me.

"Well, yes, the Blue Jays aren't like the Maple Leafs."

"Exactly. The Canadiens won the Stanley Cup and you were there, and I saw Toronto win the World Series. What are the chances of that, eh? What a year for us and for Canada. It was wonderful, we were out of our minds. We got back to Casa Loma and partied till four in the morning. And if I do say so, my salsa dancing was a big hit! I gave the whole ballroom a lesson. Jane got all the out-of-towners rooms at the Royal York. Here, look, I brought you all the little soaps and shampoos. My train home wasn't till that night, so James came and got me and took me for a drive."

"All over Toronto?"

"No. To Niagara Falls! I haven't been there since I was a little girl. Wow, is it ever magnificent! Stunning. What a Wonder of the World. The Canadian side is the best, the US can't even compare. James and I went on the *Maid of the Mist*. We got soaking wet. They let me keep the blue raincoat they insist you wear, I think Frieda will enjoy it, or you, you want it?

It's funny. And coming back, James drove us around Niagara-on-the-Lake where the Shaw Festival is. We stopped at one of their vineyards for a tour, here, for you, a bottle of their new ice wine. Then he got me back just in time for my train. Ontario, Yours to Discover!"

"But not for good?"

"Oh no. No. I'm a Montreal girl. But we shouldn't be so prejudiced about Toronto, it's pretty nice. For a visit."

"James Murphy sounds like a good guy."

"Oh he's great, just great. So much fun. We talked about everything. We never stopped, we just picked up, like it was the seventies again. He heard I almost got married two years ago. How was your weekend? How were the kids?"

"Well Frieda and Andy had a little surprise for us. You missed it."

"Yeah? What was it?"

"Nits."

"No!"

"Yep. Our wee angels both have head lice."

"How? We send them to the finest schools."

"I called FACE this morning but the principal says maybe they contracted cooties at summer camp."

"Oh sure, blame the Camp de Ballet."

"No one is immune, no one is safe from . . . pediculosis!"

"I had lice twice in elementary school. My poor mother with the lice comb, I caught them from the same girl both times."

"Daniel was a big help. Is it ever disgusting work. We were nit-pickers together. He took Andy, and I had Frieda."

"And where was mon oncle Benoît?"

"He's not always on suspension. He does work sometimes."

"Great timing. They can get a second bout of lice, you know. You can miss some nits, and they keep hatching and laying eggs. If they come back, I'll nit-pick next time. That comb has my name on it."

Heidi was belle of the ball, and I was picking nits with a lice comb. I hoped maybe the winds of fortune were changing for her.

Lars Sprüngli has the most amazing piercing blue eyes. He could be quite successful as a hypnotist, especially with his snow white hair and curly waxed moustache. I was surprised when he showed up at my house.

"I should like to talk to you about Madame Reine Ducharme, if you can spare me some time?" he said in English that was so perfect I almost thought he wasn't really from Denmark. "She is a remarkable woman."

"Yes, she is." And does she ever know a lot about poisonous potions, I did not add.

"She said you are une bien bonne amie to her."

"I try my best."

I cleared my pathetic attempts at Halloween costumes off the kitchen table and made us tea. We could see Andy and Frieda in the garden. Lars Sprüngli asked me how old my children were and remarked on how nicely they played together. I nodded yes when I could have said, Not all the time they don't! Our little cherubim finally turned into normal children, there'd been plenty of fights and tantrums since school began. I even saw the Girls of Cabin Fonteyn business rear its ugly head, starring our darling Frieda, clearly one tough little cookie, I discovered she may have given back as good as she got. Andy had proven to be a challenge sometimes, he could be so stubborn, and Benoît was dismayed that he was such a poor skater. He was afraid Andy would be the first kid in the Atom Division to ever be handed a penalty for too many falls on the ice. Andy doesn't want any lessons, he thinks skating will just come to him with practice. But their not being saintly is healthier, more normal at least. I think they were being too good because they were afraid we would send them away if they acted up. Once they were sure of us, they were Free to Be You and Me and as selfish as ordinary kids.

Lars asked, "Are you making these little multicoloured clothes for your children?"

"Yes, for Halloween. I thought I could do this, but I am not a seamstress. And they're not really sure what they want to go out as, so I'm hoping for inspiration. I was trying for a scarecrow and a crow. All this is new for me."

"Oh yes, in North America in October there are pumpkins for Halloween and children go out for their candy," he said.

"And it's next week."

He smiled at me benevolently and then brought up an ugly topic. "Canada will never bring back the death penalty?" he asked.

"I don't think so." I was relieved that he was happy about that and not disappointed, otherwise he wouldn't be a lovely Danish gentlemen but some sicko counting on a death watch.

"Then I will not lose ma belle Reine to the gas chamber."

"That's really American. I don't even know if we ever had that in Canada."

"Or the firing squad, lethal injection, the electric chair, hanging . . ."

"We had hanging, but not anymore. Trudeau got rid of it.

And I think even if we did bring it back it couldn't be for people who didn't get sentenced to it already."

"That is very good to hear."

He'd brought us presents, three big Lindt chocolate bars from the Duty Free and a box of Danish cookies.

"Children like cookies and chocolate," he said looking out at Andy and Frieda.

"They sure do, thank you, danke! What is that in Danish?"

"Tak. It is my pleasure. Well, that is all. I must go now."

"That's it, you just came by to say hello?"

"Yes. To make your acquaintance, you are very important to Reine."

"Tak. Were you in Montreal for business?"

"Not business but to see Reine again."

"Again?"

"Oh yes. This is my second visit."

Lars Sprüngli appeared to be as smitten as Reine. He seemed like such a lovely man and not some nut who writes to murderesses behind bars.

"Would you like to stay for dinner?"

"Yes, but I must make my departure to the plane. I thank you for the kind invitation. Another time?"

"Sure . . ."

But how often did a Man from Denmark just drop in?

Heidi's James Murphy came to Montreal for a day to be interviewed for a big diplomatic job. He took her out for lunch, she wore her sapphire cocktail dress.

"It would be a posting with the UN," Heidi said.

"Why Montreal? The UN's in New York."

"And all over the world. But we have agencies here. It's actually with ICAO, International Civil Aviation Organization. They oversee security measures, refugees, peacekeeping, UNESCO . . ."

"Wow. And he'd be based here?"

"Yes. Too bad they didn't offer him the roving goodwill ambassador job the Queen wouldn't let Fergie keep," she said and laughed at her own wit.

Heidi's mom had gone on and on about Sarah "Fergie" Ferguson and that self-appointed UN job, but she stopped mentioning the Royals once Heidi finished with Woodham.

"That would be great for you if James Murphy moved here," I said.

"I suppose . . ." And then she got really upset. "I can't go through this again!"

"What?"

"I've always liked him, Lenore. But Joanne was my close friend. And their breakup at Loyola was such a big deal at the time. She was the one who dumped him. And I was seriously going out with the Rat. But I should have broken off with him before James fell for Molly of McGill, who turned out to be all wrong for him. James and I got along so well as buddies. The more we talk about the past and the present and issues and life and everything, the more I realize perhaps James was the one for me. He's the Man Who Got Away."

"But now he can be the man you get."

"No. He mentioned Joanne. He knows she's single again and still in Montreal. Maybe he'd like me to help him hook up with her."

"Don't be a cupid for them. Don't torture yourself."

"Well, if that will make him happy, the heart knows what it

wants. Stupid of me. Anyway he's gone back to Toronto, who knows if he'll get the posting. He took me to Gibby's."

And this was the way she wasn't going to discuss her true feelings anymore — by talking about Gibby's. She was such an idiot about men, she made me want to scream. She was describing their entrées when my doorbell rang.

It was Federal Express. Two years ago, FedEx used to mean bundles of dirty money Fergie sent me that he won at the gambling tables. But this huge package wasn't from Florida, it was from Denmark. From Herr Sprüngli.

Heidi and I opened it together and gasped when we saw what was inside.

"Viking costumes!"

They were the most beautiful outfits I've ever seen, with fabulous horned hats. He'd enclosed a card.

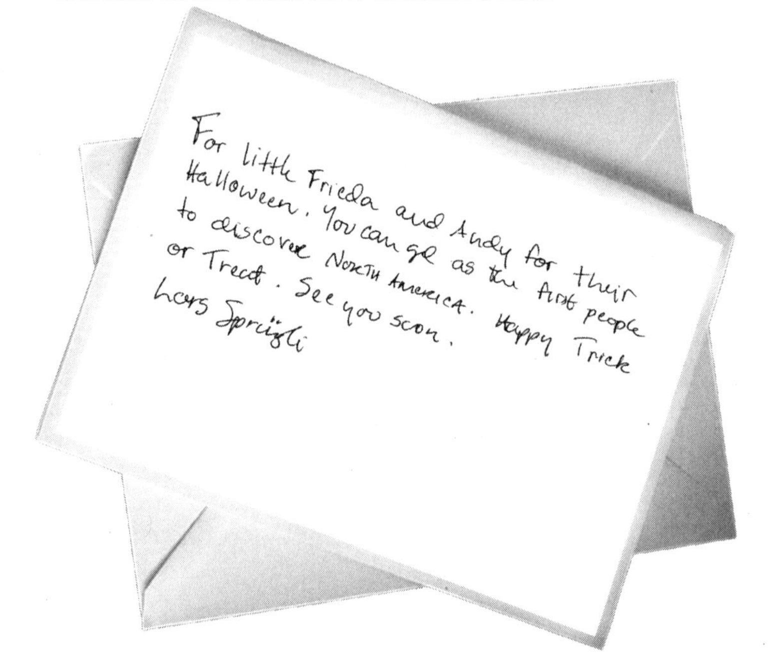

For little Frieda and Andy for their Halloween. You can go as the first people to discover North America. Happy Trick or Treat. See you soon.
Hans Sprüngli

"Well, I guess we can return those costumes we borrowed from your theatre pals in our act of quiet desperation," Heidi said.

I was madly festooning the house for Halloween the next day and Andy had his hockey net out on the street playing shinny with his friends when I heard a voice, a nasty one with an English accent.

"You there, little man, off my road," Jemima ordered.

Yes, dear hearts, Jemima Farnham was back.

"You stay right there, Andy, play on, honey, all ice is home ice," I told him and asked her, "When did you roll back into town?"

"The other day."

"Are you a granny? Has Tammy-Anne had the baby yet?"

"No, but it will be induced soon. It will have to be, it's rather overdue."

"How are things with Lord Peach and Longbreach?"

"I gave that position up."

"But you are going back to Britain?"

"Of course, as soon as the baby is born and Neville and I see the lawyers, oh no, I am not staying here."

Hurray, yippee, my spirit was skipping down the street. She fixed her glare on Andy.

"That little boy . . ."

"He's my ward," I told her. I could think of myself as Bruce Wayne with Dick Grayson.

"Your ward?"

"Mine and Heidi's. He has a sister Frieda too."

"Ohh. You're being paid by Foster Parents?"

"No."

"Hmm. Because you have to be approved for that."

"We're their guardians. Andy and his friends move when cars come, so don't worry about them."

"I don't want that rubber ball coming through my window!"

"It won't. Lighten up. He's a kid."

"Shoe's on the other foot now. Pinches, doesn't it? Let's see how you feel when people come running to you every time your boy does something they don't like," she said viciously.

"But no one is complaining to you anymore, your Blake is gone," I said.

"Thanks to your two lovers," she said.

"Pardon?"

"That Fergie man and your copper."

"Fergie had nothing to do with your son leaving."

"Of course he did. Poor Blake was shattered, he's terribly non-confrontational and he found himself in the middle of a fight."

"What fight?"

"A big melee on the street, when his beautiful new Trans Am was backed into by that Fergie man's beat-up truck."

"When was this?"

"In May, when you were off in England, I would expect."

"Fergie was here?"

"Blake couldn't give me many details . . ."

"Why not? Was he stoned?"

"Quite possibly, all right, perhaps yes. There was some element of babbling in what he said when I found him at his girlfriend's. But whatever it was, your Fergie fellow was involved. Blake was sure of that. After all, Fergie was Blake's supplier in the early days, you know, when he was growing marijuana in your yard."

That's when Andy stopped a shot that bounced off his knee pads and headed, yes, straight for Jemima's window. She screamed, the ball hit the window frame and bounced back to the street. Nothing was broken, but I was a wreck. Jemima ran back into her house and I ran into mine.

I called Viola at her new mini-mansion house on Ballantyne Street in Montreal West.

"Viola? The Miami Vice Celtic guy you saw in my backyard, did he look like Burt Lancaster?"

"The movie star?"

"Yes."

"I don't really know what he looks like."

She didn't know what Burt Lancaster looks like, proof positive she's a lesbian.

"Char, Burt Lancaster?" I heard her call.

"*From Here to Eternity*. Big kiss on a beach, with rolling waves and Deborah Kerr," was Charlotte's correct answer.

"Does that help?" Viola asked me.

"No! I need to know if the man you saw . . . never mind, can I come over and show you a picture?"

"Of Burt Lancaster?"

"No, of the man I think you saw."

"Okay. But we're not really ready to entertain.."

Why didn't Burt Lancaster ever star in a movie with Judy Garland? Then I'd have my answer. Instead I had to tell Andy to bring in the hockey net and to get Frieda, we were going for a drive westward.

Viola and Charlotte love to renovate so much they've torn their entire new home into pieces, I don't know if they'll be ready for the little Chinese baby in two years.

By the time we arrived, Viola did have a recollection of Burt Lancaster. Charlotte had reminded her.

"He was in *Judgement at Nuremberg* with Judy. I know who he is now."

I showed Viola a picture of Fergie.

"That guy doesn't look like Burt Lancaster. But he's the one in your yard. Only really tanned. And heftier."

"He's gotten fat?"

"Yeah, I guess you could say that. Pudgy-ish. Bloated."

"And he was at my house?"

"Yes. He and Benoît didn't seem to be getting along. Quite a contretemps."

"There was a car accident with his truck."

"I missed that. But I did see him in your back yard. He's the one. So that's the famous Fergie. Want to see what we've done so far? Take your mind off him for a few minutes and humour us, would you?"

They gave us a tour of the construction site that is their home, Andy was fascinated by all the bearing walls they planned to take down. He may wind up being a stagehand and an architect. Frieda was solicited for her opinion on paint colours and room configurations. I couldn't really focus, all I had running through my head was:

1. Benoît said the seedy Miami Vice guy was a possible date for Daniel. FALSE
2. Fergie's truck has been in the Lachine Canal for four months; the last time he was seen was four months ago, at my house. TRUE
3. When I was in England at the Cobbles, when Benoît was on suspension and building my new porch, he never phoned me again for days after his Jee Teem call. TRUE

Because Fergie'd been to visit! Viola said the meeting didn't look friendly. Jemima claimed Blake wound up in the middle of a fight. What went on? Why did that black cloud pass over Benoît's face on *Hello, Gorgeous*! when I mentioned Blake?

If Benoît never told me Fergie was here it was because he knew it would upset me. Or he was afraid I'd take Fergie back. What was Fergie doing at my house? Was he hoping to get back with me but got so depressed because I had someone new that he drove into the Lachine Canal? Or did the people he disappeared cars for years ago disappear him, led to him by Cheechio? Or did Benoît have a big fight with Fergie and somehow shove him, maybe kill him by mistake, and then give him a burial at sea? Did Benoît use his sailing lessons to dump Fergie's body off *Hello, Gorgeous*!? Am I going nuts?

This was just some of what was rambling, raving in my head. And Benoît was in the Laurentians on a stakeout. All he'd told me was it involved drugs and a motel. He was unreachable, and if Heidi thought she was Joni Mitchell's "Both Sides Now," I was Elvis singing "Suspicious Minds."

Frieda and Andy and I each had a pumpkin to carve, thanks to Benoît, who had taken them to Atwater Market on Friday before he had to leave for Motel X. I didn't want *Dark Shadows* thoughts of Fergie to ruin the kids' and my first Halloween together, so I tried my best and put it out of my mind. The bags of candy were made up, the house was really, really decorated, and our kids were going to be the most authentic Vikings this town had ever seen. Daniel would accompany them, they planned to trick or treat every street till they dropped. Heidi came down to my place because we were going to give out the candy together. I missed this last year, I was working every hour God sends at Festin. It's good to be la patronne now, as the boss I can arrange my hours to suit my complicated schedule. Jocelyne turned out to be a terrific manager, and her new job has left her less time to run out for a smoke. Of course, if I'd been at Festin, this night would have unravelled differently. Oh well. I did have to know the truth.

The first kids arrived just after five o'clock, well before our two headed out. But they finally went, and Heidi and I made a bet on how many children we'd get tonight.

"One hundred and fifty," Heidi said.

"Seventy-five," was my modest prediction.

"Lenore, this is Westmount, kids are bussed in because they think they'll get better candy."

Some of the costumes were quite fantastic and imaginative, lots of them were downright creepy. I was trying to keep bad thoughts away but . . .

"Are the kids' costumes bothering you?" Heidi asked.

"Well, so many of them are about death."

"It's Halloween, they're supposed to be. Oh, look who's lumbering our way, Lenore, it's Casey's friend Frankenstein. Ask him how he liked Ireland."

This didn't make me laugh, I was a wreck. I'd kept my paranoia all to myself too long, I was going to explode.

I'd been entertaining so many dark thoughts. I'd even looked for signs of digging in my yard. Why were my new shelves so strangely arranged in the basement? Why were all Fergie's things put away behind them in that cupboard?

Was it because maybe, just maybe, Fergie was in garbage bags behind my shelves? I'd even called the Charlie's Angels cops to see which taxidermied animals were in the truck. Brunette Cop Pradesh said she didn't have much of a list, the salvagers didn't go to a lot of trouble to elaborate because they weren't human and were in such bad shape from being in the water for so long.

I was really trying to keep myself together when the seventy-sixth trick-or-treater to arrive was Undead Man: glazed eyes, wearing a ski jacket with sticks stuck in it, like he'd dug himself out of his grave. I threw candy at the Undead, then I freaked out as I shut the door on him.

"Lenore! What is it?"

"We have to look in my cellar, right now!"

"Why?"

"Because I can't stand it anymore!"

"Can't stand what?"

And that's when I told Heidi all my suspicions.

"You really think Fergie was here?"

"Viola saw him in the back yard. In May. Blake had a run-in with him on the street the same day. And Benoît's been lying about it."

"Why?"

"Because . . . Fergie was in the house, in my cellar."

"How do you know that?"

"There were empty Labatt Blue bottles. And all his stuff is supposedly packed away in a cupboard behind the new shelves. I hope."

"What do you mean, you hope?"

"I hope it's his stuff there."

"What else could there be?"

"Fergie."

"Why would Fergie be there?"

"Because Benoît killed him."

"Benoît?"

"By mistake . . . by mistake! To protect me. You know what a hothead he used to be. And he's down as a rogue cop."

"Lenore, stop it, that's impossible, you're getting paranoid."

"I told you I've been going crazy! It's all the secrecy! And the lies from Benoît, his eyes going dark, him being all broody. And Charlie's Angels here to tell us Fergie's truck's at the bottom of the Lachine Canal."

"There, that's where he'd be, Lenore, if Fergie's anywhere, or churned up in the rapids or lunch for some fish on the way to Quebec City."

"I hope so. Please, I've gotta look. You stay here and give out the candy."

"No, I'll go with you. Seventy-six kids is more than enough. We can always come back to Halloween, if we can, which I'm sure we can. It's probably nothing . . ."

So we turned off the porch light and headed down to my cellar, my Lenore's Folk Art World. Once such a magical place, now Belmont Park's Haunted House of Horrors. All we needed was the Laughing Lady.

"You wanna wait for Daniel to come home?"

"With the kids?"

"Oh, right. But Lenore, if Fergie's body was behind those shelves, wouldn't it smell?"

"Not if Benoît did something to it."

"Such as?"

"He's a cop. He must know ways. Maybe he boiled it away with acid and all that's left is the bones."

"Lenore! Where do you get ideas like that?"

"You're the one who made us take the Haunts of Jack the Ripper Walk because we had two extra days in London!"

"You wanted to go."

"I was being supportive because you were heartbroken. I wanted to go to Scotland."

"There was no time for Scotland!"

I pulled everything off the shelves. We could hear ghouls banging for candy on the door upstairs. Some of them were pretty persistent, Heidi almost went up to them. "Ignore it," I said to her. Soon my collection of treasures was spread all over the floor. The new shelf moved away really easily. We pulled open the cupboard door, looked in and gasped. That's when we heard it: the front door slowly opening, then steps above us, wandering across the front hall. Heidi whispered, "They're coming in to get their candy!" But it was the heavy footsteps of a lone grown-up. We realized the light from Lenore's Folk Art World was shining up, the intruder would know we were below, whoever it was stopped at the top of the stairs, then started coming down until he was in the full cellar light. It was a policeman in a *Friday the 13th* mask.

"Bonsoir, mes belles filles," Benoît said coldly.

We both screamed, Benoît pulled off the mask.

"Pretty good, hein?"

We stared at him.

"Mon souvenir from the bad guys. We arrest them before they got to the motel, so me, I'm home. How come you're not giving les bonbons out no more? Which way did Daniel and the kids go, I can maybe join them. Hey, what did you do to my shelf?"

He rushed over to the open cupboard.

"There's nothing in there, Benoît."

He looked at me.

"Non. C'est vrai."

"You told me all of Fergie's Salute to Taxidermy was there."

"Oui."

"And all his other junk. Where did it go?"

"He took it."

"He took it? How? Did he break in?"

"He didn't have to break in."

"I changed my locks."

"Yeah, but poulette, I was working on the deck. The back door was open."

"Were you here?"

"I was at Canadian Tire. When I come back, his big truck is park in your space."

"What bloody nerve," said Heidi.

"That's nothing, Heidi. That Fergie, he's down here in Lenore's Folk Art World," Benoît continued.

"Was he looking for me?" I asked.

"No, that's the thing, that's what makes me so mad, after," Benoît said sadly. "And Fergie makes himself so at home, he's brought his own Labatt Bleu, and he's drinking while he looks."

"What did he want?"

"His junk. He's only taking what's his, he tell me."

"All his stuffed wildlife?"

"Yeah. But before them he was looking for his clothes."

"You told him I put them in the Salvation Army bells?"

"'Hey, not my M*A*S*H 4077 t-shirt!' he yells at me. I say yeah, tout ton garbage in l'Armée du Salut box."

"Did he ask where Lenore was?" Heidi wanted to know. "Or who you were?"

"He says to me, so are you the guy she's shacked up with now?"

"He always was classy," said Heidi.

"I say, she's not the kind of woman who shacks up, buddy. If only he was here because he want you back, it make more sense . . . but it's his creature he wants."

There was thumping of heavy sacks full of candy above us. Daniel and the kids had come back.

"Hey, why did you close up shop? There's still kids out there . . . hello?"

"We're in the basement," Benoît called up.

Daniel and the Fine Young Vikings came down to Halloween Night in the Cellar.

"What a mess. What's happening here?"

"Benoît is telling us a ghost story about Fergie."

He repeated the essentials, then he got back to the part about Fergie's Salute to Taxidermy.

"Only he don't want them all, he wants one called le marmotte."

"That little rat thing?"

"It was a rat thing of value," Benoît said.

"Was it like the Maltese Falcon?" Frieda asked from her perch on the stairs.

"How many of my movies have you sneak-previewed, little lady?" Heidi asked.

"Not that many. Did it have jewels sewn in its stomach?"

"Or drugs, like in *Wait Until Dark*?" Andy asked.

"No, but Fergie think it's sitting in the cellar all the time worth seventy-five thousand dollars. US."

All the bills and debts Fergie left me to pay, I almost lost my house, and I could have paid them all off and my mortgage with his ugly little rat thing?

"I thought his two-headed calf was the only thing worth money to anybody," I said.

"No, because le marmotte wasn't le marmotte, it was what he call canus opediea, a prairie dog préhistorique, and it's extinct. More than the dodo."

"No way!" Andy said.

"Or so he think because he see a nature show on TV. And Fergie, he's gonna sell it to some eccentric guy like Michael Jackson with too much money in la Florida. And I say, take it away, because I know it's not some dinosaur, it's a rat, like you. Fergie, take them all, she don't want this chez elle."

"So Fergie loaded the Salute to Taxidermy in his truck?"

"Because I make him, I even cart some to the truck for him. We have a battle because I won't let him have le marmotte, it's in my custody till they're all packed up."

"Who knows what other valuable fossils he had in his collection, unbeknownst to him," Heidi said sarcastically.

"Viola, she see us in the yard between the trips. Enfin, he's got them all in his old truck. I can't wait till he's gone for good, this is the last time I worry he's going to come back to your life and take you from me," Benoît said.

"Benoît, that would never happen, no one will ever take me from you."

"Vraiment?"

"Oh, oui, vraiment. Never again, nobody else but you. You're the only one for me. I'd be lost without you. Je t'aime."

"Everybody knows that," Frieda said.

"She's crazy about you," Daniel said.

There was a brief moment of romantic silence which Heidi broke. "When did Fergie meet up with Blake?"

"You know how Blake like to race his stupide char Trans Am up your little street? Well, he drive up like a maniaque, Fergie is backing out. And they have une grande collision."

"Fergie hit his Trans Am?"

"Yeah. And Blake is yelling at me, 'That was reckless endangerment, he coulda killed me, you're a cop, why don't you arrest him?'"

"But you ignored it?"

"Oui. I say it's no-fault insurance here, and you're the one who's speeding, you stupid punk. You're probably on drugs. You call the cops yourself, I'm on suspension. That's when the pennies they drop for Fergie and he say 'You're a cop? You the one who got the Feds after me?' And I say you better believe it, but the Yanks didn't go after you enough, buddy, because you're here. And Blake start to yell at me too because I was the one who help you find out he's the one leaving the threatening notes on your car. Both of them are fâché and screaming at me now and I say, 'Maybe I get the goods on you, but I'm not the one who smash up your véhicules.' I walk away back to la maison and leave them yell together."

"That's the last time you saw either of them?"

"Yeah. And I decide not to tell you, why ruin your nice time in England? I will always keep this mon secret. Why insult you, la meilleure femme au monde, that's you, and all Fergie come for is his t-shirt et le marmotte? He's not here to beg you to take him back, or to say sorry. I am so angry with him, I call you chez Farnham because I have to tell you I love you, but I was scare I would say too much, I'm so mad. But all I get is that lady who say, 'Sorry, I don't speak no French, lovie,' when I'm talking English to her! I keep busy, I put up the new shelf, I come up with a story. And everything is okay, but then Viola start to talk."

"And Jemima. And the cops."

"What cops?"

"Constables Malone and Pradesh. They told us they fished Fergie's truck out of the Lachine Canal."

"What? Lenny, you never tell me this!"

"Well, you don't tell me everything. You always got upset when I mentioned Fergie."

"Because he was no good. He make you so unhappy."

"And it made you unhappy to know what he meant to me."

"Misery," Heidi said.

"Exactly. He was so rotten to me, it seemed kind of fitting that he might have ended up in the St. Lawrence. That's awful of me, I know, but I wasn't upset he was dead, I'm so hard-hearted, it was such shocking news, Benoît. I was going to tell you, someday."

"Well, yeah. His truck in the water. You think he's dead?"

"The body's disappeared."

"Maybe it was a settling of accounts," Frieda figured.

"Out of the mouths of Vikings," said Daniel.

Chapter Twelve

Constables Malone and Pradesh came back because I was ready to talk. I gave them a much better statement than I did the first time. Benoît had already talked to them, they not only knew each other, it turned out they were fans.

"He should be a sergeant by now," Brunette Cop said.

"Too bad about that CSIS biz," Blonde Cop added.

"Give him another year, they'll forget all that."

"I wish you'd mentioned Benny the first time we were here, Lenore."

"I wish I'd mentioned a lot of things," I admitted.

I was a real canary now, I sang about all of Fergie's crimes, and Cheechio, and named Blake and Viola because they were the last people, besides Benoît, to see Fergie on our street. Mary and Mumtaz — the Angels, now on first name basis — were very pleased. And could see that I had somewhere else to go once they left.

"Where are you going?" Mumtaz asked.

"To a wedding," and I even told them where. I wasn't keeping any more secrets.

It was sudden but not entirely out of the blue; as Heidi says, the heart knows what it wants. She was wearing the dress she'd chosen for her going away outfit the time she almost married Emerson.

"I would have bought something new if I'd had more notice," she said.

"Me too. But hey, we're pretty elegant."

"And how often is this ever going to happen to us?"

"It's too bad it can't be in a chapel," I said.

"Yes, it will probably be the oddest ceremony we'll ever witness."

"We're more than witnesses, we're bridesmaids."

"I'm always the bridesmaid, you are la matrone d'honneur."

"I sure am. I don't take my Oscars dress out for just anything. And I'm wearing it by special request."

When we got to Joliette Prison, Herr Sprüngli looked so dapper, he wore a navy blue suit and had trimmed his moustache.

"You do us a great honour today," he said.

"Glad to help out, I was so surprised to be asked!" said Heidi.

Marie-France picked us up in the Festin Ça Roule! bus. She was a bridesmaid too, but of course. Before her release, she'd been Reine's protégée.

Reine was on the other side of the glass, while the rest of the bridal party stood in what Heidi called the Free State with Herr Sprüngli. Reine looked radiant, even in her prison blues, I'd put together flowers from her jardin for her bouquet. I figured none of us would have a chance to catch it, given the set-up at Joliette. That would be okay, this way Reine would have a lovely souvenir of today to brighten up her cell, and none of us would be under pressure to get married.

The prison chaplain was a Catholic priest. Heidi had wondered about this. "I didn't know you could have a Catholic ceremony if you were in a state of mortal sin. Reine is a mass murderess, even if she did make a good act of contrition."

Of course Heidi felt bad later. "Please forgive my lapse into being judgemental, Lenore. It's quite hypocritical of me when I was an accomplice to the event."

The vows were in French and Danish, they were husband and wife, and then Reine was led away, but not until the guards let them sneak in one quick, illegal kiss. And that was it for the honeymoon. Lars is allowed to visit but not conjugally, only in the visitation room, no contact and bulletproof glass.

Reine was thrilled to take his name, she is now Madame Ducharme Sprüngli, while Lars lives in her house and awaits her release.

"It could be a very long time . . . then again, perhaps not. Whenever it is, I shall be waiting outside the prison gates to take her home," he said.

He's very gracious. The house is so big, he felt, that Daniel would be welcome to share it with him as long as he wishes. Since he still has to travel for his business and do his protest rounds at Death Row prisons, he'll be away a lot.

What matters most is that Madame, who loves Love, is a married lady again and so very, very happy and wishing to spread the joy. As we left Joliette, a voice behind me called out, "Attention! Lenore Rutland!"

I turned around, and a prison guard threw something at me. And I caught it.

"Le bouquet?"

It came with a note embedded in it. The new Madame Sprüngli had written:

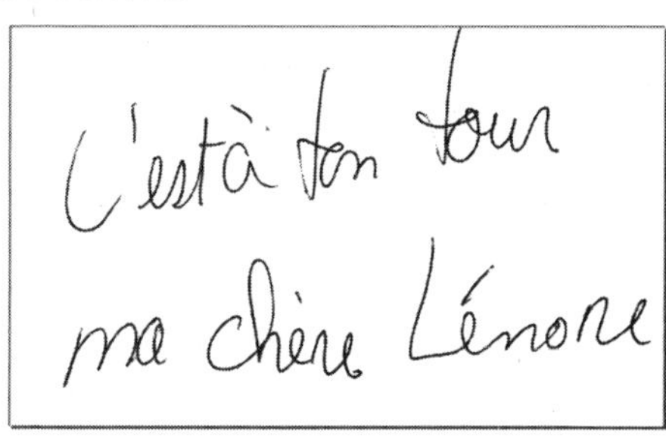

The Festin Ça Roule! bus had another major trip in November, our theatre junket to Ottawa. Daniel did the driving and Benoît, Heidi, the kids and I arrived at the auditorium just in time for the show, at my request. They knew how much reason I had to be superstitious.

Heidi's family waited for the Saturday performance so we'd all be together and get a great group rate. We were part of the Flynn Clan.

We'd missed opening night and all that drama, but Mrs. Flynn had reported the highlights. "Daddy is sensational as Eliza's father. Wait till you hear his 'With a Little Bit of Luck' and then 'Get Me to the Church on Time'!"

He truly was sensational, he brought down the house with both songs, everyone loved him, especially us. I cried when Freddy sang "On the Street Where You Live" because that song is so pretty, and then Benoît whispered, "That's how I'm feeling, Lenore, when I come to see you." Mandy Hepner, the girl playing Eliza, was so terrific that I thought they'd changed actresses when she came on as the educated lady, she was so different.

We all stayed over at the Flynns, there was a party for Hugh at their house after the show. He was in his glory. Sheila Flynn raved about one performer in particular, besides her husband. "That Mandy Hepner — Eliza — wasn't she wonderful, Daniel?"

"She sure she was. What a beautiful voice."

"She's such a lovely, lovely girl. In her thirties, she doesn't have a boyfriend right now. I never saw one around, anyway."

That's when their brother Kevin, trying to be funny, said, "I think Daniel would be more interested in Freddy."

We'd all seen Daniel talking quite a bit to Freddy after the show. Daniel X-rayed his eyes at Kevin.

"I'm seeing a lawyer."

"Why? You gonna sue me?" Kevin asked.

"What are you seeing a lawyer about, Daniel?" his mother asked him.

And Daniel answered, "Romantic issues."

"Oh, really. Is she nice?"

"No, she's not nice, Mummy. She's a he."

And that was it, out in the wide, wide open. Almost.

"You're seeing a lawyer and he's a man . . ." she started to say.

"And he's my boyfriend."

Stunned silence until Sheila Flynn, in the great timing that she alone possesses, asked, "Is he Catholic?"

All the Flynns went crazy laughing. Daniel laughed the most. I thought, oh, they think Daniel is joking, but I was wrong there.

"Is he Catholic?" is a family joke. Sheila Flynn has asked that about every suitor any of her kids ever had. Here she was in this terrible tense moment making a joke, making it easier for everyone, including herself. All the fears of melodrama and ugliness were dissolved. There would be no screaming or recrimination.

"I asked your father if he thought you were gay," Sheila Flynn told her son.

"And what did you say to that, Dad?"

"I told her you'd tell us if you were. I said, Sheila, you know how old he is, he'd have told us by now. I guess he's not gay."

"But I told Daddy," Sheila continued, "there are all these lovely girls he's never asked out. All the dancing he did with Lenore, and they're partners in the restaurant, and nothing ever happened." Then she turned to Benoît, "That was all before you, Benoît. I know you're very happy together, and I wouldn't want Daniel to break you up."

"Did you think I might be different, Dad?" Daniel asked.

"Yeah, your old man's been around. I was in the Army. And now I'm in show business, I've seen those Broadway boys. I could put two and two together when you were chatting up Freddy."

"Did you start to clue in at all, after you took us to Mirabel?" Heidi asked her Mom.

"Yes, when you hinted maybe there was another reason for his friend Gaëtan leaving him the condo. Was he your long-time companion, Daniel?"

"Not even that long-time," Daniel said, and then he broke down.

Sheila rushed over and hugged him.

"I'm so sorry, Danny."

"I miss him so much," Daniel sobbed.

"Hey, Danny, Danny, buddy, sorry, eh?" Kevin said and patted him on the back. His brother Patrick came over and silently tapped him on the back, too.

And then his father was standing over him.

"I'm so sorry, Dad, this night is supposed to be about you," Daniel apologized.

"It's about time it's about you, son," Hugh Flynn said and gave him a big hug. Heidi joined the family throng, it looked like the last episode of *The Mary Tyler Moore Show*.

"All the terrible grief you've kept to yourself, Danny," his mom said.

"Yeah, it's been terrible," Daniel admitted.

"Gaëtan was such a lovely, sweet, charming man," his mom said. "But you don't have the HIV too, do you?"

"No, that's one of the reasons I didn't tell you. I was afraid you'd worry."

"That's how Maureen Keilly found out her son was gay, when he told her he had more than HIV, he had AIDS."

This had been a very frank discussion, and I know that Patrick and Kevin and the sisters-in-law Heidi calls the Stepford Wives were happy all their kids, from Patrick Jr. to Tatum, were off in the den watching the video of *My Fair Lady*. Our two were still with us. Sheila Flynn, worried, had looked over at them every so often during this revelation scene, she does not realize how sophisticated their minds are.

Daniel seeing a lawyer was news to most of us.

"A lawyer, Daniel?" Heidi asked.

"Yes, he is. With a very prestigious firm." He named the firm, and we were impressed by just how prestigious it was.

"Their office caught on fire. It was a two-alarm," Frieda told us.

"Have you met him?" Heidi asked her.

"Oh yes. I like Joël."

When it was time for bed, Heidi, Frieda and I got the guestroom-den and les boys all bunked out in the living room. Everyone was asleep, I was so tired, but Heidi wanted to talk.

"My parents took Daniel's news quite well, don't you think?"

"A miracle."

"I knew they would, once he told them."

"You did not know that, Heidi Flynn."

"Granted, it was what I wished for on my big three-nine birthday candles. My, my, to think, my brother is seeing a prominent lawyer."

"His sister could be seeing a UN diplomat."

"Stop that, Lenore."

"Is James Murphy coming back to town?"

"Yes. Next week, as a matter of fact. For a final interview with the ICAO people."

"And then what?"

"The universe will unfold as it should."

"Your Gemini horoscope says: why not try going for a Canadian guy? You haven't had much luck with foreigners."

"Just the Brits. Miles and Woodham."

"Your fiancé was American."

"Emerson was a landed immigrant."

"James Murphy is the first one in a long time with a normal name. Go for it, go for him. You all made me go after Benoît."

"That was different. James and I have a history."

"Benoît and I had a history, we had a bigger one than yours."

"More colourful, maybe. I can't jeopardize my friendship with James. I can't make him choose me."

"You can so. If you have to settle for a platonic arrangement again, you may as well enter a convent."

"That's a sweet sentiment. If I have to regard him as a friend, I'll do so. I can manage."

"Is that why you wore the blue cocktail dress to Gibby's?"

"Drop it, Lenore."

She got up.

"What? Aw, you're not leaving?"

"Yes, I am leaving. Because I have to go to the bathroom."

I lay there pondering — was I too harsh? Should I back off and just leave things be, do nothing? Even though she's bordering on pathological? — when a little voice spoke out of the darkness.

"We have to do something about Aunt Heidi."

"What do you suggest?"

"We need to consult the Oracle."

"Who's that?"

"Her Mom."

And that's what happened. The next morning, we ambushed Sheila Flynn in the kitchen. Lucky for us Heidi likes her lie-ins, but it wasn't even seven a.m. yet. Frieda had an interesting approach.

"How come you and Mr. Flynn and two of your sons all live in Ottawa? And Heidi and Daniel don't?"

"Because Mr. Flynn's company moved its head office here. All the children had been to college by then and were on their own. But they'd visit us, and two of the boys met Ottawa girls and fell in love."

"But Heidi and Daniel stayed in Montreal because it was better for them?"

"Frieda, is this about Daniel being gay?"

"No, it's about Heidi being single."

"Would you like her to change that?"

"Yes. I want her to be happy with somebody."

"She's had such bad luck, hasn't she? Especially this year! Two useless Englishmen. That wimpy Woodham, I used to worry that Heidi's expectations were too high, now I worry that they're too low."

"Or nowhere at all," I said.

"And then Miles of Near Sheffield turning out to be a Casanova. His mother was devastated."

"She knows?"

"Poor Irene, she just wrote and told me. And sent clippings. It made the papers."

She fished in a drawer to prove it.

MILES AHEAD OF MILES —
BEST GOBSMACKED EVER!

Randy Bull Put Out to Pasture
by Slappers Sixsome

And in Irene's letter:

We coldnt belive it oursleves but there it was on telly. It solvd the mysetry of your leving so Heidi and Lenore sudden.

The powwow at the White Hart had succeeded. Sheila Flynn was worried about the "mysetry" of our disappearance, and I told her we'd found out about his evil ways just in time. When her mom showed it all to Heidi later, she was mad. "You'd think Jennie could have called or written to tell us. The best ratings they ever had? MY IDEA!"

Mrs. Flynn continued with the saga of Heidi's Both Sides Now. "And before those British boys, there was that pompous Emerson and his horrible family. One of the happiest days of my life was when my daughter said she wasn't getting married! And those are just the losers of the past few years. What can we do for Heidi, she deserves someone wonderful, because she's wonderful."

"What do you think," I asked, "of James Murphy?"

Her face lit up.

"Is James back in the picture?"

"More like on the horizon," said Frieda.

"He's wonderful. So polite, kind. Smart. Funny. He's a catch. Perfect for her, but he was dating her best friend Joanne at the time. Heidi would never be disloyal. And she was going out with that horrible you-know-who."

We explained what the present situation was, and she admitted it would cause a problem.

"They're both too shy and proud. That stupid 'I don't want to lose him as a friend' nonsense. She only met up again with him, they haven't been friends for years. This little dance could go on forever. They need a good push. How did she ever get together with awful Emerson?"

"She wanted a baby," I confessed.

"Well, she'll be forty by the time she has one now. It's still not too late."

"I don't know if having a child is an issue anymore," I said.

"Well, of course not, you have Frieda and Andy," Mrs. Flynn said and smiled at our scheming little girl.

By the time Heidi got up, we three had come up with a simple plan, it wasn't the Siege of Troy but it was close. But we knew if it failed we were in big trouble.

The next day, as Daniel drove us back, Andy had a joke especially for me. "How do you get an elephant out of the theatre?"

"How?"

"You can't, it's in his blood. Mr. Flynn told me that. Good, eh?"

"It sure is. Did you have a fun time in Ottawa, honey?"

"Yeah. And I liked camping out in the living room. Mon oncle Ben says you met on a stakeout."

"I guess it was," I said.

"An underground woman on the run was living in a house?"

Andy even knew she was Heidi's and my dance collective teacher, Frayne, who disappeared.

"And you know where they are looking for this Frayne? In her bathroom!" Benoît told the kids, and they loved this.

"Is that really the first time you met?" Frieda asked.

"I guess it was, yes, we met in a bathroom. Heidi was with me, and we thought Frayne had met with foul play."

"And Auntie Lenore, she's looking in a laundry hamper," Benoît told them.

"For what?" Frieda asked me.

"I thought her body was in there."

"She's always looking for bodies, this one," he said.

"Was there a body, all chopped up?" Andy asked.

"No, it was full of old *People* magazines."

"Did you ask Auntie Lenore out in the bathroom?" Frieda asked Benoît.

"I wanted to, but she's got her head deep in the hamper," he said, and he did an impression of me with my head way down in a laundry hamper that made me cry laughing.

"So you didn't ask her out?" Frieda asked, frustrated

"No. She was too busy picking up *People* magazines." He looked at Heidi, and she gave him a look: don't tell who you asked out instead. One of these days maybe we'll let the kids know they had One Date.

"Not then, but every time I see Lenore after that, even when she get arrested in a raid, I ask her out, to the Expos, to this, to that. She is always really too busy. But one day I am doing another stakeout because I am watching out for . . ." and he stopped telling the story.

"Who?" Frieda asked. This was something else I might never tell her. She didn't need to know that Benoît was staking out the woman known as the Queen Bee, nickname to us the Godmother, name to Frieda and Andy, Mom. Benoît was all wrong about Elspeth, but he wound up making the Arrest of the Year. Benoît told her what he could.

"Madame Ducharme, she's the one I'm watching, and Lenore help me get her. After this, we finally have our first date at Le Forum."

"So then you started going out?" Frieda asked.

"No. Because there was a big misunderstanding."

"You have a fight?"

"I was mad at her. I was a fool," Benoît told her. "For one year after that I do everything I can to win her back."

"And he did, because here we are."

"Oui, here we are," Benoît said and took my hand and kissed it. "You try getting this elephant out of this theatre."

James Murphy was finally in town, and out of absolute necessity we sent children to do a woman's work. James Murphy and Heidi were going out for dinner. He'd asked her to suggest a good spot.

"I was thinking we could go to the Golden Moon," Heidi told me.

"Is that in Chinatown?"

"NDG, right near Loyola. It's a greasy spoon, we all used to hang out there."

"An old-times-sake kind of set-up."

"No, it's just for fun."

But somehow on the night of the Golden Moon, due to a bizarre twist of fate, the colour-coded child-minding chart had failed, Daniel, Benoît and I were unavailable to be with the kids. Heidi would have to take them on her date with James Murphy, when we knew she'd be too polite, shy and scared to stake her claim because she was afraid she'd lose him as a friend.

"But they could go with you to Festin, they love to play les étudiants de Marguerite Bourgeoys . . .," she spluttered.

"No. The Hell's Angels are coming tonight."

"The Hell's Angels?"

"I didn't want to tell you. Yes, we have a Hells Night every week. They love La Bolduc."

I'd told this tall tale to Tyler John Biddiscombe, and now I'd passed it on to Heidi. It sounded like an excellent reason to keep kids away. This fibberoo came back to haunt me when I got to Festin, before I tried to rope in Heidi, but she wasn't giving up this easily.

"I don't believe you, you'd never consort with criminals."

"They don't get up to any criminal activity."

"You'd have told me before, what's this really about?"

"I'm telling you the truth, it won't be a child-friendly atmosphere this evening. Don't tell me the Golden Moon isn't child friendly."

"It's a pizza joint. Of course it is."

"Ooh, pizza," Andy crooned.

"All this time, you've been plagued by a biker gang at Festin. I don't think so, something's fishy here."

"Okay, okay. No bikers. We're doing inventory."

"Inventory in November? Even if you did, the kids could help, they'd love it." Where was Hollywood's Casey McCordick when I needed an implausible yet believable excuse?

Frieda suddenly took charge. She put on a Great Performances preteen hissy fit.

"My science project! On Great Inventors! It's due tomorrow, I thought it was next week!"

Heidi was shocked, "Frieda! How can you not be prepared?"

"I whited it out in her homework book," Andy confessed. "To be funny."

"Funny? FUNNY? What's funny, Andy, when I fail science this year?"

"You won't fail if you get it done."

"By tomorrow? How am I supposed to do that? It's got to be on Great Discoveries. Who can I do at the very last minute?"

"Marie Curie?" I proposed.

"Perhaps something Canadian like Banting and Best," suggested Heidi.

"Or on the penicillin. They made it out of mould," Andy said.

"I have to do tons of research!" Frieda was practically hysterical, she was very good.

Heidi was the professor, this was her department, this was an emergency.

"I'll help you, Frieda. James can come to my house, he won't mind, and if he does, well . . . he won't. I know him."

And being the man everyone said he was, he did more than not mind. I got a full report later.

"He brought Golden Moon take-out pizza," Andy said.

"And Frieda asked him out of the blue about the World Health Organization, for another project someday," Heidi said, unbelieving.

"Oh really, honey? FACE is really an advanced school," I said, Big Bad Acting to Frieda.

"It sure is. And then I asked James Murphy if that's the kind of job he'll have, and he says sort of, it's very complicated. And I said, 'Do you want to move back to Montreal?' and he said, 'I sure do,' and he looked right at Aunt Heidi."

Heidi blushed. "He did, that's true."

"Right at her!" Andy said, and Frieda continued.

"And then I asked him, Is this so you can be friends with Aunt Heidi again? And he said 'Yes. That's why I'd like to take this new job. I've come back to get the girl.'"

"But of course I was afraid the girl he meant was Joanne. Andy asked him if he ever went out with me in college."

Oh they are good, these two. Frieda continued her report.

"And James Murphy said, 'No. I went with a girl named Joanne, but we broke up. And then I met a girl from McGill, and we got married. But neither of them were the one for me. I came under the spell of the girl I know I should be with at a castle in Toronto. And I was there because I wanted to see her again. I hope it's never too late to change your life.'"

"James Murphy said all this?" I asked Heidi.

"Yes! And then Frieda quoted Anne Frank."

"Did you tell him about your Anne Frank ballet and that you want to be a choreographer when you grow up?"

"No. Because I don't want that for my job. I want to be a zoologist and work with Dr. Jane Goodall in Africa."

Heidi and I exchanged a look of approval.

"That's new. But what a great career choice, Frieda! You'll want to watch my *Gorillas in the Mist.*"

"I did already, Aunt Heidi."

"And *Planet of the Apes*, too," Andy snitched.

"What I quoted from Anne to James Murphy was, 'If you have a food factory, why not make candy?'"

"And I said quotes for James, too," Andy added. "I told him, 'Be your own hero. No team is ever beaten.'"

"Where did you get that?"

"Shinny rules. Mon oncle Ben taught them to me. James Murphy asked Aunt Heidi to see if they can try and be Aluminum Sweethearts."

"Alumni," corrected Frieda.

Heidi was ecstatic. "I said, I think we can try that, James. Yes, I wholeheartedly agreed."

"And I now have a Great Discoveries paper I can use whenever I need it," Frieda declared.

"You all think you're pretty clever, don't you? Diabolical!" Heidi said, very, very pleased.

"And not just us," Andy said.

"James Murphy said he crashed the Casa Loma party but Jane was all for it," Frieda said.

"It was something of a mutual matchmaking crashing enterprise," Heidi admitted. "And now, it seems we're finally going to be a couple."

"And that only came to pass because Frieda decided we had to be in cahoots with a Higher Power," I said.

"Who?"

"Your Mom!" Andy told her.

While True Romance shone over the Golden Moon, all Hells had not broken loose at Festin, and Tyler John Biddiscombe was pretty mad.

"So where are they, these biker gangs?" he demanded.

"This isn't their night," I told him.

"It's never been their night," he said, quite snarly. Jocelyne warned me that there'd been some non-participating dans le fun guests at Festin a couple of times, spies sent by Tyler.

"You think they wear their biker gear to come here? They dress up to go out for dinner," I said.

Strangely enough, he believed me. "Maybe they told people not to visit Prom Night."

"No." This fact, I knew, was true.

"Liar! They want to shut us down! They'll bankrupt us! We're not getting the people, no one will come near Prom Night."

"Because there are too many theme restaurants now in this city."

Jocelyne's never seen many people going into Prom Night — "pas de line-up," she heard from her scouts — and Nuit des Chevaliers wasn't doing that great anymore either.

"Le noveauté du Camelot Show, c'est worn off, et le prix fixe, c'est trop, too expensive," is Jocelyne's assessment.

Tyler John threatened me. "I'm calling in the cops. Unless you tell your boys to back off and give us a chance."

"Tyler John, we don't have any boys. We never did. We're successful because we deserve to be, that's it, that's all. If you go bankrupt, it's your own fault. I told you last year Prom Night was a bad idea. You want to do things over the top with knights in shining armour and high school punch bowls, you've got to get more than enough customers to pay for it all. Nuits des Chevaliers was an instant success with a one year waiting list, so what did you do? You raised the price to sixty-five dollars a person. You cut operating costs because your overhead was insane, but you can't have a jousting match with one knight and one horse."

At this point in my lecture on How to Run a Successful Theme Restaurant, Tyler detected a presence looming behind him. He turned around, jumped and swore. Our Bear du Bois is especially impressive when he stands on two paws with the other two poised in attack mode.

"Man! He looks so real."

"Like he just walked out of the forest, doesn't he? That's what my kids love about him."

"You don't have any kids."

"Oh yes I do. And they picked this model."

"Where did you get it?"

"Ponton's. He was very reasonably priced too."

"This was my idea last year, woodsy creatures for Festin!"

"Would you like to be escorted or chased out by one?"

It had been quite the evening, but, to quote our profound Frieda, "I think tonight went well, don't you?"

Benoît suggested we go up to Beaver Lake and walk around on Mount Royal. Our last visit was one of our first outings as a couple, on that glorious, bright day in January when we skated across the frozen Lac des Castors and then around the Chalet. We sat on a bench in the sunshine and I thought, What a perfect day. What a great guy is sitting here with me. Aren't I one lucky girl?

Here we were again, Benoît chose the same bench we'd had in January. We didn't bring our skates this time because there'd been so much rain, there was no ice. He was content just to be sitting there. I looked over at him and it hit me: I am over the moon madly in love with this man. But what romantic thing did I say? "I wish it looked like it did the last time we were here."

"The snow and ice will get here soon enough, ma belle."

"Right now it's so muddy and bleak. But that's November."

"We should get away. You and me, we never been on a real holiday together."

"That's true, we haven't. That's not right."

"I think we should do things right."

"I agree. Where would you like to go?"

"I think you would like Greece, maybe?"

"Greece? Why not? As long as we don't run into Elspeth and Elijah."

And I laughed because I thought he was joking.

"I mean it about Greece, Lenny."

"You don't really? It's so beautiful and sunny and far away."

"Yeah. That's why we got to go. Heidi and Daniel, they

could take the kids. We'll visit your friend Costas on Santorini."

"Santorini, really? Oh my goodness. Wow."

"I would like it to be for a honeymoon."

"Honeymoon?"

"I know to go for that raison, you got to get married to me."

"Marry you?"

"That's the deal. Oui."

This almost left me breathless, but I managed to say, "Okay. Sure."

"You don't say that just to get a honeymoon?"

"No. I say that because I want to marry you."

"Vraiment? Will you marry me?"

"Yes. When?" My heart was racing, but I could think: let's find a date and soon. He already had one.

"December 28, 2:46 p.m. This year."

"Next month? Why December 28? Why 2:46?"

"It's our first anniversary, là, when you decide to take a chance on me."

That was true, it was the moment when I called him back at the Festin entrance.

"We can find a good church. And have the reception at Festin? C'est beau! Oui?"

So that was it, all planned and decided, I accepted his terms, and he sealed it with a passionate, show-stopping, backstage-pass-outdoing kiss. I went up the mountain single and came down a December Bride-to-Be.

Jemima was banging down my door, I knew she'd be mad. I was terrified she'd retaliate and report us to Child Welfare, but I was ready for that. I have all the arguments, thanks to Daniel's lawyer beau. Joël has given us some major insights into our legal rights.

"Yes, so 'they're yours' doesn't really count as legally appointing you guardians. But as long as you have all the kids' official documentation and do right by them and the law doesn't know, you can keep them."

Even if Jemima reported us to Youth Protection and we wound up in an intervention, they'd listen to all the arguments, they act in the best interests of the children, and their best interests are us, that's for sure. I guess if any relatives ever show or their parents turn up, it'll be something else entirely, a massive legal battle for custody, but until that happens we can play what the Brits call Happy Families. I was ready, I thought, for whatever Jemima threw at me. Except this.

"I guess you're satisfied," she snarled. "Ratting my boy out to the police!"

"I had to tell the police Blake was one of the last people to see Fergie."

"Did you have to tell them to visit the body shop people who repaired his Trans Am?"

"I never did. I just told them he and Fergie had a collision."

"That made them overly suspicious. They discovered Blake's car was severely damaged, and the paint chips in the dents matched that Fergie's truck. Well, of course they did, Fergie smashed into him. But no, they said, Blake smashed into Fergie, over and over again."

"Benoît said it was just one collision. On our street."

"But the police are now inferring — they took Blake in for questioning — that it had to do with some sort of road rage."

"Road rage?"

"Yes, isn't that ludicrous? They storm-trooped in to capture Blake at his girlfriend's and dragged him out in handcuffs like a common criminal."

"But to do that, he'd be under arrest. They'd have to have something on him."

"Oh, they think they do! They say he followed Fergie on his way to that Cheechio's, then gave chase and caused his car to drive off the embankment into the canal."

"Blake killed Fergie?"

"He didn't mean to, it was road rage. He may even have confessed, but he's not responsible, he was on drugs."

"Your son killed my ex-boyfriend?"

"There's no body. I now have a dilemma, how am I supposed to start my new royal duties with my son incarcerated? I may have to extend my stay in Canada!"

"I thought you'd want to stay around to see more of your new grandchild. What was it?"

"A girl. I suggested Victoria Elizabeth, but they're going with Shania-Mariah. They're in Alberta anyway. No, it's Blake who needs me, but so does the former Duchess of York."

"Fergie? Sarah Ferguson?"

"Lady Sarah Ferguson. She needs guidance to be prepared to enter private life without further incident. I've offered and been accepted as one of her ladies-in-waiting."

Jemima will be working for Lady Fergie Sarah Ferguson. Sheila Flynn loved that, it was the best news she'd had since Heidi told her she's seriously seeing James Murphy.

I suppose I should feel at odds, here's Fergie lost at seaway in the St. Lawrence, or maybe he's alive somewhere, maybe he crawled up out of the muck on some shore like Elspeth. That Medusa could come back any day and claim her kids, but we have Joël for our lawyer, we'll go to court if we have to. She's never getting them back unless she's gone through an Aegean sea change and vows to be a good mother. Heidi feels our adopting a dog from the SPCA for Frieda and Andy is yet another true sign of our commitment, love and devotion. As if we needed a dog to prove it, we're so nuts about those kids, I wish I'd known them when they were younger.

So all of this has led me to the brink that is tomorrow. My life's fuller than it's ever been, it's like I'm the Horn of Plenty with all the fruit bursting out of it. Heidi feels we've paid our dues, we've suffered enough and deserve Good Karma at last, and like the book of shinny rules says, if you want to play, you've got to shovel. But I still can hardly believe it: Holy Moley et zut, alors! I'm getting married! The wedding came together faster and better than I ever expected. Starting when Simon Tratt got his invitation and arrived at my house. "This is by way of my RSVP. I'm not only coming, darling, I'm doing the dress."

"That's such a kind offer, Simon. But it's too short notice for you. Heidi and I are going up to Boulevard St-Hubert."

"Schlepp all over there for some kétaine schmatte, when you have me? I owe you, darling heart! After all your runway work for me at the Oscars, I can hardly breathe for all the designing jobs. I am finally world famous! And yours is going be the wedding of the year!"

I have the most exquisite dress on the planet, better than Diana's, Fergie's or Princess Grace's.

"Well, it should be, chickepen, you are our Royalty, après tout!" Jamie proclaimed when I gave him a sneak preview. The entire *Silver & Gold* Cast, except les chiens, "blew into town for this blessed event." And Casey and Calhoun get in later tonight. Everybody will be here.

Heidi as my maid of honour and Jocelyne, Marie-France and the Judys as the bridesmaids will all look sensational. Simon said for me to give them carte blanche, they can wear whatever they want, they don't even have to match each other. "All eyes will be on the bride, anyway!" I'm so happy that Frieda wanted to be the flower girl and Andy didn't think he's too old to be a ring-bearer. Benoît has Daniel as his best man and masses of people from the force as the ushers, I bet Mary and Mumtaz will be among them. I'm amazed that two orphans like Benoît and me found each other. We don't have any parents left and never had any siblings, but somehow we wound up with this beautiful family circle.

Reine feels badly she'll miss the ceremony, but she'll be there in l'espirit and knows "mon mari Lars" will give her a full account next visiting day. And I'll be round with the photos to show her through the bulletproof glass, once I get back from our honeymoon. In Greece!

Marguerite Vichy promised me that the wedding feast at Festin will be spectacular. I didn't ask any questions, I know she'll come through. There'll be lots of singing at the church and then at the reception, when Jamie joins our musical theatre folks to do our wedding songs medley with his added bonus: "Sadie, Sadie, Married Lady." Hugh Flynn promised "Get Me to the Church on Time!," and look at me, I'm singing "I've Got Beginner's Luck" at my own wedding. I can sing them all, if it takes all my life! "This Is My Beloved," you better believe it. Is there a great song about belonging, I could sing that, about all the wonderful people I now have in my life.

I was all alone and such a mess till they found me. Because of them, I'm so in love and happy, gobsmacked and grateful.

Acknowledgments

There are so many people to thank for *Guests of Chance*; the first ones must be my marvellous sister, Peggy Curran, and Laurel Boone, my fantastic editor at Goose Lane Editions.

Then un grand merci to Le Conseil des arts et des lettres du Québec for the grant which enabled me to write this book.

I was able to do research in England because I was a guest of chance at the invitation of my fabulous friends Jane Liddiard and Helen Shay and their families; I can gladly say that they do not, in any way, resemble most of the English people depicted herein.

My terrific pals James Roberts and Bertrand Simard are responsible for helping me curb my Luddite ways, toss off my Cyber Peasant cloak to dwell on the fringes of the twenty-first century; they helped me become somewhat branchée, and fixed all my French.

And then there are all the friends, family, colleagues and helpful souls who gave me ballet insight, Yiddish, encouragement, theatre schedules for 1993, their middle names, insider info about a major awards show, an even greater appreciation for Petula Clark, a tour of their sailboat, unconventional conception techniques, legal advice, their handwritten notes, and yes, as you have read, much, much more. These lovely folks are: Debbie McGlynn, Sylvia Cymbalista, Frances Silverstone, Gayle McCrory, Louise Abbott, Niels Jensen, Irene Kucenty, Heather Pope, Patricia Poirier, Charlotte Poirier Stephens, Zoé Poirier Stephens, Alan Stephens, Rachaël Van Fossen, Jocelyne Kéroack, Trevor Craig, Swifty McCarthy, Sylvie DeSerres at Fraser Hickson Library, Mary Burns, Haanita Wagn of Prairie Theatre Exchange, "Miss Hilary" Blackmore, Graham Greene, Debra Hale, Marcia Tratt, Stephen Barber, Margaret Fairhurst Dudley, Patricia Fairhurst Gerrie, Bruce Hagerman, Anna Bratulic, Ilona Martonfi at the Yellow Door, Pat Boera, Norma Jean Horner, Roy Horner, Nancy Cree, Jim Cree, Andrew Calamatas, Meredith Bain Woodward, Sheila Josefz at the Alhambra Theatre, Lorna Wilson, Alan Cumyn, Rosemary Johns, Frances Hutson, Alan Hustak, Gregory J. Reid, everyone involved in *Guests of Chance* production, editing, proofreading and distribution at Goose Lane Editions, Beverly Swift, Claire Crawford Guinn and Peter de Castel.

A borrower-be thank you to Sei Shônagon, Tower of Power, Julia Cameron and *The Artist's Way*, Enid Blyton for *Noddy*, Roger Williams, Kander and Ebb, George and Ira Gershwin, William Wordsworth, Liza Minnelli and Oscar Wilde.

And for all I have somehow forgotten to name or who want to be thanked or just wish they had their name in the acknowledgements of a work of fiction, please place your name right here_____________.

Thanks so much everybody.

Colleen Curran
Montreal
June 16, 2005